NO LONGER PROPERTY OF
SEATTLE PUBLIC LIBRARY

D0384743

NO LONGER PROPERTY OF
SEATTLE PUBLIC LIBRARY

PRAISE FOR *IN OUR OTHER LIVES*

"Theodore Wheeler weaves a compelling and complex narrative of public pain and private loss, of lives ruined by tragedy and at the same time redeemed by discovery. He shows us that people are mysteries, even to those who love them most, and that war and its aftermath reach deep into our land and our hearts."

—Mary Morris, author of *Gateway to the Moon*

"Reminiscent of the late Denis Johnson's masterpiece, *Tree of Smoke*, Wheeler's sterling novel tackles the modern world's attempt to systematically catalog the chaos of life. This clear-eyed look at society's entrance into a fully digitized world delivers a host of fascinating characters' unknowing struggles within the purview of the recently unveiled Patriot Act. As they wrestle with the old questions of what to believe in, and how to ground a life if you no longer believe in anything, it becomes clear the new information-gathering apparatus fails to understand the longing and need that propel each of them forward. An ambitious and absorbing achievement."

—Devin Murphy, author of *Tiny Americans*

"Theodore Wheeler's *In Our Other Lives* is wholly engrossing. Through the mysteries of the Ahls family, narrated through the eyes of the all-knowing servers that see, hear, and record everything in the wake of the Patriot Act, Wheeler deftly weaves the intricate, vulnerable lives of his characters against the stark backdrop of the American plains, resulting in a poignant book that's as human as it is political. Once I started, I couldn't put it down."

—SJ Sindu, author of *Marriage of a Thousand Lies*

"A captivating, thought-provoking, and sweeping novel filled with power and depth. Set against the backdrop of America's near-decade-long war on terrorism, *In Our Other Lives* offers a nuanced portrayal of public and private lives and the way those lives intersect, disconnect, and become lost in translation. Different kinds of losses and invasions radiate through this novel, and Wheeler reveals complexities of the human heart with subtle, beautiful prose that surprises as often as it delights."

—Kassandra Montag, author of *After the Flood*

"Taut, knuckle-whitening, and full of intriguing questions, *In Our Other Lives* is a page-turner that keeps the reader guessing. An FBI agent visits Omaha, Nebraska, to gather information about a radicalized young man who was either captured while on a mission trip to Pakistan or who voluntarily joined up with a group of terrorists, only to find that in this midwestern city everyone keeps a secret; that disappearances and deaths pervade their lives as surely as they do for those in the Middle East; and that the war abroad is nearer than anyone imagined. Don't miss out on this thrilling saga about a family in turmoil and the international crisis that ties them all together."

—Phong Nguyen, author of *The Adventures of Joe Harper*

"Powerful, provocative, fascinating, and deeply unsettling: *In Our Other Lives* weaves the threads that connect our lives and those who account for this haywire of memory, love, faith, reason, and understanding. I am still thinking about this one, the way it snuck up on me, and how it will not let go."

—Robert Olmstead, author of *Savage Country*

"With the pace of a thriller and the patience of a psychological study, *In Our Other Lives* depicts ordinary people consumed by tragedy and obsession. Wheeler skillfully depicts the struggles of mothers, missionaries, and spies, while always paying attention to the small, beautiful impulses that make them human."

—Jennie Melamed, author of *Gather the Daughters*

IN OUR OTHER LIVES

ALSO BY THEODORE WHEELER

Bad Faith

Kings of Broken Things

IN OUR OTHER LIVES

A NOVEL

THEODORE WHEELER

Little
a

This is a work of fiction. Names, characters, organizations, places, events, and incidents are either products of the author's imagination or are used fictitiously. Any resemblance to actual persons, living or dead, or actual events is purely coincidental.

Text copyright © 2020 by Theodore Wheeler
All rights reserved.

No part of this book may be reproduced, or stored in a retrieval system, or transmitted in any form or by any means, electronic, mechanical, photocopying, recording, or otherwise, without express written permission of the publisher.

Published by Little A, New York

www.apub.com

Amazon, the Amazon logo, and Little A are trademarks of Amazon.com, Inc., or its affiliates.

ISBN-13: 9781542016513 (hardcover)
ISBN-10: 1542016517 (hardcover)

ISBN-13: 9781542016520 (paperback)
ISBN-10: 1542016525 (paperback)

Cover design by David Drummond

Printed in the United States of America

First edition

*for my fellow travelers, Anne, Lynne, and CCB
and my mother*

He felt calm and sober, a crystal clear lucidity—
without object now—and he thought of tomorrow,
that the sun would rise anew, that they'd be
somewhere else, nothing but files would be left of
today and of the day before.

—Uwe Johnson, *Speculations about Jakob*

FILE 1

ELISABETH HOLLAND

19 SEP 08 TO 29 SEP 08

[19 Sep 08; the day the video aired]

Elisabeth Holland sensed there was bad news the same as she had at other times—she woke early, started coffee, set out her scrubs, waited for the phone to ring—but this morning something was different in the way her internal organs were arranged. The world had shifted underneath her while she was asleep. Elisabeth felt it on the horizon. The sun rising, yes, but also that something vital had changed inside her and out.

This time it was her mother who called to tell the news.

—*Did you see?*

—*See what?*

—*He's alive. They found him.*

Elisabeth continued fitting the sleeve into the percolator and added three spoons of dry grounds from the canister. The phone was on speaker, on the counter, while her mother rushed to tell what had happened. The call was something Elisabeth must have dreamed about dozens of times, hundreds of times; and it was, she admitted this freely to a woman she worked with at the hospital, that she daydreamed all the time that someone she'd lost would return to her. And in this moment— her mother rambling, repeating the same words, *they found him*, and Elisabeth unsure who was found and who had done the finding—she questioned if she was woman enough to handle the news she'd so long hoped to hear, or if the news would overwhelm her.

—*Is it going to be okay?*

—*Oh, honey. I don't know. Sometimes things happen for reasons we can't understand.*

—*Don't say it's God's plan. I'll hang up if you say that.*

Elisabeth forgot about the coffee to rush across her apartment and turn on the TV, then she saw. Tyler in a glitching, wavy video, a ten-second clip looped on cable news. The title read: "Missing American Found; Turncoat?" The cable-news anchor verified that the man's identity had only just then been confirmed by the government and that the man in the video was Tyler Ahls. Elisabeth knew the man in the video was Tyler Ahls. Her kid brother, missing in Pakistan nine months by then, supposedly on a missionary trip. Under a *doppa* cap and patchy beard, Tyler: the block shape of his head, his stringy ginger hair falling long down the sides of his skull. His gray eyes, his gaze slightly diverted, always, because he was timid.

—*It's Tyler.*

—*Yes! Tyler!*

There would be thousands of questions to ask and answer because of that video of Tyler Ahls in an Afghani cave. But Elisabeth didn't worry about all that. In this moment of simultaneous joy and dread, Elisabeth felt sorry for herself. She hung up the phone and returned to brewing coffee as the weight of her mysteries puzzled in new design on her shoulders. That she married and lost love young. That she only briefly was a mother before that too escaped her, that her son died, two months old, and she'd lived alone since then. That her brother, her parents—she'd never known what exactly to think about them. She watched the drips drop into the pot, trying to grasp what that video was going to mean for her family, for her parents and for Tyler. If Tyler really was alive, for one thing, and if he could ever come home; and if it would have, in fact, been better if he died hiking, like they believed he had while evangelizing in Pakistan, instead of being in the hands of terrorists; or if he was one of them. (She hadn't yet seen the ransom video of Tyler, the curious demands he made, so she didn't understand why the newscasters wondered if he was a turncoat.) Elisabeth struggled to keep her mind on anything. She thought of her husband. Maybe it was wrong of her, but when her mother called and said *they found him*, Elisabeth thought, she'd hoped, it was her husband who'd been found. Her husband (Nick Holland) who was also missing, for three years by then. Nick ran off on his own volition and nobody was looking for him. Elisabeth didn't know this at the time (how could she?) but Nick would show up in Omaha not long after this morning.

Once the pot was brewed, she poured herself a cup, stirred in two spoons of sugar, but didn't sip. The aroma made her gag. She poured the entire pot into the sink, unthinking, washed it away with clean water from the tap, then took a Coke from the fridge because she needed something sweet. She sat at the table and tried to put herself in the right frame of mind to go into the hospital where she was a nurse. She emptied the can in a few swallows. The taste, the sugar, was what she was thirsty for, so she opened a second can.

It was strange to have Nick Holland drop into her mind—when her mother said *they found him*. What Elisabeth thought of, that moment, was Nick holding their baby. The look on his face, that sly, almost unwitting smile, Nick so pleased with whatever joke he was keeping to himself—because her mother had put his son in a silk baptismal gown, what he'd called a dress. She and Nick lived in a one-bedroom ground-floor in Chicago then. Her dad poking around, an armchair flipped over on its top so he could fix where a spindle unglued out from its joint. Her mom practically pacing, manic, trying to explain the historical significance, the family lore, trying to explain the three generations of the pretty white gown she brought to put on Caleb.

Nick was the one who dressed the baby in the gown, who slid white silk over newborn head and tightened the pleats with a sash. All with Deb Ahls trying to interfere over his shoulder, all without the baby crying.

Elisabeth's parents, her mother especially, weren't comfortable with the fact that Nick had no religion. That he was godless, as they called it. Elisabeth even concealed how Nick was never baptized. *Of course he was,* Elisabeth lied, on the phone to her parents when she called to tell them she'd married Nick. *Everybody in Nebraska is baptized,* which is where Nick came from. This had to be the reason the Ahls rushed down to Chicago the instant Caleb was born, Elisabeth's mother clutching the paperboard box that held the silk gown like it was a religious artifact, like it was the Shroud of Turin she dug out of their attic in Wisconsin. Already the Ahls didn't like Nick—he was eight years older than their daughter; she was only twenty-three when she married him—and his godlessness made this gap harder to stomach. Still, couldn't they have left that gown in the car?

Nick's bemusement at the situation delighted Elisabeth. He was quietly perplexed as he listened to Deb Ahls go on about sacraments—baptism, reconciliation, etc., etc. Nick strolled to the window with the baby to look where a guy was trying to tip a Chevy Metro over a snowbank without getting high-centered. City plows had barricaded in all the cars on the block, so Nick watched the sedan rock and its tires sink into the snow as he fingered the pleats and bleached lace that brocaded Caleb's chest. This was the Nick Holland that Elisabeth loved. Cowboy Nick, tall and lean, with a scuzzy beard. Exhaustion bowed his shoulders, his back, because he returned to the warehouse where he worked only a day after the baby was born. He didn't have to do that, but that's how he was—*how I was raised,* he'd say, to remind Elisabeth that he came from hard workers, farmers, that he'd risen before the sun most every day as a teenager, or so he claimed. Nick, who that day, unbathed in blue jeans and plain white tee, barefoot, at half past noon on a Thursday, woke only because company was at the door. Of course, the baby had disordered his hours—why shouldn't he sleep when he had the chance?—and in Chicago he always worked nights.

6

It wasn't clear to Elisabeth why she remembered Nick this way. His glancing over his shoulder at her, Caleb asleep in his arms all of a sudden. "Well," he said, looking at Elisabeth but speaking to her mother, "we're not running out the door right this minute to dunk him in holy water, if that's what you expect."

With the same sure hand, Nick slipped Caleb out of the gown and swaddled him in swaddling and set the baby in the bassinet without waking him.

How did a guy like him know how to do a thing like that? Nick claimed he never even held a baby until the OB put Caleb in his arms in the delivery room. Elisabeth's legs still spread in the stirrups and there's Nick with his son in his arms; Nick joyous, laughing, hair in his eyes, an infant cradled in his elbow. Was that a natural component of the cogs that made Nick Holland tick? Dusty good looks, a strong mind for trivial knowledge, a soft and assured touch with infants? And if this was so, this last component, then why did Nick run off and leave her and the baby so soon after that day?

Elisabeth couldn't finish the second can of Coke she grabbed for breakfast. She felt sick; she'd had too much sweet too early. She went to brush her teeth and gulped from the bathroom faucet. Water helped a little. What use was there in starting off her day with a stomachache?

She wanted only to brush her teeth with her head in the sink until it was time to go to work, so she wouldn't have to walk by the TV again, wouldn't have to see her brother's face squared in by a news crawler. She wanted to hold tight that image of Nick and Caleb at the window with the light coming in on them, to remain aloft on the brief flutter of her heart when she thought it was Nick who was found alive. And, for a change, she could hope someone else might have to answer for everything that had gone wrong.

A federal agent came to question Elisabeth about Tyler. She'd talked to agents from the Omaha field office already but more germane was that Special Agent Frank Schwaller arrived on assignment from the Chicago field office on this date. Schwaller had a unique mind his superiors hoped would be suitable in this case, to ask about her brother, to decipher if there was a viable threat—that is, if there was capability behind the threat Tyler mentioned in the bizarre ransom video that was emailed to the world media. In the video he demanded *the president atone for atrocities carried out against Pashtun people*, his words slow and over-enunciated. Tyler glanced at his feet when he spoke over the four edited minutes. Tyler from the waist up in a collarless linen shirt, his shadow slanted on a white bedsheet hung behind him, his face glossed with sweat as he made strange claims. *I am a missionary here to help ordinary people, an apostle sympathetic to all people. Sure, that means my Muslim brothers too.* He was shivering as well as sweating. *These are the most neglected people in the world, it's not more government and war these people need, but the Good News.* He struggled to look straight at the camera, as he had his whole life struggled to look the person across from him in the eye when speaking. *My captors demand the American government do what is necessary to leave this land and free all prisoners from Guantánamo Bay, or else I will never be free to see my family again, and there will be graver consequences, more bombs, attacks on American soil. We must spread the Good News.*

Most hostages refrain from making threats in their ransom videos. In real life, Stockholm syndrome is not as strong as you might think, particularly for someone who isn't a Muslim, as Tyler claimed he wasn't a Muslim. Why did he say such things? He was supposed to be doing missionary work when he disappeared, but Tyler had a history of getting off track, of his intensity being diverted, of religious extremism (something he shared with his parents). His whole life he had been radicalized, if you believe Christians can be insurgent. Watching that video, especially the full twenty-minute version, not just the clip they looped on TV, you had to wonder: Why had he been put up to this? Why did he go along with his captors?

It was Agent Schwaller's job to determine if the Ahls family had any insight as to why Tyler made such statements. This meant the agent had to dig deep into the life of Elisabeth Ahls Holland, besides what was already known about her. That her brother went missing in December 2007 while hiking an insurgent-occupied mountain range situated between Pakistan and Afghanistan. That she was a nurse in Omaha, twenty-six years old. That she'd grown up zealously Christian in Wisconsin, had gone to college in Chicago to escape all that, then moved to Nebraska to escape further, was more or less estranged from her parents. She'd given birth to a child but was childless, her son having died three years prior, aged only two months; she was still married, technically, though her husband hadn't been seen in years. Agent Schwaller would talk to her half a dozen times in all, that week he was in Omaha. He stopped by Saint Wenceslaus Hospital first thing. Elisabeth was doing rounds on the third floor when Schwaller came to find her.

Sandy Laika, the charge nurse, spoke to the agent first. Sandy was tall and slim and approaching middle age, with a severe tan and long black hair and high, prominent cheekbones.

Theodore Wheeler

"What's the problem?" she asked. "Trouble with one of the patients?" which happened from time to time that the authorities stopped in to check on a lead if there was a gang member being treated who was flagged in a database, or some foreigner, an immigration thing.

The agent was skinny and tall, and his legs unfolded awkwardly as he walked. He had this half grin, like he was fighting to look serious, to not acknowledge how ridiculous he appeared, plucking his dark sunglasses from his face, slicking back his hair. But, still, he had a government badge with a foil hologram. It was legit. He had some questions for Elisabeth Holland, if Elisabeth was around.

"This is her shift, isn't it?" he asked. "Has she ever mentioned her brother? His whereabouts or activities?"

"No. She's said nothing about that." Well, that wasn't true. "Just that he went missing," Sandy added. "Last year, wasn't it? Tyler got lost climbing a mountain? But now that video."

"Yes. That's right," Agent Schwaller said. "Her brother was lost in an accident. Is that what Ms. Holland told you before the video surfaced?"

The agent recognized Elisabeth when he met her. She wasn't small but was shorter than some, was squarer. She'd played soccer her whole life, until sophomore year at DePaul, when her knee was taken out by a midfielder from the University of Dayton who was trying to take the ball from her. Elisabeth told this story a lot when she went out drinking with Sandy Laika and the other nurses after shift change. How much she'd loved playing soccer. How she earned a scholarship, had moved to Chicago to follow the opportunity. She'd looked her best then, she thought, mumbling this private thing into her drink—then thumbing through photos on her phone to show action shots of her on the pitch. She looked different now, but not so dissimilar. In her shoulders, her brusque stride, she still moved like an athlete.

10

The Bureau did some checking in Chippewa, where she grew up. An agent from Milwaukee dug up some interesting rumors about this Elisabeth Holland. The junior agent really pleased folks up in that town bar, letting them pour out stories about the Ahls tribe. Lis Ahls is what they still called her. *All's well that ends well*—that's what the report said. They were glad she left after high school, and hardly ever returned to that place her family ran by the highway, Apostle Crossing. The people at the bar claimed it was a religious shrine and that it really brought in the dough. *A mil a year,* one guy said, but he was laughed out of the bar by the others, saying that.

Apostle Crossing was a roadside attraction: Christian-themed dioramas, statues carved from stumps, placards that told stories about the lives of the disciples, organized as separate thematic "stations," all of it packed on a six-acre plat, a third of that graveled for the parking lot. Gerry Ahls built Apostle Crossing by himself, nearly, all the exhibits anyway. He was a skilled craftsman and carved the statues by hand. There was even a station dedicated to Tyler, *and he just a boy of seven, pure of heart,* with a photo of him as a bedraggled boy (more Pig-Pen than Charlie Brown) because it was Tyler's vision that inspired the park, from a dream he had when he was seven years old. Sure, the thing made money when it was open during the summer, but you wouldn't confuse it for Valleyfair; there were no roller coasters, no trams, no funnel cakes, no corn dogs. It was a roadside amusement, a smallish diversion that left pamphlets at hotels around and contracted group rates for retirement homes and church youth groups and Bible studies in Southwest Wisconsin, sometimes even the Twin Cities. This is where Elisabeth and Tyler grew up, the house off to the side of the property near the road, behind a stand of birch trees—so everyone in town thought they knew the Ahls family well.

That Lis, locals in the bar told the junior agent, *she has more than one guy on her conscience. One boy for homecoming, a different one for winter ball.* And wasn't she asked to prom her freshman year too? Sure she was. By a senior, an All-Conference forward in boys soccer. She liked to wear overalls with a belly shirt underneath in ninth grade. Otherwise she wore her Adidas shorts in class. Ones the boys could see up. Did she know they were looking? Sure she did. Then off to Chicago, thinking she's something special at DePaul, freshman this and that, until she lets some dirtbag knock her up. *Were they married before or after she got pregnant?* Nobody remembered. She never came back to Chippewa, not after that. And her poor folks. They might believe what they're selling inside the gates at Apostle Crossing—they might not—but no parents deserve two kids like they got.

That's what they said in Chippewa. The junior agent had quite a time. The locals were buying him drinks by the end of the night, once he gave them the chance to talk.

Agent Schwaller spoke to Elisabeth only a short time that first day. He waited by the nurses station until she returned to the counter, looked him over, and didn't say a word. She was much shorter than the agent, sleek and petite in her eggshell-green scrubs, but the difference in height didn't bother her. She was nervous, but not intimidated. It was obvious Sandy had warned her—*he's FBI, asked about your brother*—so she didn't say a word, just stood next to the agent and looked him in the eyes until he spoke.

"You're Elisabeth Holland?"

Even then she only blinked and nodded at the agent to affirm. He didn't cow her. His blue eyes, his arms too long for his body, a little softness in his chin. She didn't want to be bothered by any of this, not by this agent who, by all looks, took himself too seriously.

"How long has your brother been gone?"

"A while, I guess. About a year."

"You haven't heard from him during this time?"

"Not a word," her ponytail swaying as she shook her head.

"No emails? No postcards? Would you tell us if you were in communication with him?"

"I guess. If you asked about it, like you're doing now. I'd tell you the truth."

"Do you know how to get in touch with Tyler?"

"I'd call him right this second if I could."

Elisabeth broke eye contact with the agent, looked to the corner of the nurses station. A phone was ringing on the countertop; though if she wanted to answer the phone, she probably would have. She was going into herself. Schwaller must have been sure he had her thinking in a deeper, more subliminal way. That's what he wanted. Maybe Elisabeth had overlooked something simple about the events of Tyler's disappearance and the key to this mystery was coming back to her; maybe this would be an easy assignment, after all—if this thing she'd overlooked came rushing out of her, a phone number, a contact, a way to reach out into the ether and find someone who was lost. Elisabeth was thinking, remembering, staring where a cardigan hung over the back of a chair with a pack of Camels in the pocket, where there was a blinking red light on the ringing phone, where the caller ID said UNKNOWN. A tear welled in her eye, in the left one. Schwaller thought he had her.

"Have you talked to any of his acquaintances since he went missing?" Schwaller asked.

"Not for a long time."

"Do you know his approximate whereabouts?" No. "Has anyone asked you about him? A stranger who approached you online?" No. "Do you know where he'd go if he was scared or in trouble?" No. "To the best of your knowledge, has he ever been to Iraq before?"

"God no! Why on earth would Nick Holland be in the Middle East?"

"Who's Nick?" the agent asked. The agent looked down to his notepad.

Elisabeth was set aback. She slipped up, said her husband's name when they were talking about her brother. Somehow she was confused again; something must have made her think about Nick. How he smoked Camels. How he used to call her late at night, but she never knew where he was calling from, and the number on the caller ID changed more or less weekly.

"Who's Nick?" the agent asked again.

Elisabeth looked to the agent and straightened. Her neck flushed, the red spreading to her collarbones, her face. She took a deep breath, stared at Agent Schwaller a moment to catch herself. "I thought you meant someone else," she said. "We're talking about Tyler, aren't we?"

"Who's Nick?"

She turned away, gazed at a corner of the nurses station, a cabinet door where clipboards hung from pegs; she moved a paper chart from its folder to the desktop like she needed to get back to work. "Nick's my husband," she said. And then, "I have nothing else to tell you."

Schwaller, of course, was more persistent than that. He lingered around the floor awhile, then tried to corner Elisabeth in a patient room, not more than eight minutes later.

An old man lay sleeping there, his wife holding gauze to his head. There was more gauze taped where he was bleeding, but besides that the old man looked fine. The computer said everything was normal. Did his wife want some water? Yes. Elisabeth went and got the wife some ice chips and a pitcher of water and smiled at the woman.

Agent Schwaller waited in the doorway, where he got in the way, where Elisabeth had to squeeze past him to go in and out—his hair combed back, his long chin, the black suit he wore and the briefcase he carried to show something about himself.

"I can help you," Schwaller said. "I understand it's intimidating, having a guy in a nice suit up where you work asking embarrassing questions. But I'm on your side. This isn't me trying to bust somebody. Your brother. Tyler. Say he really did get lost hiking and ended up abducted by some bad guys, say that's the truth, and it's a big misunderstanding how he ends up making threats from a Haqqani bunker. Wouldn't you want us to rescue him? If it's possible, we can bring him home. Forget the ransom, nobody's withdrawing troops, but there are resources coming to bear on this."

"What are you talking about? Wasn't it worth it to look for him when he was missing before the video? Tyler is an American citizen, you know."

The agent stumbled into that one, played his hand too forcefully. It was too easy for Elisabeth to slip around him in the doorway and lead him back to the nurses station, where she could sit on one side of the counter and he had to stand on the other, where she could dissolve her gaze into a computer screen.

Schwaller set down his briefcase, took off his suit jacket, unbuttoned his cuffs and rolled the sleeves a turn or two, to his forearms.

"What about your husband?" he asked. "You brought him up, just now. You said his name: Nick. What if I tracked him down? Would you be interested in that? You'd maybe help us find who we're looking for if I could track down Nick?"

She looked up from what she was typing, threads of hair falling from where she'd tied them. This weakness again, this look of struggle in her eyes. *Who is this Nick Holland?* the agent wondered. And she too must have wondered if something strange was happening. This was the second week in a row she conjured Nick out of thin air.

Elisabeth said she'd try to help. But not at work. They could arrange another time.

"That sounds super." Schwaller pulled out his BlackBerry and asked what worked for her, to come by her place to talk.

"This is good," he said. "I need to know what you know. There's no threat. I'm not after you. Tell me about your brother. Tell me about Nick, and I'll make things happen. I'm in the business of finding people. But first I need to know everything."

No matter how astute Agent Schwaller was, he couldn't know everything about Elisabeth Holland, no matter what he claimed. There would always be obscurities in files to which Schwaller wasn't allowed access, things he wouldn't ever know—phone calls; emails; heartfelt confessions over dinner, at a bar, in bed at a hotel with a cell phone set on the nightstand to listen. Thousands of audio files, video files, every moment within reach an unwitting confession—almost always benign, merely personal, private, merely what was in Elisabeth's heart, but a confession nonetheless. Schwaller had witnessed some of these moments—not as many as an NSA analyst on Oahu would have, but some—Elisabeth hopping out of the shower to get ready for work, Elisabeth breaking down in tears when she watched Christmas specials in her apartment, on the phone with her mother, on an elliptical at the gym, in a bank lobby clutching a deposit slip, dressed up with her hair done at a bar alone, on dates with men she met online. And though this might sound gratuitous, honestly, if you had all this information, all this access, could you look away?

How did Elisabeth even end up in Omaha? Start there, that's in her file, in audio captured from her phone when she wasn't aware it was recording, a fruit of modern surveillance, from things she confessed to her friend Sandy earlier that summer, at a wine bar after work, more than a bottle in when Sandy asked how Elisabeth ended up coming here from Chicago. Did she move to Omaha for work? Sort of. Did she move for love? No. Far from it. She said:

It's complicated. Sure, there was nursing school. That kept my mind off all the other garbage. But there are nursing schools in Chicago too, right? It's not like God sent a sign, like I prayed over my troubles and He told me to do this and coming here was a leap of faith. It kind of was, except, all along, I planned to go to nursing school after I was done with soccer. And I did, right, eventually. If I leave everything else out (say I went to DePaul, I went to nursing school, I got a job at Saint W) then the story is really simple. Forget all the sad stuff. Leave out when my husband took to the hills. Leave out my baby. I could leave out the part when—this is crazy—my mom insisted I shouldn't be left alone in my condition, and when I wouldn't let her stay, she sent my brother to Chicago to keep an eye on me. Good old Deb called ten times a day to tell me, "Isn't it about time you move on," and "Your dad met a nice man at Bible study this week." I didn't want to go back to how things were when I was a kid, Tyler poking around in my shit all the time, my parents in my business. That's why I picked DePaul over Marquette in the first place, when I went to college. Chicago isn't in Wisconsin. After Nick, after Caleb . . . the distance wasn't far enough anymore. When I found a nursing school in Omaha that would admit me on short notice and apply my credits from DePaul, I jumped at that. I packed everything in a week. Tyler was still with me in Chicago. He didn't like how Saint W is in Nebraska. "Isn't that where Nick's from?" he said. He always tried to get a rise out of me. "Doesn't his dad live out there on a bean farm or something?" But it's way out there, where Nick grew up. It wasn't like I was going to bump into him or anything, like Tyler should give a fuck about that. (Elisabeth Holland, Mobile Audio, 11 Jun 08, Omaha 68114. Uncorked Wine Bar.)

Tyler was the one who researched the procedure at the courthouse downtown: what was required to divorce someone who ran off and disappeared, if you couldn't serve them the papers by hand. The aggrieved spouse had to post public notice—the *Tribune* or *Sun-Times* would do in this case—and if the offending spouse didn't respond after a certain period, the court would consider the offending served and the aggrieved could get her divorce.

That's what you want, isn't it? Tyler asked. *Don't you want your last name back?*

Elisabeth didn't file for civil dissolution or post notice, and she refused to explain herself to anyone who asked why she wasn't moving on. The truth was that she didn't want to think about herself without Nick Holland, without Caleb Harrison Holland, what they'd called the baby. That's who Elisabeth wanted her family to be. She didn't want to think how she'd lost both Nick and Caleb, and so quickly. How she was married to Nick a little over a year before he slipped out, how she held Caleb fewer than a hundred times before he stopped breathing in her arms one night, or how she was sleeping (both times) and hadn't noticed that Nick and then Caleb were leaving until they were already gone.

If filing for divorce meant her parents and brother were her only living relations, then no, she wouldn't file.

Elisabeth sold most everything when she left Chicago. Her mom (when she came to help Elisabeth move) threw out the rest of Nick's things, what he'd left behind: disposable razor blades and shaving gel; a half-eaten bag of Corn Nuts; CDs; his liquor. When Deb Ahls saw the booze she called it Nick's liquor because that's how she saw things. It couldn't belong to her daughter, for goodness' sake, not the Crown Royal, not the Stoli, not even the PBR. Elisabeth drank the PBR in front of her mother to piss her off, the time she came home and noticed the medicine cabinet was half cleaned out, Nick's white tube socks gone from the dresser, his blue jeans from the closet. *You have no right!* Elisabeth screamed. Of course Deb Ahls had no right. But that's what moms do.

The rest of it—DVD player, blender, toaster, mixer—Elisabeth sold all that on Craigslist, then made a deal with a secondhand store to pick up the sofa and double bed—which was the easiest way to handle that, since the salesgirl had a book that told what price to offer for each. Elisabeth didn't have to appraise how much she wanted for her and Nick's things, like she did with all the baby stuff. Pregnant women came, grandmothers-to-be pulling along, so excited to flip through what remained of everything Elisabeth bought for Caleb or received at the shower, rattles and diapers and butt cream and a grooming kit with tiny nail clippers. *You took good care of this,* a woman might say. Then the woman would notice there wasn't a kid around, and no nursery, no debris a growing boy would leave in his wake, nothing like that at all in the apartment, no toys except for those for sale in the boxes. The woman would realize.

The crib, the boxes of miscellany, most of it still in its packaging, pacifiers, nursing pads, blankets with blue cartoon elephants, the bouncer seat, the high chair, the circular pillow so baby wouldn't fall off of Mommy's lap or twist his neck when nursing if Mommy went to sleep, the rocking chair, the bottles, bottles upon bottles. Elisabeth thought she'd need so many for some reason, and she hadn't opened any of them.

At first she liked the feeling of weightlessness, one similar to when she went to college, after she set up her dorm room at DePaul, the fifty minutes it took to unpack her duffel bag and few boxes, whatever fit in the back of a friend's Ford Ranger, her CD player and notebooks, her toiletries crate and ibuprofen. That was that. No longer weighed down by everything she left behind in Chippewa, off to college like a jet. Elisabeth wondered if she'd feel the weight vaporize when she left Chicago, going to nursing school this time. What she couldn't fit in the car she sold cheap. Her mom waving from the curb, waving the keys, her mom and brother staying behind to give the keys to the super. It was all fine. Elisabeth felt the weightlessness for a moment in her head and shoulders. For a moment, she did feel it, freedom, and then her neck stiffened, she mortified at liberation, then the freedom was gone.

Agent Schwaller was prompt the evening he came to interview Elisabeth. Three hours after her shift at the hospital, so she had time to shower when she got home. After her shift she usually stopped somewhere for dinner—the local agents already knew this, following her. Sometimes at Taco John's, sometimes Bronco Burger. Sometimes she went straight home to heat something up, but she liked stopping for fast food. The workers at the Taco John's knew her. The local agents saw this through the window, how she was greeted when she walked in. *The usual? Or you mixing it up today, honey?* She'd get her food in a plastic bag to go. She'd fill a cup with Diet, grab some packets of hot sauce, and return to her car, a blue Pontiac, late model. She had a place down on Thirty-First Street, which was in her personnel file, on her tax returns. She'd been renting the same place more than three years, which says something about her, about the stability she craved. MOUNT VERNON, it said on the outside of the apartment building, but it probably wasn't called that anymore, not officially. It was just apartments. Two bedrooms in hers, a kitchen and a bath. She lived there alone. There was a Lutheran church next door. She put her car in the church parking lot (which was fine with the church, every day but Sunday) and unlocked the security door, her drink and the plastic bag with her food together in the same hand, her not-key hand, then she walked up the stairs to her apartment.

All afternoon Schwaller rehearsed questions in his head, anticipating her answers and where he could press her further. He dressed as exquisitely as he knew how. Black suit brushed free of lint. Black sunglasses cleaned of smudges by a microfiber cloth. Black shoes shined, with black laces straight. But his tie. His black tie he flipped in the four-in-hand style so it hung crooked on his neck—a knot with a greater degree of style, he thought, than any other he knew. He shaved and aftershaved in his hotel room. He got ready to astound this Elisabeth, to awe her.

Schwaller was different and he knew he was different. His Austrian ways and appearance—that's how he thought of it, even though he'd never been to Austria and was only part Austrian blood. His rail of a body. His light hair left longish, wet straight back across his skull. His steel-blue eyes. Most people have little clue how they actually look in the eyes of others—if Schwaller asked someone to describe what they look like, which he did sometimes, they almost never got it right. Maybe they sheepishly admitted to some shortcoming when pressed. *Oh, shortish, I guess.* A little doughy, lately. Chickenlegged. But they lacked self-awareness to a large degree. Most people didn't know how to use what God gave them—not like Schwaller did. He was a rail; he was steel; there was intensity to his composition, the thin pink lips, his unblinking, scanning eyeballs, with a farcical whimsy in his half grin, the way he unfolded his hands, long fingers unbending, and invited you to tell him the truth. You might tell him more than you planned, because he was odd. Odd but tough. Not the kind of guy you meet every day. He knew this. What Schwaller was not, on the other hand: he was not scrawny, his arms were not too long for his body, his legs did not awkwardly unfold as he walked, he was not ugly, not unappealing in the way he insinuated his interests into yours, along with the interests of his bosses. This isn't how he saw himself. Although you might see these negative qualities if you meet Schwaller, that's not what he counted on.

A lesser person might be overcome by their peculiarity. Schwaller was not a lesser. He was more than his parts.

Elisabeth had him sit in the TV room. On TV the Brewers and Cubs were playing, but she turned the game off when they sat on the sectional—Schwaller and his briefcase on the long side, Elisabeth alone on the short.

He said nothing, just looked her over. How new she appeared wearing anything other than her nursing uniform. (Or her soccer uniform from college. He'd seen a few photos of her in action, sweaty and straining, kicking at the ball with an opponent sniping from behind, and the team yearbook too, that was in her file. Although Elisabeth was younger in the photos, you could tell instantly it was her, the roundness of her face and those dark eyes.) Schwaller said nothing, he didn't fish in his briefcase, just stared and waited for her to volunteer some anecdote or another. She didn't. He remembered that Elisabeth had dealt with investigators before—the coroner in Cook County, the police and state detectives, as happens when a child dies—and from her ordeal she learned to refrain from saying more than was requested. She wasn't going to spill her guts just because an agent of the law was sitting on her couch. But there was the baseball game she was watching before and probably wanted to get back to. Would she check the score, Schwaller wondered, if he waited long enough? He stared at the dark screen until Elisabeth also looked to see what he was staring at, and he waited, tried to guess if she worried how the inning ended, if the score changed, and if her mind wandered somewhere else.

"So," she said. "As of last week we all thought Tyler fell into a gorge and died. What could I know about anything?"

Of course the Bureau knew all about Tyler Ahls's supposed hiking accident in an occupied valley near the Khyber Pass. Bearing that in mind, Agent Schwaller wanted to know all about Elisabeth. Who she talked to. Who she slept with, worked with. "It gets a little fishy," he promised, "you start digging into anybody's life."

Two large windows cut rectangles into the room, onto the coffee table and the floor that was scrubbed smooth through the varnish, the coffee table clean too, not a grease stain or watermark. Schwaller noted how Elisabeth kept house, how the magazines were ordered, DVD cartridges stacked and organized in a tower, even the big windows were spotless and reflected back the scene in the room, the two of them sitting there.

"When did you see him last?" Schwaller asked. "Your *brother*."

"Two years ago," she answered, which wasn't true. "Wait. Not that long."

"It couldn't have been," Schwaller corrected her. He reached into his briefcase and flipped through his small notebook until he found what he was looking for, held his finger to the spot on the page. "Want to try that again?"

"You're making me nervous," Elisabeth explained, her face flushed, her skin glowing, from keeping a straight face. She didn't want to talk about this stuff with Agent Schwaller. She looked out the window when she spoke, said, "Last year, then, I don't know exactly."

If you know how Tyler is, it makes sense. He didn't say anything for months, then calls one day and says he's got to go away. "When do you leave?" I ask him. "Tomorrow," he says. "Where this time?" "Peshawar," he says. But that didn't mean anything to me. He'd been to Pakistan a couple times before this, but I had no idea where Peshawar was, not until we knew something wasn't right. When he disappeared, I went back to Wisconsin to see my folks. They already had a guy going through the details, some sleazy PI from the Twin Cities. I don't know how they found this guy. He did nothing good. Pulled out some maps, pointed to the Khyber Pass and showed how it was the road to Kabul. If Tyler told me he was going to hike a mountain trail where a war was being fought, I probably would have guessed something was wrong. But maybe not. I worried, right, but this trip was supposed to be the same as the ones he took before. I wished him luck, told him Vaya con Dios and all that. But he didn't call home like the other times. The PI put us in contact with a guy in the State Department, but that did nothing. They only wanted to know why he was a missionary there to begin with, and that's a question we couldn't answer. How do you tell some guy from DC, "Oh, you know Tyler, that's how he is." No matter what we said, they made it seem like Tyler was up to something illegal. That's all I know. There was nothing else my folks could do. It cost a fortune trying to find Tyler in Pakistan, money my folks don't have, by the way, no matter what anyone says. (Elisabeth Holland, Mobile Audio, 29 Sep 08, Omaha 68105. Mount Vernon Apartments.)

Maybe she wasn't so strange, Schwaller thought. If somebody interrupted you at work and said your brother might be mixed up with a terrorist network and your shift not even halfway over yet. With her experience. With the way she'd had a family once, her own family, if you can call it that, Nick and the baby, and then lost it all so quickly, so heartlessly and plain. Maybe Elisabeth worked different than most people. Maybe she didn't expect to see anybody again, from day to day—maybe she couldn't.

"Explain it to me," she said. "Why do you think Tyler would join up with terrorists?"

"A white kid? Is that what you mean?"

"No. An American."

"I can't get into the reasons with you," the agent said, which is what he was supposed to always say, to not get drawn into conversations about capitalism or the war on terror. Since Elisabeth was a suspect's sister, he should have stuck to the questionnaire, even if that wasn't his style. Even if it killed Schwaller to keep his mouth shut, that's what he should have done.

"Why not him?" he asked Elisabeth. He sat up straight on the cushion, unbuttoned his jacket, let his eyes widen a little wild. "I mean, look up the definition of the word *traitor*. It's not an attractive business to begin with. Then you add in what these terrorists do, the scum your brother is mixed up with. The hijackings, sure, but that's just the tip of the iceberg. Take what they do overseas. Car bombings, shootings, burning bodies and decapitations, revealing vital information to animals who will end up on the wrong side of history. Suddenly a guy like your brother isn't so harmless. Who cares if he comes from Wisconsin?"

"But you don't know if he's mixed up with those terrorists. He's a Christian."

"Who cares if he loves Jesus! Don't you think there are Christian terrorists too? Ever hear of Eric Rudolph and the Atlanta Olympics? Give me a break. You start adding stuff up—now the only thing that matters is possibilities, probabilities. What does the intel say? That's important. Could this guy be a terrorist? *Sure he could!* Take a peek at most domestic terrorists and see what ratio of them are white Christian men, okay. We have to dig into everything. What's it say about him that his parents quit their jobs to run a roadside religious attraction? What's it say—and pardon me for being coarse—that his sister is clinging to a broken marriage? Maybe it doesn't add up. Maybe Tyler isn't a threat and was coerced into making that video. But until we know for sure, we've got to keep digging."

Elisabeth seemed to wake up when he finished, when he finally stopped to take a breath. She stiffened, stood, asked in a different voice, "Have you had anything to eat?"

The agent smiled. No. He hadn't.

She rushed to the kitchen between breaths, fiddled with the controls to get a burner going under a pan. "Do you like chicken? That's all I have."

Schwaller waited on the couch, unsure if he should follow her, or if that could be deemed inappropriate, if he cornered her in the tiny kitchen of her apartment. He kicked himself for getting carried away explaining his work when he should have let her talk—sometimes his discipline lapsed those days, retirement was in sight for Schwaller, when a late promotion could really boost his pension—and now she was hiding, had changed the subject, bent in her fridge.

There was a big-sister quality to Elisabeth, he noted. What must have compelled her to jump up and start dinner, beyond the fact that it was dinnertime and she was tired of hearing him pontificate? Maybe she felt better flattening a chicken breast with a mallet and dredging the filet through flour. The way she'd picked up the house and made sure he was comfortable, asked if he wanted anything to drink, and offered choices, "Coke or Pepsi?" She took care of things. Schwaller had two older sisters who lived in Racine, and they did the same thing when he visited: stuck him on the couch and got him things. They knew how to make a man feel useless. It was nice. An old-world quality to it, which is how they must do things up there in Wisconsin, he figured. Or it could have been something else: Schwaller thought about the report on Elisabeth that came back from Wisconsin, how she had a bit of a reputation up there, how men streamed through this very apartment after she moved to Omaha, but never for long. She did seem to have a type—men who didn't stick around. Now she agreed to meet the agent alone, she prepared him a meal. The agent doubted, really, that anyone was this hospitable, not without angling for something deeper.

He stood to snoop from one side of the apartment to the other, the scene familiar to him from images he'd seen in her file; he stretched his head around the jamb into the bedroom, where a dressing mirror was tacked to the door, where pairs of flats and white sneakers aligned in an open closet, where stuffed animals were arranged on the bed, and one in particular (a velveteen rabbit with droopy ears) sat on the dresser. Her bedroom was clean and organized, save for a blue sports bra draped over the side of a hamper. There were photos of Elisabeth on the walls, in frames on the dresser next to the rabbit. Her in a slim wedding dress, her kicking a soccer ball in knee-high blue socks, her holding an infant in a rocking chair, her and the baby-faced teen version of Tyler Ahls—a kid who barely resembled the one whose bearded face was on cable news. Elisabeth looked normal enough in the photos: the type of young lady Agent Schwaller knew fifty of, and liked them all. She was conscientious, clear-eyed, neat, pert.

On the other hand, the dining room was a complete mess. Newspapers everywhere, photocopied pages from *NYT* and *WaPo*, *OWH* broadsheets, with rectangles traced by a Sharpie around pertinent articles, about a local controversy in Nebraska that took up most of the space on the page: the state was allowing parents to leave children at hospital ERs and legally give up custody. It was surprising. The agent thought the clippings would all be about Tyler, but they weren't, they were about these kids being abandoned. Schwaller had heard about all that; he kept track of all the news he could, especially when in some-place new. So he also knew that late last week a man named Cary Junger left nine of his own kids at the hospital where Elisabeth worked.

"This is a strange coincidence," Schwaller said, peeking in to watch her at the stove. "Your brother showing up on the news. All this stuff with those kids."

"What do you mean?"

"Your brother ran away when he was a kid, didn't he? When he was in college. And now you're mixed up in that again, aren't you?" Schwaller nodded to the stacked newspapers, where Elisabeth was in the process of pasting articles about these kids into binders.

"That's not a coincidence," she answered, "what you're implying."

"Maybe I'm wrong." He laughed. They sat at the table and she made plates for them: chicken schnitzel, cottage cheese, sliced bread smeared with butter.

"*Guten Appetit!*" Schwaller said, beginning to eat. "It's just, and I know this sounds funny, but I mention coincidence because I believe in the universe—that everything is connected, that there's a purpose when atoms collide. If your brother is found—and he will be, no doubt—at the same time those kids are being abandoned by their parents, there has to be a connection. And you're at the center of it, aren't you? Like invisible forces coalesce around you."

She squared her chicken with her fork and knife, still squaring as she looked up at him, a half smile on her face. "That's still not a coincidence."

"Oh, sure," he laughed. "I see what you're saying."

Schwaller might have been embarrassed by all this, but he didn't allow himself to believe that any step he took was a mistake. Everything he did was process.

He ate the chicken faster and faster, rushed each morsel to his mouth as soon as he cleaved it from the breast. He was an insatiable eater, despite being so slim, and was really knocked out how Elisabeth made this chicken. The way she went about it. Flattened cutlets, golden-brown breading, a mix of herbs and spices, paprika, sage, parsley, other flecks he couldn't decipher or name, ones he could only taste and know they were good. Did she keep these ingredients in her apartment? Had she gone out to buy them because he was coming over?

The agent let his guard down tasting the chicken. It was good, and he was so hungry. He didn't know Elisabeth could cook. Why would he? That wasn't relevant to her family's case, wasn't noted in her file. The fact that she usually ate fast food *was* noted in her file; Schwaller had observed that himself. (He was getting off track, hadn't said anything for a minute as he sat chewing, collating his thoughts, how what he'd said before about coincidences wasn't intelligent—he could admit that. Still, he couldn't help himself, he had to be true to his nature. He remembered something that had occurred to him months before: that *file* was an anagram of *life*. He found that to be a wonderful coincidence, a true twist of fate, as he understood the word.) Schwaller wondered, chicken melting on his tongue, why did Elisabeth waste her time with fast-food tacos if she could cook like this? He was going to ask but stopped himself. That would be going too far, a question personal to him and not a directive from *The Agent*, as he saw himself. He calmed down, sliced deliberately, pressed only on knife strokes away from his body, directing away from his suit, his nice shirt, because if the knife slipped, the cottage cheese could slop his ensemble. He chewed slow and took a drink of Pepsi, pointed to the plate with his knife, gave Elisabeth a thumbs-up. "This is good shit."

He must have seemed like a bumbler. From what he told her, his bosses didn't trust him with real work anymore, or even the lesser tasks of something important, and this arrangement was fine with him. It was sort of true. A lot of his job was checking backgrounds on prospective hires, foreign service mainly. Determining who'd smoked pot in college, who still did. Who had ties to leftist groups. Maybe this work was exciting once—in the sixties, seventies, a Soviet kind of paranoia—but who cared now? Schwaller admitted as much. He had a reputation as a savant among other agents, from his time on the UNABOM case, so he was allowed to coast a little. He was allowed to be odd. It was an odd profession, if you thought about the actual mental calculations that went into his performance.

"Put any person in an extreme situation and they might go sideways," Schwaller said, aloud.

Elisabeth looked puzzled. She hadn't followed when the agent jumped to this new yarn without her.

"There's protocol we follow, a questionnaire," he explained. "We collect facts, opinions. Data. Input. Maybe something damning comes out of it. Usually not."

"These are the things you're asking me? A questionnaire?"

"Not really. This is different—it's finding out about people. Seeing if you and your family are good folks or not. Your brother shows up in a video. We got to check it out. No secret about that. I'm being transparent with you; I'm not trying to trick you. Maybe you know something that will help us find him while he's still alive. And you will tell me."

She laughed at him. "This is a waste of time, that's what you're saying."

"Sure, I don't want to be in Omaha, but I think you'll tell me something important, Nurse Holland. You know a lot. You can help."

"I already told you everything. If you're waiting for more, you'll be disappointed."

"What about your husband? That's why you asked me up here, right?"

Elisabeth sat back and breathed in sharp. She'd forgotten. "Yes, you promised to tell me where to find Nick."

"I said I'd try, but nothing has come up on Nick," which was a lie. "I'm looking, like you asked." She shrunk in her chair when he said this—Schwaller staring at her with his silly winner's grin. "Did you ever tell him what happened to your son? To Caleb?"

"No."

"Do you think he knows?"

She pinched her lips and glared at him. "Is that what you came to ask me?"

He smiled. "So, yes, I'll reiterate: the more you can tell me about Tyler, the better chance I have of finding Nick."

"As far as I know, they haven't spoken in years."

"This is how it works. Trust me. It's all connected. I won't bore you, but the thing is, there's a file to fill. There are questionnaires to complete. Input, basically." Schwaller beamed proud as he said this, as if what he said made any sense. "There's a footprint we follow. Emails, texts, phone calls, IP addresses. I don't know exactly how it works, but it does. How I think of it is, there's a chief inspector up there somewhere, in a secure complex at Fort Meade. All data goes through the chief inspector, every story, all the input that's created. The chief inspector holds every whisper inside himself. Like God. That's how I like to think about it."

"But there's no input," Elisabeth said. "That's what I've been trying to tell you. I don't know what Tyler's been up to."

The agent didn't bother explaining again, not if she couldn't understand. *It was all input.* Everything that happened could be recorded and coded. Everything that could be known and filed was known and filed. The servers, he wanted to tell her, the servers knew everything.

FILE 2

AGT FRANK SCHWALLER

09 Sep 08 to 11 Sep 08

Schwaller arrived in Peshawar at night. He'd been to the Middle East—as a probationary member of Director Mueller's Baghdad field office, two years before, and before that in Israel, Jordan, Beirut, on vacation—so he was used to flying overnight, especially in great deserts where the noontime heat caused sandstorms to churn violent enough to bring down an airplane. Schwaller understood it was safer to fly at night, climate aside, how even commercial jetliners were wise to operate under cover of darkness rather than risk being shot down by friendly or unfriendly fire. It's complicated. Everyone knows.

Coming in after midnight produced a peculiar feeling, the landscape a thousand shades of black; when, standing outside the airport, Schwaller could only make out distant obsidian knolls of what he knew were mountains; when he was travel weary and hopped in the car of a man who claimed to be his fixer. The agent could be gullible sometimes—he knew this about himself. Even in the States, getting an airport taxi felt naive to Schwaller. Goaded into an unfamiliar car, protected only by the assumption that all was usual, that if he told a driver where he was going and promised to pay, then the driver would take him as safely as could be managed, that the driver wouldn't take him into the hills to rob him.

It was like being a lamb, he thought, hopping in a car like that, trusting, tired and weary and willing. Schwaller didn't like being a lamb.

In the parking lot of Peshawar International, he watched soldiers check each car inch by inch, how gun-mounted trucks idled every fifty feet to track with the barrels of their rifles the packing and unpacking of luggage. Only three days before there was a suicide bombing outside Peshawar—the explosion killed thirty-five at a police checkpoint and left a three-foot-deep crater in the pavement. This didn't bother the agent, he was used to danger, he thought of himself as brave; and he was drowsy, disoriented, standing atop a curb in the middle of the night with sodium lights blaring above him. He couldn't help going along with what was expected of a traveler. The people around him loaded trunks with baggage, including the Pakistani PI, his fixer, who loaded the trunk of a Toyota Corolla with Schwaller's suitcase and told Schwaller to get in.

Schwaller sat in the back seat, as was his custom when he had a driver.

"What's the problem?" the Pakistani PI asked. "I have bad breath?"

There was no problem, Schwaller assured him. It's safer in back.

The seats were wrapped in clear plastic, plastic the agent heard crinkle when he sat down and adjusted his legs diagonal to fit, that clung to his clothes in the muggy air and blocked his hand when he reached for the seat-belt buckle that was underneath. He asked what the plastic was about. "To protect the seats," the Pakistani PI said. And the seat belt? "You don't need it."

Schwaller was a little surprised when the man sat directly in front of him, but of course it was Schwaller who foolishly sat on the right-hand side of the Corolla, behind the driver. He was being unnecessarily dramatic, Schwaller knew. He should be pals with the fixer. The fixer was friendly, a middle-aged man named Khan Khalili who was clean-shaven and leathery, who wore a gray linen suit and, everywhere he went, held a cell phone in his left hand. The phone never rang, not that Schwaller saw, but the fixer was ready if his phone did ring.

"Don't you ever put that away?" Schwaller asked, pointing to the phone, to the screen on the clamshell that lit up now and then when Khalili moved his hand. "Is your wife a jealous woman?"

Schwaller had to lean around the driver's seat to see Khalili's amphibian face in profile. He was a portly man with white-infested hair, who had big ears, whose left front tooth was chipped in half, his face green from the glowing dash. Larch trees whipped by in the dark, out the dust-dappled windows of Khan Khalili's Toyota Corolla.

"It's not like that."

"Like what?"

"No one is waiting for me," Khalili said, which Schwaller knew to be untrue. Khan Khalili was married, with two prepubescent sons. He was a private investigator and a fixer for foreign journalists and governments, and his family owned real estate in the Danish Abad neighborhood and part of a small restaurant in University Town. This was in his file.

Maybe Schwaller should have been disconcerted by Khalili's lying, but that was part of the relationship, as far as Schwaller understood. There was a certain amount of falsehood that must be accepted—falsehood Khalili likely saw as nuance. Why must Khalili tell a foreign agent about his wife, his sons, if he didn't feel like telling? Wasn't that fair? Regardless, the agent decided to tell a lie himself. Instead of calling out the PI to set the record straight, Schwaller played along: "That's too bad you have no family," he said. "I have two sons, eight and six." (This is how old Khalili's sons were, of course.) "Fatherhood is a joy," Schwaller said. Not exactly a lie, though not exactly true, coming from his mouth.

"Shall I take you to your hotel?" Khalili asked in response.

In the morning Schwaller arranged for a taxi to pick him up at the Pearl Continental, where he was staying, where his room had a balcony and vines grew over the building from potted plants that surrounded the outside walls. There was a pool, a free breakfast of cold cuts and soft gray cheese, a dozen kinds of gourmet juice, roe and dried fish, because Russians stayed here, Schwaller deduced. You could eat poolside if you wished. Schwaller wished. He stuffed himself with cold halal chicken sausages and overripe fruit and stale bread. A large buzzard circled over the top of the hotel, but Schwaller didn't let that ruin his appetite. Even though he felt like drawing the blackout curtains in his room and sleeping off his jet lag, he headed toward University Town in a taxi to trace the steps Tyler Ahls took in Peshawar.

There are plenty of mysteries in the files, but no dispute that Tyler Ahls traveled to Pakistan in August 2007 and was last seen shortly before Christmas that year, traveling west to the Afghani border in the passenger seat of a bright-yellow Suzuki wagon operated by a man who was a known associate of the Haqqani terrorist network. There was so much chatter about Tyler Ahls, it was no shock to the agent when that video was intercepted by CIA. (This was months before it would air on TV, though it shouldn't come as a surprise that several agencies secured copies well before then.) The Ahls name was on Schwaller's radar, certainly. The flights Tyler took to Central Asia, including two previous trips to Pakistan. How he quit ROTC because of philosophical differences, which happened to some people—gung ho as a freshman, then by sophomore year soapboxing on the quad about how capitalist imperialism will destroy the world, how we're enslaved to corporations, how we had it coming on 9/11, etc., etc.—and you could only speculate why somebody like that volunteered for ROTC in the first place. That's how it was with Tyler Ahls. Things soured. The same thing happened with his religious upbringing, it's noted—coming of age at that Bible park his parents ran outside Chippewa, where charter buses brought church groups, youth groups, senior citizens, every weekend, seven months a year, to walk graveled paths and take pictures with their arms around wooden statutes of apostles, while Tyler argued the finer points of divinity with a Lutheran pastor or some know-it-all in an American Legion hat with gold garlands glued on the bill.

After he dropped out of college, Tyler traveled the world, a few of these so-called hiking trips he went on to Tajikistan, Kyrgyzstan, China. This is 2002 we're talking about, when Tyler borrowed library books about the Silk Road and mujahideen. Everyone in the Bureau had their eyes open for someone like him. All these adventure vacations. Sightseeing the Axis of Evil. At the time of his disappearance, Tyler was teaching English in Pakistan. It's verified, a gap-year job, common enough. Maybe most kids don't go to Peshawar for a gap year, but Asia, sure, plenty of floundering college students do that. He retained certain rights at that point—freedom of movement, for example—and since he wasn't yet suspected of being a traitor and had a visa, he was allowed on airplanes bound for Pakistan. Modern Language Spoken School in Peshawar vouched for him with a letter that offered employment; he had a copy of his contract and eighty-five dollars in cash to buy a passport stamp at Peshawar International. While there, he hiked a section of the old Silk Road, along the Khyber Pass, which also happens to be a passage to Kabul. Then no word. No emails. No phone calls. He leaves his job without notice, goes missing. Disappeared maybe, maybe he fell in a river and drowned, but no one finds a body, there's no trace—like maybe he was abducted against his will, or maybe Tyler Ahls found the place he was looking for, after all.

It was a surprise to Agent Schwaller how easily Peshawaris went about their lives, four days after the attack at the police checkpoint, like they had forgotten where on the axis they fell. The merchants in stalls, the boys on mopeds or driving auto-rickshaws behind plexiglass like in a ball turret. But the middle class, them too, what there was, in Camrys and Accords and BMWs, well fed and wearing gray suits. Reading newspapers and nibbling toast behind the washed glass of a café, or with legs crossed in colorful plastic bucket seats that dotted the sidewalk, drinking tea. Peshawar was leafier than the agent expected, with trees lining almost every street. Some spots reminded him of Detroit, where he grew up. The flat blacktop pavement, the steel streetlight poles, the overgrown flora on greenbelts between roads—where sometimes refugees hung sheets of clear plastic over the branch of a larch tree until they could find a better shelter, just as some people did back home in Michigan that year. Most Peshawaris had no more connection to global terror than Agent Schwaller's own sisters, he realized, married off, relocated to tend to the broods of an insurance salesman and a chiropractor, in Racine, Wisconsin. And here he saw Peshawari women in head scarves, married off to insurance salesmen and chiropractors, perhaps.

He wondered what it was like for Tyler Ahls, walking the streets alone like Schwaller just then walked a street in University Town only half-crowded with people, with Pakistanis. Would Tyler have been jarred by all this? Would he have had second thoughts about coming, whatever he'd come to do? The driving on the left side of the road; all the honking cars, the constant noise, the terrifying, unthinkable traffic; the beards of the men; men in long shirts sans collars that draped loose over their loins; a spindly peach tree that grew from the cleft in a stone wall; how policemen wore machine guns and neon-yellow vests; waking to a muezzin calling *adhān*; the streets littered with white plastic cups—like communion cups in the Methodist church Tyler visited a few times back in Chippewa, except here it was espresso taxi drivers drank from these cups and not grape juice—and everywhere street urchins rummaged for plastic and aluminum cans and bits of wire to sell at recycling centers.

Did Tyler Ahls have visitors while he was in Peshawar? Did he make friends among the locals? Not really. He frequented a restaurant called Tikka in University Town; Schwaller would check that out. Tyler placed numerous phone calls to his mother via a magicJack device, and one to his sister. Tyler emailed at three-month intervals with one Nick Holland, his brother-in-law, which was benign at first, to the other agents, but stuck in Schwaller's mind. The content of the emails wasn't all that interesting (exchanged rumors about family members, some discussion of David

Koresh and the FBI, speculation on whether Nick had worn out his welcome with the Ahls family, and if Tyler had done the same) but the fact that Nick worked for the Midland Pacific Railroad was very interesting to Schwaller. Why did Tyler stay in touch with Nick, even from Pakistan, when he barely talked to his own family? It was curious. Did this have something to do with Nick's employment with a major freight hub?

Was it a waste of time for Agent Schwaller to go to Peshawar? A waste of money? Not to him it wasn't. Generally, he hated fieldwork—so dusty, inelegant—but he wanted to see what Tyler Ahls had seen. In University Town, Schwaller went to Tikka, the restaurant on Old Jamrud Road where Tyler Ahls was known to visit.

Schwaller could see why Tyler was drawn here. Tyler didn't have friends in Peshawar. From all outside appearances, a stranger could find friends at Tikka if he wasn't shy. There were snooker tables in back, a television played soap operas, every table was dressed in brocaded cloth and topped with clear plastic, and the large room smelled, generally, like a warm place. Tikka was mostly empty when Schwaller arrived, but it was early, still morning. Three older men in aprons, in the kitchen, tended to tandoor ovens; along an ell-shaped, red-velvet sofa, four young men with cell phones and trimmed mustaches drank bottled water and eyed Schwaller as he strolled in to sit. Schwaller assumed they were waiters, but none of them stood to help the agent. They paused to consider who this man was, this stiff Westerner in black sunglasses and black suit, sweat clouding on his collar already, his legs crossed as he flipped through a menu. Agent Schwaller didn't worry about looking like a foreign agent in that getup, as many of the professional men here indulged a significant degree of formality, with aviator shades and silk cravats, with shirt buttons undone and bushy chest hair exposed to function as a cravat.

The youngest of the waiters, a gawky teenager in wire-frame glasses, brought a fork and knife because Schwaller was a foreigner.

"Do you recognize this man?" Schwaller held a photograph of Tyler—Tyler from the videos, his stringy hair peeking from under a doppa.

"He's the American that asked about crossing the border."

"Yes. He got lost hiking."

"I don't know about that."

"What do you mean?"

"Just that. I don't know. I'm not certain." The young waiter was a little coy, how he smirked, sarcastic, not intimidated at all by the agent jumping in with questions. He was kind of charming in his way. How he stood tall and spoke loud with an accent that had a fair amount of empire in it, how he adjusted his glasses on his nose before he spoke. This surely wasn't the first time he was asked about Tyler Ahls. "He seemed okay," the waiter said, "but why come to Pakistan? And why Peshawar? We thought he was one of you. That's what Uncle thinks."

"He *is* American."

"Not what I meant. CIA."

"I'm not CIA."

"Isn't that what you all say?"

A bitter taste filled Agent Schwaller's mouth at the suggestion that he was anything other than FBI.

"Did you ever see Tyler Ahls around the neighborhood? Outside the restaurant?"

"I saw him around."

"At mosque?"

The waiter smiled. "Sure. He would go pray. But he isn't Muslim."

"He'd go and pray? Did he know how?"

"Talked to Hindus and Christians too, don't you know that? This is how he was."

Schwaller said, "Hmm," though he knew all this. It was in the files. Tyler Ahls regularly attended All Saints Church within the ancient walls of the old quarter, not far from Schwaller's hotel. Tyler's family thought he'd given up his faith, but that wasn't true. He claimed to be *all of the above*, generally, and a Christian specifically. Tyler spoke about sharing *the Good News* all the time in Peshawar, as he did in his ransom video, and spoke about doing his own translation of the Bible into Urdu and tribal Pashto dialects. So while Tyler Ahls wasn't typical, most agents accepted that he was a Christian of some unique sort. On more than one occasion he showed off bits of scripture when he was at Tikka. Tyler believed he was doing something important.

"He came here a lot?" Yes. "What? Every week? Every day?" It depended, but enough that they called him *Tyler al-Masīḥ*, the waiters did, because *al-Masīḥ* is a surname for many Christians. "Did he ask you to call him *al-Masīḥ*?"

"Not at all," the waiter said. "My uncle started that."

"A term of endearment?"

"Not at all."

"Did Tyler always eat alone? Would anyone you know call him a friend?"

"No one ever called him friend," the young waiter said. "Not how you mean the word."

Something caught the kid's eye when he said that, so Schwaller followed to see what the waiter saw: there through the window was Khan Khalili getting out of his Corolla, rushing to the door of the restaurant. Schwaller wasn't a bit surprised to see Khalili. Maybe not before noon, but the agent knew Khalili would find him at some point, once Khalili figured out the agent was checking his sources. This was the restaurant his family owned a piece of, but he'd left Tikka off the itinerary the day before, so, yeah, that's the first place Schwaller went.

Khalili sat down across from the agent. He took the initiative and ordered for the both of them. "Let's keep it light," he said, grabbing the menu from Agent Schwaller to tell the young waiter what he should bring to the table—Shinwari tikka, bhindi okra, *doday* naan, Mountain Dew.

"Do you like Pashtun food?" Khalili asked. "Have you tried it before?"

"Sure," Schwaller said. "What's not to like? I like everything."

After finishing with a single cup of tea with biscuits, then fennel seeds, Khan Khalili offered the agent a ride. "Yes, wherever you want. Your hotel? Or wherever, you tell me, but yes, your hotel, that's best."

"My hotel," Schwaller conceded. He didn't like having to argue with Khalili.

On the third day, Khalili drove Agent Schwaller to Khyber.

They traveled immediately west of the city, through the Jamrud bazaar, the high earthen walls of the Sikh fort at Jamrud; under the white bricks of what looked like an ancient gate at Bab-e-Khyber that marked the entrance to the Khyber Pass; out onto the loess-dusted, two-lane Torkhum Highway to the wide-open plains and big sky of tribal lands, a sky as cerulean and ominous here as it was in Montana when Agent Schwaller got his start tracking Ted Kaczynski. They headed, at Schwaller's request, to a spot just short of the checkpoint at Torkhum, where Pakistani tribal land opens into Afghani tribal land, with two towns straddling the border, both called Torkhum. "Like Derry and Londonderry," Schwaller observed to Khalili. He sat in the front seat this time, feeling more diplomatic than his first night in Pakistan.

Despite the winding road and traffic heavy with shipping trucks and short buses and NATO, and that Schwaller kept telling Khalili to drive slower, it took little more than an hour to reach the border crossing. Khalili stopped his Corolla atop a ridge four miles short of Torkhum, at a spot that resembled a trailhead where winding dirt paths spiraled into the hills to places unimaginable. It wasn't really a trailhead. There was a footpath that led into Himalayan cedar and parasol pine and junipers and yews, a rocky depression where Tyler Ahls was purported to have journeyed into the Hindu Kush range in the general direction of Tirich Mir, though Tyler was certainly not trained nor equipped to climb Tirich Mir, the highest non-Himalayan peak in the world. Schwaller believed

Tyler Ahls actually stayed in the vehicle that transported him to Torkhum until the vehicle snuck him across the border to Afghanistan.

"Tell me," Schwaller said, the two of them out of the Corolla, descending into pine trees in single file. "Where exactly was Tyler Ahls supposed to have drowned? What river?"

It was dry there, but not so much of a desert as you might think from the quantity of dust kicked up on the road. Now that he'd asked, Schwaller saw a couple lesser tributaries of the Kabul River from their vista. Khan Khalili pointed out a few others, but where he pointed the streambeds were dry, and all Schwaller noticed was how the landscape had a lukewarm, khaki color when warmed in the sun. This was the traditional route taken by invaders coming into Peshawar. Darius, Bābur, Alexander, the Brits, etc., etc. Schwaller thought about this when they were driving up here: how many great civilizations crossed this road to invade the subcontinent, but first Khyber. Schwaller considered it a privilege to stand there and peer through tree trunks into the rocky valley.

"Look there," Khan Khalili said, pointing west beyond Torkhum. "That's Afghanistan."

Schwaller's jaw dropped once he was aware of the border. He went silent. It wouldn't be until he was back in the Chicago field office that he could comprehend what he felt, when he explained to the junior agent in the cubicle next to his what it was like standing on a mountaintop overlooking the Khyber Pass, Afghanistan, Osama.

It was a peculiar sensation, I'll tell you. I've been in weird spots, but to see Afghanistan, the highway a dusty incision in the mountains, off to Jalalabad, then Kabul, bin Laden hiding in one of those mountains. I was in New York on 9/11. Did you know that? Downtown working a job fair, of all things. I told you this already? Back in a closet at home I keep the suit I had on that day. It's stiff with white dust from the Twin Towers. I'll never have it cleaned. When I was up there with the fixer, I got to thinking about the reason why I keep doing this, the real reason why I was in Pakistan. The bodies falling from the towers, and they weren't just bodies, they were citizens. That's what I thought about—how we were going to get the fuckers responsible. I was overwhelmed by the sight of Afghanistan. I'm not so vain I can't admit that. To look at the land and feel all the trouble it caused. You know what I mean. That bin Laden was out there. (Agt Frank Schwaller, VoIP, 15 Sep 08, Chicago 60608. FBI Field Office.)

Khan Khalili refused to go further, which was fine by Agent Schwaller once he took a deep breath and remembered why he was in Khyber. Already he was planning what he'd do once he returned to Chicago. He wanted to steam the dust out of his skin over the course of a long morning in his own shower and to saddle a bar stool in the hotel lounge next to his building, to meet a woman, a stranger only there on business, with nothing else to do but introduce herself to a man like Schwaller at the bar. He considered the case too—being led down a mountain path, noting the aroma of pine trees, how the air was both damp and dry in that exact spot at the edge of a glade, if there can be a glade in Pakistan, where there was a clearing along the mountain path amid parasol pines. *Yes,* Schwaller thought to himself, *this is a glade.* And, yes, the case. How it was certain Tyler Ahls had disappeared—but what was murky was Tyler Ahls's intent. Schwaller pushed every angle in his mind while he hiked along the path after Khalili. The Ahls family was so strange to him, these people he thought of as radical Christians. Though *radical* was the wrong word, he was stuck on the term. Even then he knew about Elisabeth Holland, how her baby had died, in Chicago, and it felt meaningful in some inexplicable way that Schwaller was also from Chicago, that he was going about his life in the Windy City the very moment Caleb Holland expired, but felt no movement in his soul. Not in the way it turned Elisabeth upside down, certainly. Schwaller knew nothing about Elisabeth and Nick then. Three years later, stumbling down a mountain path in Pakistan, he resolved to learn all he could about them. Maybe that was a trail that hadn't yet gone cold.

FILE 3

NICHOLAS HOLLAND

10 MAY 08 TO 11 MAY 08

14 MAR 04 TO 17 JAN 05

It was almost unbelievable that Elisabeth didn't know her husband was in Omaha. This is why Schwaller supposed they were lying to him—if Nick lived within two miles of her apartment and she really didn't know. Schwaller wondered how that was possible.

Elisabeth kept to herself most of the time. Put in long hours at work, volunteered for holiday and weekend shifts, filled in so other nurses could get their kids to soccer. So what if she never ran into the man? Did Elisabeth frequent the same dives as rail workers? Did Nick shop for hand towels at Bed Bath & Beyond on a Sunday afternoon? Omaha is not such a small place, what, a million people, thereabouts, and it sprawls into the prairie. You're not going to just happen into somebody, not if you're running on different tracks.

But Nick knew she was there, didn't he?

Yes. Someone tipped him off to where Elisabeth ended up; he parked his car outside her building on several occasions but didn't buzz her apartment. That's interesting. That's strange. That's Nick Holland for you. What else can be said about a guy like him? He did a lot of strange things.

Nick always cut across the tracks when he was working on a bridge. It was no trouble for him. Three and half years he worked on railroads.

Welding, torch cutting, all sorts of things. On bridges over rivers. He volunteered for the dangerous work, and not because he was paid better for taking risks, but because he didn't mind being up there. He liked hanging off bridges, stepping from tie to tie and seeing muddy water rush underneath the timbers. If he was alone, if the supervisor wasn't watching, he didn't wear the lifeline either. That's just how it was. The work was easier his way. He complained more or less constantly about lifelines: all the time wasted putting on straps, safety testing straps, untangling straps, ordering new straps. Time wasted threading cords under his legs and through metal hooks on his belt and shoulders. Still, you might do something stupid, you might go in the river, and you're not going to swim with all the gear on. Nick understood this. You'll sink. Doesn't matter who you are. It doesn't take much to slip, not when it's foggy, clutching to those slimy wooden ties. Original issues, Nick called them. He walked women out there when he worked in West Texas, to scare them, to show off, pointing out spots that had been gashed over the decades, to the place some Irish drove a spike in a hundred years ago, and now it's up to Nick to hold the bridge together. With his fingertips for balance on a rusty, graffiti-covered bridge, holding on for dear life sometimes. If it's windy. If it's raining. Nick's lifeline back in the truck.

Still, he knew what he was doing. He took his job seriously. Three and a half years he was up there. He wouldn't just fall in a river.

The agent would think about Nick a lot. He was thirty-four when Schwaller met him: a repairman specializing in bridge work, a high-wire act; lived in Omaha a single month, at the Kellogg Rooming House downtown; itinerant before that, Wyoming, Texas, Colorado, Missouri; born on his father's farm, which was strange how that was handled—his parents didn't bother with a birth certificate until he was nearly a year old. That's what Nick Holland's file said when Schwaller got it. Broad in the shoulders and of normal height, kind of narrow in the hips, like he came from a line of cowboys. He did come from the range, the northernmost region of Nebraska, the Sandhills they call them. It seemed to Schwaller there was more to Nick Holland than anybody let on, and that deserved some scrutiny in a case like this. Nick was quiet, gloomy, but not sad. Confident in his quiet, like he kept things to himself. That was a virtue where he came from, so maybe meant nothing.

The interesting thing to Schwaller was that Nick's name was all over Tyler Ahls's inbox, starting in spring 2005 up until the point Tyler disappeared in the mountain wilderness outside Peshawar. Sure, they criticized the government in their correspondence. Dick Cheney jokes were an obsession of theirs after Cheney shot a friend in the face while hunting quail. But who didn't make a joke about that? Did it mean Nick wanted to see harm come to America, or that he and Tyler were making plans? Of course not. Mostly they talked about the growth and development of Nick's son, which was an inexplicable conversation to come across for those who were observing them.

In Nick's file there was this thing with a baby, three years before. In the report, the coroner emphasized there was nothing to indicate blunt trauma or smothering in the way the infant died. Elisabeth insisted Nick was gone when all this went down; he abandoned them a few weeks before the kid died. They were still married on paper (even in 2008) but hadn't seen each other in years. She didn't have a clue where Nick was, thought he was out west, living in motels back out on the range, out where there still was range. Schwaller wasn't going to be the one to tell her otherwise. She never bothered to get a divorce in all this time. Another strange thing. She wouldn't say for sure why not.

Nick called Elisabeth in the middle of the night, in the months after he left her in Chicago. He called and didn't say anything, just waited on the line.

Waited for what? For her to speak, to recognize his silence, and then?

Who can say what he was waiting for? Maybe he was merely calling to call. Because he should call, and he wanted to. Of course he wanted to call. You think he was just a bastard—and he was anyway, even if he sent money (which he didn't) even if he sent toys for the kid (which he didn't) even if he called every night to check on things, to see how his boy was doing, and the boy's mom too, to see how she was doing, the so-called love of his life.

He called, sometimes, but he didn't speak to her, didn't check on them. He didn't ask if everything was okay.

The one thing Nick knew was that someone was answering the phone. And then, after a while, no one was answering the phone.

[10 May 08; four months before the video aired]

Nick Holland drove everywhere the years after he left Chicago. This was obvious when you tried to track him down. He'd never been on an airplane his whole life, and once he was getting steady paychecks from Midland Pacific he only paid cash at filling stations—which was smart, Schwaller himself only used cash unless Bureau accounting required otherwise—so that made tracking Nick through financial records difficult.

This much is known in his file, from his employment records: Nick Holland took a week of vacation in May 2008. He was thirty-four years old.

He went to see Elisabeth's parents that week, after he saw a magazine article about Tyler vanishing in Khyber, the April 2008 issue of *Outlands*. This was three years after the phone line in Chicago was disconnected. It had been that long since he'd talked to Elisabeth, or even heard her breathe. It had been more than nine months since he heard from Tyler—now that Tyler was missing, the only two who could tell him anything were Gerry and Deb Ahls.

Nick got a promotion with Midland Pacific a year before, to bridge inspector. Rose above track-laborer classification, had health insurance, AD&D. He wanted to start a 529 college savings plan for Caleb and needed an SSN to attach to the plan. Of course, he didn't know Caleb's SSN and that gave himself an excuse to go to Chippewa. He half hoped Elisabeth and Caleb would be there in Wisconsin. Maybe Elisabeth wouldn't want to see him—she might want to keep Nick as far away as possible—but he suddenly needed to know where his boy was. He wanted to stop being such a shithead about everything and give the kid some money and maybe say hello. He wanted to see the kid.

That's the most likely explanation for why Nick drove to Chippewa to drop by his in-laws', Schwaller supposed. Maybe the scope of his desires was wider than this, but the magazine article, the 529, that would have been enough of an excuse. For the three years prior, the only member of the Ahls family Nick spoke with was Tyler. It would have been suspicious that Tyler went missing, given what Nick knew—that Tyler was aware of the geopolitical danger of moving to Peshawar and hiking the Hindu Kush, that Tyler's emails were increasingly erratic, made frequent references to David Koresh and John the Baptist, and how Tyler wanted to be part of their tradition, his own destiny as a missionary, a revolutionary (as he saw it), though Tyler had trouble explaining how three trips to Pakistan fit in his vision—or how hiking foothills there made him either insurgent or evangelist. Those years, in their emails and phone calls, Nick trusted it was the truth when Tyler said that Elisabeth wanted nothing to do with him. More than anything, given Tyler's state of mind, Nick wanted to find out if what he was told was true or not.

The Ahls looked much older since Nick saw them last. The kind of thing Tyler mentioned all the time in his emails (*the folks are getting old fast*) but Nick had to see it for himself before the image he had of the Ahls in his mind could alter. How Gerry Ahls had lost weight, was looser in the cheeks, stooped more in his shoulders, had less color in his skin and hair; how Deb Ahls was shorter, Nick was sure of this, and she scowled all the time, though her scowling could have been caused by the fact that her deadbeat son-in-law showed up at her door unannounced during a rainstorm and invited himself inside. Maybe that's why Deb Ahls scowled, and why all the color drained from the old man's face.

Both of them came to the door to stare at Nick. Deb peeked around her husband, portable phone in hand, like she might need to call emergency. "Jesus," Gerry said under his breath. Deb smacked him on the arm for swearing, a reflex.

Gerry reached out, shook Nick's hand, and pulled him into the house in a single continuous motion. "Is it raining already?" he asked, taking Nick's wet coat to shake off the drops. Deb gave Gerry the stink eye for inviting Nick inside, but she didn't scold him. She retreated to the living room and sat down on one of the chairs there, the same floral-print upholstery they'd had for years; she crossed her legs and let the portable rest on her knee. Nick hadn't expected they would let him in. He worried they wouldn't talk to him at all, that he'd get a punch in the nose for showing his face around here.

You can't say the Ahls were happy to see Nick, but what else were they going to do? It was raining outside, and wasn't there thunder on the other side of the hill, and hadn't a woman on the radio promised it was going to storm? Didn't their dog, Cooper, a bloodhound, come rumbling down the stairs to say hello to Nick? Didn't Nick bend down to rub the whining dog's ears, to let the dog lick his face, because at least the bloodhound was happy to see Nick? Even if the cordiality was a false front, it was as much of who Gerry Ahls was as the fact that he parted his hair on the right and wore Lee jeans and had silver fillings in his teeth. So long as Nick Holland was his son-in-law—which he still was—then Gerry could swallow his spleen and ask the man in to have a seat.

"So what happened?" Nick asked.

The Ahls looked to each other and frowned more deeply, Gerry with his hands in the pockets of his trousers, holding himself straight and silent, waiting for his wife to speak.

"What do you mean what happened? To who?"

Nick smiled. Elisabeth's parents had always played games with him.

"Tyler," he said.

"Oh. Tyler," Mrs. Ahls said.

"He said Tyler," Mr. Ahls said.

They told Nick what happened—a slightly less nuanced version than he read in *Outlands*. How Tyler went hiking in Pakistan. Tyler claimed things were safe where he was going, and the Ahls were inclined to believe him. He was always right about these things before, his previous trips.

"You know there are terrorists there?" Nick asked them.

"Oh, we know now," Deb Ahls said. "A PI told us after the fact. But terrorists had nothing to do with Tyler's disappearance."

Nick must have believed what they said. What did it matter if they thought something else happened? They believed Tyler fell in a canyon and no one could save him because he was alone. (The video hadn't yet showed up on the news, so that was the only story any of them knew.)

Apostle Crossing was still closed, and it was quiet outside. How strange seeing the park again must have been for Nick, thinking how he was related in a small way to all those carved wooden statues, with moldering leaves at the bases of the displays. It was a mess, and the Ahls would open for the season before long, before Memorial Day—that's usually how they did it. The place looked more ridiculous off-season than it did in summer. All the banners in storage, so there were bare wires strung all over. Jesus and the Twelve Apostles with the fake plastic olive branches around them still green and leafy, a Palm Sunday display with its meaty fronds, but the real trees, oaks, just then budding. The corner of their house visible from behind the stand of slender birches that divided it from the park. And no people around, no tourists. In the middle of it all was a stone structure with a photograph of Tyler as a boy, on a placard that detailed the park's origins. (Tyler had explained this to Nick in an email: *And then there was me. My sad chubby body, my freckles, a ginger. It felt impossible that God cared what happened to my life. That was the same year I had my dream about Apostle Crossing.*) Visitors often thought all this was Gerry's vision, but that wasn't really the case. The genesis was attributed to Tyler.

"Have you heard anything about Tyler since the article came out? Any new tips?"

"No."

Nick asked where Elisabeth and Caleb were living, but the Ahls wouldn't tell, saying instead that it wouldn't be a good idea to tell. So Nick hung around, made small talk for an hour while the storm moved over them, until it was almost seven and past time to get some dinner on. "Why don't you stay for supper," Gerry said, his voice slow and reliable.

It was obvious Mr. Ahls hadn't talked this over with Mrs. Ahls, from the appalled look she aimed his way, how he shrugged and mouthed *why not?* It wasn't clear to Nick why they asked him to stay, or why that was better than being forthright, than telling him where he could find Elisabeth and where he could find Caleb. He didn't know what they were dancing around. The Ahls must have realized that Nick didn't know what had happened to Caleb. They wouldn't want to be the ones to tell him. Still, with that being the case, why did they invite him to stay?

"There's T-storms," Gerry said. Nick didn't mind driving in a storm, but storm or not, dinner or not, he wouldn't leave until he heard what he'd come to hear.

There was thunder all through dinner.

"Did you plan it this way," Deb asked, "so we couldn't tell you to hit the bricks?"

Gerry laughed, like she meant it as a joke, but Deb didn't laugh, and Nick didn't answer.

In that little old dining room in their little old house, they had hardly changed a thing. The same plates from their wedding, with the purple serving dish Deb Ahls filled with string beans at dinner. Even the tablecloth, worn through so Nick could see the squares of stitching, its gruff threadbareness so apt for the Ahls. Gerry offered to say grace once food was on the table, and the three of them connected hands on the tablecloth with eyes closed until old Ahls was done thanking the Lord for the food and shelter and their health and, yes, even for the unexpected company. "Our prodigal son-in-law" is how Ahls phrased it. And with that, amen.

After eating, Nick and Gerry sat in the living room and watched the weather on TV, the splashes of red and orange and green pixels. They gestured at the map slowly, tentatively, tried to predict which way the lines of storms would drift and how bad the damage would be. Gerry asked Nick if he had a plan for getting around the storm, because sometimes roads flooded up there in the hills and lakes when it poured, when a red blob of radar overtook the county.

At dinner and watching the weather, Gerry kept looking at Nick. He never cared much for Nick, that's no secret. Nick never really expected him to—he married Gerry's daughter, she didn't invite her parents to the ceremony. What should anyone expect? Still, Gerry is a quiet guy. Nick had the idea Gerry never once spoke his mind about how he felt about anything. The way he looked at Nick, full of pity to the bursting point. He should have hated Nick, after everything Nick did to his daughter, after Nick took off. Then Nick showed up asking for help. Gerry should have punched Nick in the nose or slammed the door. But he didn't. Gerry had this look in his eyes. He felt bad for Nick.

"Why don't you stay?" Gerry asked. Deb was in the kitchen drying the dishes, and she'd be out any minute to tell Nick it was time to hit the road, storm or no. "This isn't letting up any time soon. You head up now and make a bed, then leave in the morning."

Nick had to share a bed with the dog because the dog had taken over the attic room as his own. Nick didn't mind the concession. He knew Cooper from before, his smooth, bronze-colored coat and jowly way of bellowing hello. The bloodhound curled in a hollow made in the quilt when Nick entered the room that Saturday evening. Nick went to bed early, around nine, and had to bow around Cooper when he lay down, which was fine. It was cold in the spare room, so they kept each other warm under the quilt. After an hour the dog straightened into Nick's body to share the mattress.

If Nick had trouble sleeping up there in the attic room, it wasn't the dog's fault. There was a birch tree outside that tapped the window with the tips of its budded branches. From time to time a branch screeched the glass and made Nick's ears ache at the surprise, at how he strained to hear every little bit of sound then, the murmuring of two voices in the room below him. The storm moved across the sky, later, beyond the birch branches, when it was no longer above them. Nick saw lightning connect cloud to cloud, far to the north, but by that time he couldn't hear the thunder.

[14 Mar 04 to 17 Jan 05; when Caleb was conceived to when Nick left]

Why did Nick leave Elisabeth and Caleb when they all lived together in Chicago?

He wasn't a bad father; in fact, he was good with Caleb, better than most new fathers with an infant, better than most experienced fathers. Both of them wanted kids (she surer than he) once they were married. Elisabeth found an entry-level job with an advertising agency that specialized in direct-mail campaigns. The gig didn't pay much—less than Nick's loading and unloading pop bottles at a warehouse, as a matter of fact—but she was insured and maternity leave was in the benefits package. *It's better to have them young,* Elisabeth said. *Who wants to be in a wheelchair when your kid graduates high school?*

It was almost disappointing to Nick how fast he knocked up his wife. He'd hoped it would be drawn out, making love without worry over the course of a year, maybe two. But it happened so quickly— probably the second time they tried to make a baby. Just like that.

Do you think it will be a girl or a boy? Elisabeth asked him that March, after she showed him the positive. *What will we name it?*

Nick quit smoking once Elisabeth was pregnant, and tried to quit drinking but was less successful at that. Still went out with friends after work, to the Touch of Class Lounge, because the beer was cheap and he was thirsty and frustrated and scared by what was happening back at the apartment, where a child was growing inside Elisabeth's abdomen. Not yet a child, a peanut, with a tail and eyes like a tadpole. Sometimes he came home late from the bar with an off-sale bottle and Elisabeth could hear Nick and his friend, Donny-from-work, when they were halfway down the block, their piercing, belligerent voices. Donny had long hair and a scraggly beard. Dreadlocks grew in his beard, that's how scraggly. He was the kind of guy who set up shots of Malört on the bar while Nick used the pisser. They were shouting, jovial, about how Donny leaned out of his minivan at a stoplight and pissed right there in the street. Nick walking along, swinging the off-sale bottle (more Malört) in its bag until the plastic gave and the bottle birthed out the bottom to the pavement and broke. Booze spread over the concrete. Nick still invited Donny in. They drank the cranberry vodka in the fridge until Donny finally left. Nick stunk like beer and vodka and cigarettes when he lay next to her, but he swore, later on, that it wasn't him who was smoking, as if that was the most important thing.

The parking lots out where he worked were all abandoned. Trees grew through cracks in the asphalt, even at the place Nick worked, so tractor-trailers had to slalom trunks. Silver maples, along with a few black walnuts and trees of Heaven—Nick would have noticed, he knew things like that.

He was plagued by the idea that Elisabeth and the kid could both die during a botched delivery. And what he'd do to get by in case that happened.

On his days off he rode the El, like a tourist. Even though he'd lived in Chicago a few years, he was awed by the city. The constant noise, the tight spaces, the idea he should be afraid of the people around him. All these things—being made a stranger. Chicago was very different from where he grew up. Especially the winters out west on the farm, the silence conspicuous—no cicadas, no June bugs, no thunder, just his feet scuttling along an iced-over field. In the city there was always the noise of things bumping into each other, the steel on steel of the El.

He rode the El to Rogers Park to look at the clinic there. Just to look. Rode south to the Loop before it returned back north, the Red Line, because it passed Wrigley, and before that DePaul, right next to the field where Elisabeth used to play soccer before her injury. Nick never saw her play—that was her prior life, the life of Sports-Lis—but he liked seeing the field, seeing campus, that neighborhood where they went on dates. As quickly as the train stopped it started again, and DePaul was a memory, Wrigley Field a glimpse out the smog-streaked window of an El car. Sometimes he stayed on to the end of the line, that mysterious Howard mentioned on the loudspeaker, to see if such a place actually existed, and who, if anybody, made it that far. Howard did exist. There was a strip mall there, a grocery store.

That day, it is noted, Nick got off at Loyola and grabbed a coffee at a Dunkin' Donuts under the El, then walked around bombed-out parking lots. It wasn't such a bad place, Nick saw, once you got away from the station. The buildings small, mostly two story, and he could see the sky, the low, dreary clouds. He strolled slow and sipped his coffee, and he arrived so quickly the clinic sort of snuck up on him. There was a storefront. Nick didn't know what he expected—activists, picketers, Evangelicals—but there was only one girl sitting out front, her hand bound in rosary beads. The girl wore a navy-blue peacoat, pink snow boots, and sat on a rectangle of cardboard to keep warm, warmer anyway, because she'd probably prayed there before and froze. Nick stopped and stared, but the girl acted like he didn't exist. He didn't. That is, he didn't matter. Not a solitary man looking at the red brick of a storefront like he'd never seen red brick before; a man staring at a building like he'd never seen a building, one shared by a handyman and a dentist and an abortion clinic. It was only an office—the windows with shades pulled tight from ceiling to floor, and no shouting Evangelicals with gritty photographs of bins filled with baby legs, baby arms, chubby baby faces.

Only that girl with the rosary, who was so cold on the pavement she kept her eyes closed. Nick set his coffee on top of a blue postal-service box and waited ten minutes before he went home. He wanted to see a woman go in the clinic, wanted to peek through the open door and see what happened to the woman, if she was sucked inside, door locked behind her. Maybe the clinic was closed. It was a Monday.

In the years after, he confessed only to Tyler, in an email, about the day he rode the Red Line and got off at Loyola and the thoughts that raced through his head.

Nick forgot about all that before long. The idea didn't return until after Caleb was born—until he held the kid every morning before Elisabeth got out of bed—and Nick would want to die, remembering how he rode the Red Line up there to the clinic.

Everything went well during delivery. It was all so usual. Elisabeth screaming *you will never fuck me again.* The doctor asking Nick to step aside. Nick waiting to sever the umbilical cord. Nick held the baby before anyone—the baby dressed in blood and wax, still connected to its cord that was still connected to Elisabeth, until Nick was handed silver scissors and cut them apart. Then he backed out of the way as a nurse weighed and measured and sucked fluid out baby's mouth and locked a security box around baby's ankle. Nick was the one who told the nurse that the baby's name was Caleb Harrison Holland. Nick figured he would call the boy Cal someday, when the boy was older, when the boy could walk. Cal Holland, which ran together in a single lilt in a way wonderful to Nick's ear.

Nick returned to work at the loading dock the next day, before Elisabeth and Caleb were even home, then started working third shift because they paid a bonus for that.

He'd get home early in the morning to watch Caleb smile in his crib, the way babies smile. Stretching the muscles of his jaw and cheeks, face to face with his daddy as the first light of morning cut through warped vinyl blinds in the apartment, where Nick had taped plastic over the windows to keep the cold out. When Nick changed a diaper, he'd lift Caleb by the ankles and hold him with his neck twisted while Nick wiped. He wasn't going to hurt the baby wrenching his arms into a onesie—somehow Nick knew how far babies could bend and twist without breaking. Nick scooped up the baby and walked around the living room, back and forth, until baby wanted to eat. Then Nick laid him in bed next to Elisabeth.

Nick was in a panic, these mornings, because he'd thought bad things before the baby was born. He'd gone to the clinic and debated if he should ask Elisabeth to take care of things. The thing that needed taken care of was Caleb Harrison Holland.

Nick struggled to level that wrong, if there was a way. Most mornings—except the morning he got in his car and drove west until he hit Cheyenne, Wyoming—he'd sneak down through the door to watch Caleb breathe in fits. Nick didn't know if it was normal for babies to breathe like that, to struggle at everything, because a baby doesn't know how to do anything, not even how to breathe or nurse, not at first. Nick would put his hand on Caleb's chest to feel the boy breathe, the heart beat, and he'd see how much Caleb looked like him, just like everyone said—*No denying that one's yours*—the big ears, the wispy cowlick. Nick kept a hand on Caleb's chest. Rubbed the other along the blue blankets, the blue onesie, the blue stuffed animal that played lullabies from a mechanism inside its gut, the velveteen rabbit Nick bought for Caleb from the hospital gift shop, one with button eyes and black-thread whiskers and long ears pert with stuffing. Nick hyperventilated those mornings, sometimes, trying to understand what bubbled up inside his chest, and he'd have to pull his hand away from his baby's body and go to the kitchen to make coffee, to stand there and force his eyes shut to stop them from leaking and wait for the first sizzling drop from the percolator.

He'd bring a travel mug to Elisabeth so she could have coffee in bed while she nursed Caleb. Elisabeth told Nick he shouldn't do that (caffeine made it hard to produce milk) but she enjoyed coffee. Sometimes Elisabeth was sad and exhausted when she woke, and she moaned about her ass bleeding. Other times she smiled. She told Nick he could lie next to them if he wanted. So he did. He snugged in behind her and held the both of them, Elisabeth and Caleb, and listened as Caleb guzzled his breakfast. Nick was cold and tired. He'd been working all night. The bed was warm.

He was a ridiculous man. A lost man. Nick could have been saved. All he had to do was stay.

The Ahls slept in late and were still asleep when Nick ate breakfast in the murky morning light. He let Cooper out and grabbed the paper from the driveway, then sat in the kitchen with a slice of cinnamon bread and grape juice he found in the fridge. Cooper by his side the whole time.

During that Christmas five years earlier, when he first met the Ahls, Nick spent a good deal of time with the dog because he was so uncomfortable in this house. If Nick was petting Cooper, he didn't have to join the conversation, didn't have to see Deb raise her eyebrows or emit a scandalized little laugh when Nick told how he was reared by cowhands or why he hadn't finished college or how he didn't mind working near Midway Airport, because there were bars there that never closed. It was foolish to tease his future mother-in-law, even if he hoped she'd have a better sense of humor about things like that.

Of course, Elisabeth didn't warn her parents that she was bringing a man with her; she didn't even tell Tyler, and then they were standing at the door together. This drifter-looking guy in a secondhand brown coat with fur around the collar, his thin mustache, his arm around their daughter. Nick didn't show his age then, not in his skin, but he was clearly older from the way he stood, embarrassment in his posture because he couldn't possibly explain how he was with a young woman like Elisabeth. And she with a smirk on one side of her taut, flushed face, her arm around his waist, like Nick being there was to punish the Ahls for something—for their being the way they were. Though the Ahls didn't like Nick, he gave no cause for animosity, except he needed a shave and more or less refused to talk about his own family when Deb asked at dinner. Elisabeth tried to assure them that Nick was *a hard worker at a job that isn't exactly stimulating* and *he had a full ride to college once* and *he makes me happy* and *who's talking about getting married? Did I say that, Mom? Maybe I want the person I love to meet my family.* Bad noise like that. Of course, maybe Deb knew more about the way these things end up than her daughter did. (They'd marry a week later, on New Year's Eve, at the Cook County courthouse. Tyler was the witness.) When Tyler asked Elisabeth if she wanted to go on a walk after dinner, Nick said it would be okay. He and Gerry sat down to watch football, the Hawaii Bowl, Nick on the couch with Cooper stretched over his lap.

The house hadn't been touched since that visit. Its quaint, homey accoutrements. A *Peanuts* calendar that hung next to a crucifix by the kitchen telephone, Deb's scribbles on certain dates, a nub of pencil that hung down the wall on a string; the spot in the pantry where a sack of kibble was kept; framed Norman Rockwell covers of the *Saturday Evening Post*; porcelain trinkets and commemorative beer bottles lined on a curio in the TV room, with the beer downed years before during Wisconsin Badger Rose Bowls, and older ones from the year the Brewers took the American League pennant but lost the World Series in seven to the Cards. The house was full of curiosities like these—oddities that constituted life itself to the Ahls.

Nick and the bloodhound went for a walk in the forest. He'd always liked large dogs. The way Cooper crashed into the cold water of the creek had a cleansing effect on Nick, on his outlook. He let Cooper off the leash once they were around the privacy fence that separated Apostle

Crossing from the woods. They followed one scent and then another and another until the dog circled a towering fir tree and gazed up the mottled trunk at nothing. Nothing Nick could see.

It was strange how Nick spent that morning playing with the dog. Strange how he spent the night with the Ahls, that he'd eaten dinner with them. Nick wasn't there to visit. He'd come to ask questions about Tyler, about Caleb and Elisabeth. But for reasons of his own, Nick didn't ask those questions. He didn't ask if Tyler had been lying to him. All of it so strange—when you scan through Tyler's emails, his letters, transcripts of his calls, like Agent Schwaller had scanned through them—you'd see how Tyler talked an awful lot about Caleb Holland. That is, he spoke to Nick about Nick's son on numerous occasions, at regular intervals. And not baby Caleb, but six-month-old Caleb, year-old Caleb, etc., etc. Tyler told stories as if the boy had lived. (*He swims by himself now . . . His hair is dark, straight, coarse like Lis, and his nose has a point to it, is narrow, like Lis . . . When he asks about his dad I tell him you're working far away and can't come home . . .*) So peculiar. Would Nick have known if Tyler was lying or telling the truth? Evidently not. Not if he didn't have contact with Elisabeth those years. Tyler was the only Ahls Nick spoke to until he went to Chippewa that spring.

Close to the Ahls's house there was a sugar maple that had been damaged in the storm. Half its limbs hung broken to the ground, though the maple wasn't such a big tree, its bark still smooth. Since it was a nice morning, Nick decided to cut the damage out in pieces. He found a bucksaw in the shed to start after the smaller branches, climbed to the fork, and set to work. He smelled sap as he sawed, and that fueled him, sawdust flittering gold to the ground in rays of light. The sound of his boots gripping the tree where its bark feathered. He worked alone, for a while, until Gerry came to see what was going on. "It's a Sunday," Gerry said, a little amused. "Day of rest, you know."

Nick felt pleased with pruning the tree, so he didn't stop, and soon enough old Ahls came grunting from behind the shed with a long ladder because Nick couldn't reach the branches far above the fork. Gerry held the ladder as Nick climbed, and the ladder swayed some because of the way Nick had to jerk the bucksaw back and forth. The swaying didn't bother Nick one bit. Nick was used to situations far more dangerous than this.

They worked like that a long time, Nick and Gerry, Cooper lying in the leaves, dozing with his head on his paws. All of them silent except to grunt, or when Nick cursed because the bucksaw teeth ate through the web of his left thumb. Both men looked to the house to see if Mrs. Ahls might tap on the window and object to the profanity. But she didn't tap; she didn't even split the shades with a disapproving digit.

Some neighbors came along the road around lunchtime and got out of their car to see what sort of work was being done.

"Cutting off the dead ones?"

"Yep," Gerry said. "There's a lot coming down."

"Cutting it up for firewood?"

"Yep."

"I see," they said, and got back in the car and drove up to where they lived.

Gerry explained how quite a few houses had been built up there along the road in the forest. Most were new, so those people wouldn't have any idea who Nick was, and maybe they thought he was Tyler, the real prodigal come home. The neighbors wouldn't come out and ask if the mystery man was Tyler Ahls. They'd wait to hear through their channels.

"Nothing else was here ten years ago," Gerry said. "Just our house, Apostle Crossing. Things change a lot."

With the damaged limbs down and in segments, they piled the logs in a wheelbarrow, then stacked them against the side of Gerry's woodshop. Then Gerry asked Nick inside so he could show off what he was working on. Nick sat on a stool, the dog by his feet, and worried the gash near his thumb the saw had made. Gerry held up a few pieces, a birdhouse, a comments box, a replacement head he was carving for John the Baptist. "Keeps me busy," he said.

Elisabeth wasn't like her father so much, not in terms of personality. Gerry was difficult to talk to about serious matters—too defensive about his politics or theology, too guarded about his emotions. You had to work to bring him out. It's because too much had built up inside him. His shame, his dashed hopes, the disappointments of his life. Or so one could extrapolate. It was different with Elisabeth. She liked to talk about failure and how optimism sometimes betrayed a person—but how failure was no reason to give up hope. She told Nick this more than once: *Don't give up hope,* even about stupid things, like when the guys at the warehouse were assholes. This sounded odd coming from an apostate like her, so close to *don't lose faith.* Nick thought it was because of her soccer days and the national squad she was on, team spirit, cheering on her teammates, the belief in each other, but it could be she was like that because she was young when Nick knew her and her dreams hadn't yet been taken from her.

As he sat on a stool in Ahls's workshop and waited for Ahls to speak, Nick's hands shook.

"We hired a PI to track you down in Chicago," Gerry said. "But you were long gone, weren't you? Stepped out for a pack of cigarettes, is that how you do it?"

Gerry stood with his back to Nick, moved his planes and awls and blocks around the workbench, cleaned up without actually putting anything away. He grabbed a chisel and pressed the head with the meat of his palm to etch grooves into a piece of scrap wood, one groove close to the next, for no purpose. Nick wondered if Gerry was finally going to curse him, if he'd say something that should have been said for a long time now—a scolding Nick had been waiting for, to be told off by one of the Ahls clan once and for all, like he deserved. But maybe Gerry Ahls had given up all that. Maybe Gerry really did try to walk in light and exile hate from his heart.

"I don't think that PI we put on you is worth much," he admitted, peeking out the one dusty window in his workshop. "Two times we used that fella, and both times he comes up empty."

Gerry laughed without smiling, then picked a straw-bristled brush from a hook and swept curled, blond-colored shavings off his bench to the floor. The bristles were worn down, Gerry had used the brush so much, what had been his own father's brush.

"She kept your name. Goes by Lis Holland, and that means something about what she wants," he said. "If I tell you where Lis is, do you promise to check on her once, then that's the end of all this? You'll leave her alone? Because, you know, she's better off without you."

"I want to see Caleb. I have money for him."

Gerry looked away from the workbench to read something in Nick's face. "I'm only telling you because you should know," he said. "Elisabeth went to Omaha. She works at Saint Wenceslaus Hospital and lives in an apartment building at Thirty-First and Jackson Street called Mount Vernon. Remember your promise. One time. That's it."

In the workshop, Ahls told Nick about Caleb.

Nick acted unaffected in the months after this, like he knew nothing—what a strange man he was—so he wouldn't have to talk about the fact that Caleb had died, and how embarrassing it was that it took Nick three years and coming to Chippewa to hear what happened to his son. That whole morning and the night before, Deb and Gerry Ahls avoided the subject. But then Gerry and Nick sat close in the workshop. The space heater kicking on, Gerry cleaning the tools that had been handed down through the generations of his family but would be handed down no more.

"I don't know how this happened," he said.

"What do you mean?"

"Nobody telling you about Caleb." Ahls hooked the brush to the pegboard, then swept at the workbench with his hands. "Didn't you ever question," he asked, "why you never heard a single word about how the boy was growing up?"

Nick with a devastated look on his face. Confused, with just a whit of what was coming. "I haven't talked to Lis in years," he said.

"It happened right after you left. He never got a fair start."

"What does that mean?"

"He died."

"Caleb?"

"We tried to find you. That private investigator was supposed to track you down and tell you, but he didn't have a clue where you were."

All the color drained from Nick. Ahls should have warned him that bad news was coming, told him to get down from the shop stool he sat on, but Nick didn't waver, didn't fall. He asked where Caleb was—if he was buried in Chicago.

"He's buried here," Ahls said. "I'll take you."

Gerry wanted to tell Nick everything about the funeral—what Caleb looked like in that little white casket, how Gerry himself made the box in his woodshop and all the particulars that went into it, how it was native spruce he used, boards he took from the house Granddaddy Ahls built when he came from Alsace-Lorraine. Boards Gerry ripped from that house when they tore it down in 1975. He saved the lumber for a special purpose all those years. He'd tried his best, under the circumstances, to make the ceremony special. Of course they all did. Why wouldn't they?

They had the service right there in Apostle Crossing. Deb insisted. They buried Caleb in the family plot on the other side of the hill.

This was something the folks in Chippewa liked to talk about. The little white coffin with silver finish work. All sorts of rituals, the witnesses said. "Ave Maria" sung in contralto, sure, that's usual. But the coffin was on display for three days at Apostle Crossing. Why would they do that? What did they expect would happen? What miracle? Then at the funeral. Deb Ahls wanted to wash the baby's feet before the burial. They're not even Jewish, but that was what she wanted. They lifted the coffin lid one last time. They took the booties off the baby's feet. A little washtub there—this with the pastor and the guests waiting outside in the cold. Elisabeth couldn't take it. She grabbed the little guy and held him. They tried to put him back in the coffin, but she wouldn't give him up. She held his stiff little body. Collapsed to the ground holding him until finally the pastor talked some sense into her and got the coffin closed for the ceremony, and then they finally got the coffin in the ground. They didn't even do the thing with the washing of the feet.

Gerry didn't mention any of this to Nick. But it has been noted.

Nick left Chippewa that morning, after Gerry drove him over the hill to the Ahls family plot, to the grave under a boxwood tree. Nick went back to where he was working in Missouri and put in for a transfer. This too is noted. He put in for a transfer to Omaha.

FILE 4

AGT FRANK SCHWALLER

01 OCT 08

If he knew where she was, did Nick go see Elisabeth first thing once he got to Omaha? He had her address, the name of the hospital where she worked.

Agent Schwaller would ask Nick this, but Nick didn't say, just smiled and acted dumb. Schwaller knew Nick had gone to Saint Wenceslaus that September, but Elisabeth was out to lunch at that moment; Nick spoke only to the charge nurse, Sandy Laika, and for some reason never went back to the hospital after that day. The agent could only speculate. Was there something else behind Nick's visit?

Schwaller redoubled his focus on Nick after Elisabeth said the name—that first time the agent was at Saint Wenceslaus, when she inexplicably mentioned her husband. (*God no! Why on earth would Nick Holland be in the Middle East?*) Nick Holland wasn't hard to find. He was working under his SSN for Midland Pacific and had been for years. Track laborer, repairman. He did line work out in Wyoming, Colorado, Texas, until he was transferred to Missouri to try his hand at bridge inspection. That's when his employer discovered his real talent: hanging from the underside of a bridge. Nick could have been foreman if he wanted the headaches that came with cozying up to management. Refusing a supervisor position seemed so typical for Nick, once Schwaller got to know his history. That undercutting of self. The striving for mediocrity.

Schwaller knew Nick was working in Omaha, that he'd transferred there a month before. He tracked Nick to the repair yard one morning. Spotted Nick loading a truck with tool belts and safety gear, orange vest, hard hat, brown-tinted safety glasses, hammer drill, rubber and steel mallets, a blue water jug with MPRR stenciled in red spray paint on the side, a bag of ice dumped in the cooler.

"Are you Nick Holland?" Schwaller asked. Nick didn't answer. He looked Schwaller over, then went back to loading the truck.

"Holland!" the foreman barked at Nick, hustling to catch up in his disheveled foreman's way. "You got to talk to this guy before you head out. He's law enforcement. Tell him what he wants to know so I don't have to worry." The foreman stomped back over the gravel to his trailer on the other side of the yard. Didn't even wait for Nick to respond.

"It's funny you're in Omaha," Schwaller said. He was in his black suit and black wayfarer shades. The sun was rising, nearly 7:30 a.m. From the way he dressed, Schwaller looked like he'd been up all night playing baccarat at Rick's Café Américain rather than in a double bed at an Embassy Suites in downtown Omaha. "Do you know why I'm here?"

"Nope. You going to make me guess?"

Nick was brawnier than he looked in the photos from his file, which were old, of course. He had big forearms and squared shoulders. His fingers stubby and knuckled. His skin tanned dark, his hair bleached. Working outside will do that to a man, Schwaller supposed.

"Tyler Ahls. Tell me what you know about him."

To his credit, Nick didn't miss a beat. He gazed into the cooler a moment before he spoke, kept calm, stirred Gatorade powder into the water, then reached in a hand to break up clumps that floated on top. "What's this about?"

"Has it been a while since you heard that name?"

"Sure it has."

"So you don't know Tyler's general whereabouts?"

"Asia. Isn't it Asia?"

"Or if he was previously associated with any anti-American, or, say, anti-Western groups? No? I don't suppose you would know anything about that."

In a postmortem to his superiors, a month later, Agent Schwaller would try to explain himself, and the tack he took in questioning Nick.

Maybe it was simple of me. I didn't want to pick on the man. It was obvious he wanted to be done with me and get out to his job—not that I particularly cared what he wanted. Now, would it have been a coup for me if Nick Holland was still in contact with Tyler Ahls? Certainly. A bridge inspector for a major rail line connected to a terror suspect? Of course. But what was there to go on? Nick was a flake. He'd never been to AfPak—he'd never even been on an airplane. Nick didn't believe in anything. No religion, a college dropout, abandoned his wife, his kid. If this was a narcotics case, smuggling, a guy like Nick Holland would be suspicious. But not global terror. He didn't fit in with a bunch of true believers. Though he kept in touch with Tyler, didn't he? And he seemed fairly motivated to speak to his wife about something, right? There had to be something going on. (Agt Frank Schwaller, Mobile Audio, 21 Nov 08, Washington, DC, 20535. J. Edgar Hoover Building.)

"You know how much is involved in getting track time to start a bridge inspection?" Nick stood with one foot on the cab tread and lectured Agent Schwaller on the bureaucratic annoyances of working for Midland Pacific. The truck was loaded and ready to go, an alarm dinging because the driver's-side door hung open. "Go up to the office and look at the charts the dispatchers have to work with. These lines run twenty-four-seven, with trains coming along every forty minutes, and that's if it's slow. We're talking a small window. I've got to get out on that bridge and do a visual. If there's time, I can drop down and do a sound test on the column pylons before the next freight comes through, but I won't cut it too close with something like that. There's no way I'm using a cherry picker with time that tight. I'm climbing." Nick glared at the agent. "You're eating up my window. What do you really want to know?"

"Why don't you talk to your wife?" Schwaller smirked, puffed out his chest a little, felt his neck pop into alignment as he tilted his head to look Nick in the eye from around his shades. "Is that out of line to ask? Because I saw her yesterday, in the course of investigating her brother, and Elisabeth Holland—she still goes by your name, you know—she has no clue where you could be. Isn't that odd?"

"Fuck off." Nick pulled himself up by the steering wheel and turned over the motor.

"She got a restraining order against you?" Schwaller leaned in the truck window so Nick couldn't drive away. "Why not simply pay the lady a visit? She's your wife."

"I made a promise."

That didn't make sense to Schwaller. He must have wondered, a promise to who?

"Where did you go when you left?" he asked. "Where did you disappear to? Is there any chance you met up with Tyler on a mountainside in Central Asia?"

"Tyler was a good kid," Nick said. "If folks had let him alone for ten minutes, he'd of been fine. It's a damn tragedy what happened to him. He was trying to get away from something, but he couldn't do it."

"That's an idea you identify with? Running away from people?"

Nick stomped on the accelerator and tore into the gravel and headed to the bridge.

Schwaller tracked Nick to a river crossing near Plattsmouth. Spent half the morning trying to get up to the bridge. The agent was a remarkably slow driver. He was deliberate, careful, rarely went over fifty miles per hour on the highway and often under thirty in the city. He had a lot on his mind and didn't want the fact he was driving to distract him. He couldn't keep pace with Nick and was late getting to the bridge. That, and he got stuck on a dusty gravel track he thought was an access road. It provided access somewhere, just not to the deck of the rail bridge.

Schwaller slowed under the bridge, pulled his car next to a steel guardrail that protected the edge of a weedy slope. Below that, the muddy Missouri shined white with glare across its surface. Four bridges spanned the river at this spot. Two for the railroad, one for light car traffic, and the fourth, the newest, the most aesthetically space aged, cradled a natural gas pipeline.

The agent saw men working through his binoculars. He picked out Nick and watched a while, leaning out the window of his rental car because he didn't want to dirty his oxfords in the gravel. There was trash all over, close to the water. Crushed cans of Busch Light in the weeds, toadstools that grew out of a deflated muskrat corpse. An abandoned trailer with its door hanging open, shattered glass clinging to a window frame, soiled rugs rotting in a pile out front. Some of the stuff in the weeds was unrecognizable it was so putrefied. Cinder blocks, radial tires, a drawer from a desk, five-gallon tin buckets with the bottoms rusted through. Somebody had spray-painted OK across the corrugated steel of the trailer the last time it flooded. OK meant there were no bodies inside. It unnerved Schwaller to think about the kind of people who lived in the middle of nowhere, like Ted Kaczynski had before they captured him in Montana. Across the Missouri there was a campground where a few RVs plugged into hookups, near a wooden dock that was anchored to a sandbar at the eastern edge of the water. Two fishing poles stuck out of the sand with their lines drifting into an eddy, but nobody was there to reel even if a fish did bite. Nobody Schwaller could see.

He backtracked. Followed a street through Plattsmouth, one that put him on a narrow toll bridge. He paid a dollar at the booth to cross and ended up in Iowa. At least he could park his rental along a ditch near the tracks on the Iowa side, where he waited by two Midland Pacific trucks. There was a crew of six on the bridge. All six of them glanced around inspecting, marked chits on clipboards—*Doing a visual,* Schwaller figured—Nick pacing back and forth, fidgeting with the yellow Kevlar straps that snugged over his shoulders and between his legs, with the carabiners that jingled on his belt, a cigarette dangling from his lip as he asked the others what they saw. Suddenly a timer sounded and Nick told everybody to get off the bridge because their window was about to close. A train was coming.

When Nick hopped down, he went directly to the ditch where Schwaller waited.

"You never talked to her all this time?" Schwaller asked.

"No," Nick said, not one bit surprised to see the agent again. It would be difficult for Schwaller to sneak up on anyone connected to Tyler now that his video aired on the news. "It's been years since I talked to my wife."

"You never called?"

"Not really. Not how you mean it."

Schwaller almost asked Nick about Caleb right then and there. Maybe, he thought, ask: *Didn't you ever talk to your son on the phone? No? Do you know for certain he's alive?* Maybe that was too crass, even for Schwaller.

"Why do you keep bothering me? I told you I don't know what Tyler got up to. He was supposed to be mountain climbing. I don't know a thing about that video."

"Sure, I believe you don't know much. But don't lie about Tyler. We know he sent you emails. You used your work account to reply. Didn't you think somebody would be watching?"

"What are you talking about?"

"Your correspondence with Tyler Ahls." Nick could be coy with the agent all he wanted, it wasn't going to work. "What were you hoping to get out of talking to Tyler?"

"If you snooped in my email, you should know."

"Humor me."

Nick sighed, sucked his bottom lip in under his front teeth. The agent must have had him speculating what was already known and what there was left to hide. "He told me about my son," Nick said, looking down to his boots. "I guess you know about my son."

"Do you still talk to Tyler?"

"Not since he's missing."

"If Tyler contacted you again, would you respond?"

"I don't know. It would depend on what he said." Nick didn't blink. He put his hands on his hips and elongated his body to stretch his back. He was telling the truth.

"Tell me," Nick said. "Don't you have a job to do besides bothering people?"

Schwaller stopped, eyebrows raised. "What do you think I'm doing? This is my job."

Nick snorted, flicked the end of his cigarette into the gravel, then checked his watch. There was a train coming, they could feel it, hear it inching out the cutout in the bluffs, so intensely loud as it passed that neither said a word because all sound was washed away by the hydraulic hiss of the railcars, the glare of the horn as the operator blasted hello to the repair crew. All those railcars painted in the familiar black and green of the Midland Pacific. These were grain cars, Schwaller knew that. Growing up in Detroit, he had an uncle who used to sneak him into a massive switchyard, this when Schwaller was eight, nine, ten, so he could watch and listen, to pass the time on a Sunday afternoon. Schwaller felt like it was something special to be washed over by the roar of a train, a slow-moving one like this, a noise that seemed to go on forever, trapped and amplified by the river bluffs, loud enough that Schwaller didn't feel his body, not like he normally did, the whole world an erasure, until the train passed.

"Why did you leave?"

Schwaller took his sunglasses off and put them in the pocket of his jacket. He sat down on a rail, the steel still warm from the train. The other workers hustled back out to their positions to resume the inspection, but that question froze Nick.

"She cheat on you? Was that it? You worried the baby wasn't yours?"

"No."

"She not let you go out drinking with your friends?"

"It wasn't like that."

"Nag you to make more money?"

"Look." Nick put on his hard hat. "The clock is ticking. If you're out here, I'm going to put you to work."

Schwaller laughed. He'd almost had Nick, he thought. Schwaller wasn't even sure why he pivoted away from Tyler to ask these questions. It was that nobody cared, he told himself; he wouldn't get in trouble for picking on a man like Nick Holland. Agent Schwaller could do what he wanted—and he wanted to see what he could get out of this man, out of these people. They were challenging him, weren't they, mocking his skills as an agent. The agent kicked the ballast so a few rocks tumbled down the long grassy hill to the water.

"You looking for a job?" Nick lit another cigarette and angled his body back to the bridge. "As far as I can tell, this federal investigator thing isn't working out for you."

"Of course I'm not looking for a job," Schwaller said. Then, in the next breath, on his feet and following, "You don't think I could handle it, do you?"

"Why not. But it doesn't pay well." Nick unhooked all the straps he'd been fighting to get straight and tossed them in the bed of the truck. He stood straighter, smiled at the agent, happier in only orange vest and hard hat and tool belt, without all the extra. "It looks simple, doesn't it? Walking back and forth, watching the signals, observing the condition of concrete and steel and wood. Are you at all perceptive? That's important. There's a lot to do, and you can't spend much time on one thing before you move on. And it's dangerous work running around on rails. Everything is greasy out there—new guys never think about that. These are freight trains we're talking about. Oil, grease, diesel grime. One slip is enough to finish you. There's shortages up and down the line—if you're looking for work, they'll take you today. This could be exactly what you're looking for, to get out of this FBI racket where all you do is ask dumb questions all day. Rail work might be interesting for you. Fresh air. Exercise."

Agent Schwaller excused himself. He went back to his rental and whipped around to the county road and over the bridge built for cars, back to the Nebraska side over the river. He watched Nick from his rental to see how the work went. Muttered "Fuck you" in Nick's direction, flipped him the bird from behind the dashboard. After a while the agent went into town and got a burger at a café, then came back. Nick was still at it on the bridge, alone out over the river while the others ate lunch in their truck. Schwaller could barely see him because he'd moved on to inspecting the subsurface of the track. Nick hopping from position to position on the rail ties, probably thinking he moved slow, that he was careful, because there was nothing to catch him if he slipped. To Schwaller, it looked like Nick rushed, moved too fast and something bad was going to happen. Nick dropping down to smack a pylon with his rubber mallet, putting his ear by the steel to decipher the quality of reverberation. If there was a catwalk, Schwaller didn't see one. But there had to be at least a ledge to stand on. Nick up and down again. A hand hooked around one of the rails to steady himself. Even the guys in the truck shook their heads. They didn't laugh about Nick. They were pissed. Maybe they heard of this guy, Holland. Maybe they worked with him before. Nick way out on the bridge, only water underneath him, a hundred feet down. Those other guys getting nervous. Sitting back in the truck with the windows down, then Holland crawls out there again—just to show off, just because he's an asshole. Didn't even put his cigarette out. He was good, but they'd seen good before. A guy like that, one of these days he'd get the whole crew in trouble for breaking the rules. And all he had to do was put on the straps. That wasn't too much to ask.

Schwaller watched all afternoon from his rental. He didn't ask another word of Nick. Just took notes and tried to figure out what was going on and if he should care or not. The agent had no idea whether it was a misguided instinct to think Nick Holland was somehow important to the rest of the wide world, but he wanted to find out.

Schwaller saw Sandy Laika at his hotel every night he was in Omaha. She popped up in the course of the investigation a few times. Sandy was the charge nurse on Elisabeth's floor—they'd met when Elisabeth was in nursing school and were friends outside work. The agent figured Sandy knew more than she let on, that she might be a pivot between these misfits, so Schwaller had her tailed. Who did Sandy meet? She met Nick Holland. Counting Nick's trip up to the third floor of Saint Wenceslaus, they saw each other half a dozen times over a month. It made Schwaller's head hurt trying to figure how everything fit.

Before all that, Sandy had grabbed Agent Schwaller at the hospital, his first day in Omaha, as he got in the third-floor elevator to leave. "My shift ends soon," she said. "You want to meet somewhere?"

"You serious?"

"Yes, for coffee."

"How about drinks?"

Sandy stopped at home to change into a denim skirt and white tee shirt, then met Schwaller downtown at his hotel. She looked lost when the automatic doors split so she could enter, Schwaller watching from across the lobby. She was tall, he had no trouble spotting her. She must have been nervous meeting a man at a hotel, the way she wandered rather than ask where to go at the front desk; how she hurried, her legs bending at the knees because she was in a tight outfit, that skirt; how it was difficult to move without her clothes bunching, so she kept her long arms at her sides. Still, she was resolute, her limbs loose and lithe enough to give the impression of confidence, with little fear stiffening her joints. At thirty-nine she didn't let a little shame stop her, even if she was embarrassed to walk the perimeter—all the open space of the lobby, an artificial brook that wound round the hotel babbling over pebbles—until she found who she was looking for. Agent Schwaller waited at the bar like he said he would, sipping a Knob Creek on the rocks.

She had what he was having, once she found him. She asked: "Why are you bothering Lis about her brother? As of last week, she thought he was dead, don't you know that?"

Of course the agent knew all about Tyler. (He had just returned from eating chicken schnitzel and cottage cheese at Elisabeth's house, but he didn't mention that to Sandy.)

"It's a good one, the Ahls stuff," Schwaller said. "Sometimes they put you on a case, you never know. But this is invigorating. If I close this case, I'll be proud. I'll have done a good job and served my country."

Sandy tilted her head at this, confused, whispered, "Yikes." Talking to the agent appeared to make her uncomfortable in her clothes, how she flattened her skirt and pinched the hem of her shirt between her fingertips. Her tee shirt was tight, she surely wore it for a reason, but she kept looking down at her chest, her abdomen, to see if its white material was see-through. It wasn't, not much, only how her complexion produced a bronzish shadow under the bleached-white material.

Schwaller kept track of the tab that night so he could pay. They weren't drinking much anyway. Sandy wasn't going to get drunk, he realized, like he thought she might. She seemed to actually like talking to him, her honey-brown eyes on him, how she only looked away to redo her lipstick as he went on and on about his job and his perspective of global events; he talked about capitalism, the war on terror, the thirst extremists had for murder. "These factors influence everyday life in the modern world," he said. "They make things a family matter, for a family like the Ahls, if Tyler has in fact been converted to the Axis of Evil. Or, you know, if he's in trouble."

He sat with his foot up on the middle rung of his bar stool, trying to draw her out. Their drinks had been empty half an hour and she still listened, swirling the ice in its melt, waiting to see if he'd order her another. He could have bought a third round, but he didn't, not right away, not while they conversed on important things like the strength and vitality of the nation and what he was doing personally to make that strength endure.

"What kind of evidence do you have on the Ahls?" Sandy asked him. "I know you can't tell me. But what do you hope to find? Are you checking out everyone? Or just the Ahls?"

"That's dangerous, Nurse Laika. If you know I can't answer, then why ask?"

"You wouldn't be checking out *me*, would you? Or my mother, for example?"

He laughed. "As a matter of fact, if you didn't notice, I *am* checking you out. Your mother, on the other hand, I'm not aware of her."

That Sandy had been so eager to meet Schwaller became a very curious thing. He thought she was attracted to him or knew something about Elisabeth Holland she wanted to tell, or both. Still, if Sandy didn't sleep with him that night—and he wasn't so sure they should sleep together, ethically, if she was an asset—then he would become very interested in what she was hiding. This was a new mystery in the mind of the agent, which happened sometimes when he picked up a case, that the variables grew exponentially faster than the constants. Of course, like everyone, Sandy did have something to hide.

Schwaller asked what she knew about Nick Holland. Had she heard of him? What kind of guy was he? Had Elisabeth mentioned anything about Nick? Anything he'd done?

"Oh, not really. He was her husband, I know. That was all before Elisabeth moved to Omaha. I never met the guy."

"You haven't?" He eyed her, brought his glass to his lips to buy a moment, confused why Sandy would lie about Nick. "I don't understand the attraction to a guy like Nick. I know a bit about him. I shouldn't tell you this, but we've been on Nick Holland a while." Schwaller held a finger to his lips and shushed. "Tell me, what did Elisabeth see in him? He isn't such a great guy. Kind of a loser if you ask me."

With no hesitation: "Maybe he said dopey things to her. 'Lay next to me. Rest your head on my shoulder.' Maybe he said stuff like that when she was feeling bad. Called her 'pretty baby.' And she liked that kind of stuff from a man."

"She tell you this?"

"What? You think women talk to each other or something? No, no, no—"

"Okay. Dumb question. But seriously. Why? If you know so much about it: Why did she love him?"

"You think she's ever stopped loving him?"

"That's another question. Tell me, though. This is a thing I can't understand."

Sandy bit her lip, smoothed the hem of her shirt to her hips. She looked sad having to think about Elisabeth loving Nick, and how things worked out between them. The way her voice went raspy all of a sudden—still teasing, flirty, but weighted.

"Isn't it enough if she loves him? How am I supposed to know why? Doesn't he have a nice face? Didn't he go to the trouble of meeting her family?"

"Anyone could do that."

"No. You're wrong. Not everybody is good at those things."

Schwaller slicked back his hair. He smiled and sipped from the melt of his highball to shut himself up, because Sandy was about to say something good. She sat up straight. She looked him in the eyes.

"Maybe all those things don't matter anyway. Maybe Nick listened to her. Or their bodies pieced together nice and he kissed her how she liked. You know? Maybe his cock fit her just right. Not too small, but doesn't hurt. The things you don't forget about a guy. Love is like remembering how these things feel."

"Muscle memory. The data locked in their bodies. That's what you're saying?"

"You're stupid, aren't you?"

He replied with a wink.

Sandy looked annoyed at this kind of joking. She sighed, narrowed her eyes at the agent. "Why do you ask all these things? I don't like it. Does the FBI really care if Lis and Nick had true love?"

"Let me ask. Does Elisabeth know Nick is in Omaha?"

"What do you mean?" Sandy asked.

"Come on. At least you know he's here, right? You know Nick." Schwaller laughed, played with the end of his chin as Sandy squirmed on her stool. "You claim to know nothing, but I think there's more than you let on. I think you know a lot."

"You're mistaken. I only know what you tell me. And what I told you before."

"Okay. You sure you don't know Nick, though?"

"I don't know him."

Of course, Schwaller knew she was lying. But he didn't know why she was lying.

You see a man like Nick Holland—his baked features like adobe, his shoulders hard, and his disposition as difficult, unyielding—it's hard to imagine him ever charming a young woman, hard to imagine anyone loving him. Maybe he's always been a shithead, as his file suggests, but more than likely he wasn't always such an asshole. Not like he was to Agent Schwaller by the bridge, for no reason.

Nick had a softness in his voice, in his tenor, in the way his tongue worked the language slowly. You can intuit some sensitivity in a voice like that—and perhaps, years prior, a capacity for empathy, for love, etc., etc.

Such inferences may have been too much for Schwaller. In any event, there were things about Nick Holland the agent couldn't know—things only perceptible to the eye of God—like when Nick took Elisabeth to Goose Island to look for geese on their first date, then junkshopping in Wicker Park because she liked doing stuff like that. By the end of the day she had a DARE tee shirt, an owl-shaped napkin holder, and a wire basket for her Schwinn. A decent haul by all accounts. They stopped in at a place that served red beer and the night went on from there.

Nick worked in shipping then. He loaded trucks at a facility for a soft-drink bottler out by Midway and Bedford Park. He'd been at it a few years, after he left college eighteen credits short of a degree, not that it mattered by then. Elisabeth was a month away from graduating herself. She majored in life sciences, had contributed on a project researching the reproductive cycle of aphids, that was the feather in her cap. She wasn't such a strong student; it didn't bother her that Nick was a dropout and looked like a dirtbag. What she liked was hearing Nick talk. His patient way of laying out a sentence. His soft voice, the way he slipped into an accent when he wasn't paying attention to the way he talked, his *g*'s dropping, the lilt of cowboy poetry sneaking in. He wasn't such a yokel—what college he had, he got on scholarship—but he was unrefined. He didn't know how to act in restaurants: if he should unfold his napkin when he sat down or when the food arrived, if he was allowed to pour his own wine, if he could use his finger to dislodge the nub of meat from a mussel. Maybe these should have been red flags Elisabeth noticed. But the way these things work, his lack of pretension would have been endearing. And if you look at her file, it's not like she was a debutante home from finishing school.

Sure, there were pieces of Nick's character in his file, data any agent with proper clearance could study. How Nick was raised alone by his father because his mother ran off when he was six and the woman (Cathy Wulfe Holland, only twenty-six herself when she ran) ended up incarcerated thirteen years at Women's Correctional Center in York, in a cell once occupied by Caril Ann Fugate, coincidentally, as was documented in a 1985 article from the *York News-Times*. (*It didn't scare me one bit, sleeping there.*) Deputies picked up Cathy in a backwoods trailer on a Ponca reservation, a few counties over, after she ran off with a young man. She was cooking PCP in the trailer, from a recipe that consisted of egg whites, food dye, and a distillation of peppercorns. (A powder resulted, as was her intent, even if what she made wasn't PCP by chemical delineation.) She and her young man also smashed out windows at veterinary offices looking for horse tranquilizers, which was more clearly illegal. Most of Cathy's life was documented in public files in various courthouses across north-central Nebraska, and in newspaper articles that all featured a photo of her with permed hair and lots of makeup—how her first marriage ended in divorce when she was four months pregnant with Nick, and her second marriage (to Harry Holland) began only three weeks later. She died of a stroke not long after prison, at the age of forty-one. (A year before Nick dropped out of college, it is noted.) Cathy managed to stay out of the public record her last couple years and left a notarized and legally binding demand to give everything of value to Nicholas Holland after her creditors were done with what remained of her. When she died, Nick got her car, the same Buick he still drove, the same he fled in from Chicago. A bit heavy-handed, that, but Nick's life tended toward melodrama, even if he was simple in style, dress, demeanor.

It fell to Harry and the farm help he employed to raise Nick. Those helpers weren't great men, but they felt for Nick, a little boy abandoned by his mom. Duty tugged at them, obligation, a code of honor they were bound to follow. They taught him manners and kept him fed and let him sit up in the cab of the tractor sometimes to look at old issues of *Playboy*. They did a nice job, all things considered. Nick played eight-man football, third base for the Legion team, graduated co-valedictorian with a big-hipped girl who had frizzy braids and wore a plaid cowgirl button-down in every picture. Among the books he moved to Elisabeth's place in Boystown were two high school yearbooks, their latex covers grimy from the rooms he dragged them to since leaving the farm, dorm to dorm, studio to studio, city to city, along to Chicago. The yearbooks were important to him, though he hardly resembled the kid in those pages. Nick Holland of Jackson Regional Senior High was president of the German Club. (*You speak German?* Elisabeth asked him. *Ja. Ein kleines bisschen.*) Chubby in the cheeks a little, smooth-faced and enthusiastic. This Nick, he wore a black Stetson to prom. In most photos he stood without particular distinction, in the back rows of clubs and on the sidelines, but his familiar figure was tall and broad-shouldered and worried in the eyes, so Elisabeth immediately said, *That's you. There you are.*

Did his school counselors identify him as depressive at the time? Does his file say anything about that? Did he do drugs? Did he attempt suicide in high school? Was he an outsider?

The file has nothing to say about that. His medical records are bare beyond his height, weight, his inoculations, that he contracted bronchitis in junior high. He was a dedicated student, an athlete of some distinction, as far as small towns go. He was solid.

By all accounts, Nick enjoyed living in Chicago. Sometimes that country-boy Nick emerged—staring up to the vanishing point of a skyscraper on Michigan Avenue, caught on a security camera, his gait a little bow-legged. He was polite to strangers, always *please* and *thanks* and *watch your step, ma'am, it's slick there,* pointing out icy spots to ladies crossing the street. He learned courtesy without a matronly influence in his childhood. Harry and the hired hands watched out for Nick and taught him to ride a horse and drive a truck and keep a dip of Copenhagen in his lip without swallowing. Along the way these rough and wandering men must have taught Nick to say *please* and *thanks* and *watch out the baling wire don't lop your thumbs off.*

He could be endearing sometimes, especially when Elisabeth met him.

It was on a south shore beach across the state line when she looked in his eyes and knew she could love him. This was Indiana Dunes State Park. Elisabeth made him drive her there. Nick stood on a seawall by the bathhouse and smoked a Camel while he surveyed the landscape in his green checked flannel shirt, a breeze brisking away the smoke on a line as soon as it left his nose, the same direction the breeze blew his hair back to reveal the soft spots in his hairline. Elisabeth with her digital camera raised to take his photo. They walked the beach where sand was smudged with clumps of tall grass and lone bare trees poked through here and there. She pulled along to a gap where two dunes split and a path led to the water, a little windbreak of dogwood shrubs and sapling cottonwoods and grapevines where they could see the lake, the light blue of the nearer water at the shore and the dark blue beyond, where the water was deep.

Elisabeth took off her hoodie once they settled into the spot, then her jeans. She wore a baby blue bikini, her legs and arms and cleavage erupting with goose bumps as she folded her clothes and put them into the grocery sack and dropped her cell phone on top. "I told you it was too cold for a bikini," Nick said, pointing at her goose bumps. But she didn't listen. She unclasped her bikini top and it fell behind her. Why not? She'd done this before, on beaches in Italy, on pontoon boats in the Dells. Leaning back on her hands, her body luminescent, shining pale in the sun. Which is why she wanted some sun, her chest more windburned than tan, a Windy City red that blotched her skin. She had a little fold of belly she didn't bother sucking in—her after-soccer paunch, her ice-cream-when-she-wanted-ice-cream, her pizza-and-beers-on-weeknights.

Nick glanced at her chest. Did a double take, then stiffened. She'd remember how his face burned red—she'd tell this to Sandy Laika, years later—how Nick scanned the beach to see if anyone else was seeing her or if the show was for him alone. "Don't blush," she told him. "Nobody sees." He looked at her right in the tits to show he wasn't a prude, even if he couldn't look her in the eyes. "I'm not blushing," he lied. Like he hadn't seen her naked a dozen times. Like she wasn't already in a bikini. "They're only nipples," she said. "I can cover up."

"Don't do that," he said. He stood and lit a cigarette and walked to the edge of the hollow. There was a person nearby, after all, a guy in a rugby jersey who threw a stick of driftwood to his dog, and the dog fetching, coming closer.

"It doesn't matter." Elisabeth laughed, Nick looking out at the guy playing fetch with a black Lab. Nick stood in front of Elisabeth and smoked, then rutted a hole with his boot tip to bury the cigarette when he was done.

She reached back to string the bikini top under her breasts and straightened the straps so she didn't get pinched when she redid the clasp. In a minute she put her clothes on too. She wasn't mad, just baffled, amused. Was Nick that jealous? That strange? That much of a prude? He didn't act like a prude when they were alone. But that was different. He seemed older all of a sudden, which he was. Nick was eight years older than Elisabeth.

He joked about it once her clothes were on. Shrugged, embarrassed, that contrite laughter in his eyes. "When we tell our kids," he said, "maybe we leave that part out."

What did Elisabeth want when she took him to the dunes? For Nick to propose?

No, she didn't want that, not exactly, not then—though she would have said yes if he had proposed at the dunes, if he'd done it the right way. If he brought a ring and stopped her while they walked the beach and got on bended knee and recited all the ways he adored her. If he'd done that, she would have married him that instant. But Nick didn't do anything the right way. At the dunes, he stared out at nothing and held a paperback copy of *Steppenwolf* with the pages rolled over the spine.

One of them had to say something. Just being practical. If they wanted to stay together, they had to start thinking a little farther into the future than next weekend. That's normal.

She just told him. "I want us to move in together."

His eyes cut to her behind his sunglasses, his brow wrinkled. He folded *Steppenwolf* over a finger to hold his page. "When's your lease up? A month?"

She nodded, speechless now, like it had taken every bristle of courage to burst out those seven words.

"All right," Nick said. "Me moving in with you?"

She nodded.

They felt the sand shift underneath the blanket and stared at the shore as far as the shore stretched, which really wasn't all that far.

"We're moving in together," Elisabeth said. "I'm happy."

In the evening, after work, Nick returned the truck to the repair yard and drove his own car back to the city. His Buick. He went home and showered before eating at a barbecue place around the block from the Kellogg Rooming House. There was a restaurant up front at the Smoke Pit and a lounge in the back. You had to take a different door to get to the lounge, as it was separate from the restaurant even though they shared the same name and the same staff as far as Agent Schwaller could tell. On the roof was a billboard that read HAPPY ANNIVERSARY in faded red paint, and below that in blue, without explanation, FOREVER IN BLUE JEANS. The people here were odd, Schwaller had deduced that already, and their mysteries were many.

Nick spent an hour eating dinner. Sat by the window, had a pulled pork sandwich and baked beans and a cola, wiped his mouth with a red paper napkin after every third bite to smear sauce off his lips. Before he left, Nick stopped at the counter and waved to the kitchen to say thanks. The cooks waved back like Nick was a regular there, like Nick was a good guy.

He drove west on Farnam Street until Turner Park, then turned down Thirty-First, a block or two, until he was outside Mount Vernon Apartments. He parked down the block, on the other side of the street, and stayed in his car. He was there forty minutes, cigarette smoke essing out the window of his car, but he never opened the door, never got out.

(Elisabeth didn't come home, she was at work, it is noted.) Nick drove to the Kellogg Rooming House and went upstairs until it was time to head back to the repair yard in the morning.

There was nothing Schwaller could do. Maybe pick Holland up for illegal surveillance, for stalking. He wanted to arrest Nick right then, but there was no complaint on file that accused Nick of stalking. His wife didn't even know if he was alive, let alone parked outside her apartment building, watching her window.

I should have given up on him, sir, but I don't get embarrassed doing legwork. My gut has been right on more than one occasion and that buys me the right to act on a hunch. Still, by all rights, I would have been happier in the end if I had conceded and recorded a final statement from Elisabeth Holland and headed back to Chicago to report what she said, that there was nothing of even slight interest going on in Omaha. That's believable. That's correct. But there was a mystery there, even if I couldn't connect the dots to show it was criminal. These strange characters all connected. A nurse, a rail worker, a turncoat. Like a bad joke. Still: How did they come together? They probably weren't all part of a terrorist cell, but my job isn't to decipher what's likely. My whole career I've worked in the belief that nobody disappears without a trace. How could anybody go on if they were resigned to the opposite? (Agt Frank Schwaller, Mobile Audio, 21 Nov 08, Washington, DC, 20535. J. Edgar Hoover Building.)

FILE 5

TYLER AHLS

*09 A*ug *02* to *23 S*ep *03*

Since age eleven, when he first discovered the Silk Road in a creased *National Geographic*, crouched browsing in a back corner of a musty public library, Tyler Ahls wanted to see for himself the mountains and deserts of the Xinjiang region of China, to arrive by horseback to the oasis city of Kashgar and lose his body to the frenzy of an open-air bazaar. Although he wasn't on horseback, Tyler did travel the Silk Road after his freshman year of college. This was his first big hike in Asia, his initial breach into the Muslim world.

Mostly he waited out that expedition in Tajikistan, not China. When he departed, he didn't tell his family where he was going, not exactly, though he wasn't evasive about his itinerary either. There were no visible borders atop a mountain range, that was all. *Nationality, denominations, they don't matter up there,* or so he said.

Tyler flew in and out of the old Soviet airport in Dushanbe via Frankfurt, spent a few weeks in camps low in the Pamir Mountains. He entered China by truck but didn't stay long. The people he was with (adventure travelers he met on internet message boards) progressed along the typical Silk Road highlights in Xinjiang, but, for some obscure reason, Tyler didn't. He waited out his visa near Tajik National Park. He told all this to his family when he returned, but their ears were unable to contain these words—Pamir, Dushanbe, Tajik, Xinjiang. The Ahls had no conception of these places, so, to them, Tyler was cagey about what happened there. Tyler with windburned features that matched his red hair, in the midst of growing what would become a very natty beard; he swore he'd return to these places soon.

The fun part for him was learning how to travel alone. Who he could trust in a train station; what food made him sick; when it was polite to eat with his hands; trying betel nuts after a market woman shoved a leaf full to him, then buying a new toothbrush in Tajikistan because he ruined his trying to scrub off the red fibrous gunk and leafy flotsam embossed on his teeth by the betel nuts. Mostly he rode in the back of trucks with the rest of the group. He was rarely alone until he extricated himself from the adventure travelers (who were watching out for him) then hung around base camps with diarrhea for weeks without scaling a single peak in the Pamir range. He was so nauseous, so sick, that's why he didn't go on the full trip, why he stayed down in the villages and encampments, where at least there were privies and 7UP in green glass bottles and a chalky purgative an elderly village woman formulated that only served to irradiate his excrement to a near-glowing fluorescent pink.

Certain agents, Schwaller among them, later postulated that Tyler's connection to this region of Asia came out of his sickness on this first trip. Tyler was so close to something he believed was holy, only to be betrayed by his body. He was compelled to rely on faith that these mountains, this region, were where he belonged. Of course, Tyler was extensively trained in matters of faith—some say radicalized. Some voice must have awakened inside him that promised, if he came back, if he returned time after time to mountains of great spiritual significance, risking more of his body each time, then he'd be rewarded hundredfold for his audacity, for his willful oddity.

Tyler made dozens of attempts to explain himself to Nick, in phone calls, in emails like the one he sent shortly before he took his last flight to Pakistan.

I wanted to be alone. That's the long and short of it. In addition to having the runs all the time and making the truck pull over again and again so they could watch me empty my gut. It was exasperating being with the same group of four people all the time. Stopping on a mountain plateau, seeing a peak in the distance, that was good enough for me. The hardcore hikers didn't understand. They said stuff to me. You can't say you were here unless you climb or you're a liar. I didn't believe them and I still don't. I remember when Lis went to Paris with soccer and she didn't go up the Eiffel Tower. Seeing is believing she told us. That peeved Mom and Dad. That's how they are, like, did Lis get their money's worth? I get what Lis meant. It feels good to walk up to a monument and not touch it. The point is to feel how you're far away from home. (Tyler Ahls, Email, 06 Jul 07, Chippewa 54729. Apostle Crossing.)

Tyler emailed all sorts of thoughts like these to Nick Holland, after Nick fled from Chicago, during the two years they corresponded. Nick, as you might suspect, often had second thoughts about how he ran off from his family. Tyler tried to console Nick. It was his belief that Nick did the right thing, fleeing. *For men like me and you, the world is better off without us. Men like us belong on frontiers.*

Gerry and Deb Ahls financed these trips on the promise that Tyler would work off his debt at Apostle Crossing when he returned. (Every summer, in exchange for airfare, he took tickets at the booth, cleared the grounds with a leaf blower, mended fences, oiled the statues with Penofin so their wood didn't crack in the sun, haggled with youth pastors and explained how the park's discount structure worked; he'd be gone months at a time, then show up with a beard and long hair, board up in his old room and keep to himself like he was trained to silence. *The other guys couldn't hack it,* he'd hyperbolize to Elisabeth on the phone, *so I hoofed it alone the rest of the way. One month up, two weeks down.*) Tyler had so much trouble at college, his parents thought a month hiking the other side of the planet would serve him well and refocus his priorities, his Christian faith, that it would help him appreciate all he had at home in Wisconsin. The Ahls must have thought Tyler would end up back in school after his trip.

Tyler hadn't let on to his parents how bad things were for him at Whitewater—though it's documented in the record. How, after earning an ROTC scholarship, he struggled to keep up with the demands of being a cadet; how there were reports of confrontations with professors and classmates, specifically whenever the wars came up, whenever 9/11 came up; how he ignored requests from administrators to take down a handwritten sign he taped to his door that first fall semester, one that read WE HAD IT COMING in red Sharpie over a photo of United 175 exploding into a Twin Tower. As you might suspect, life on campus was difficult for Tyler after that. What a senseless thing to do. There are videos of him marching on campus in his ROTC uniform—presenting the colors before a football game, rifle at his shoulder, in a gleaming silver helmet and camouflage fatigues. Even in the photo for his student ID he wore his uniform. Imagine how his WE HAD IT COMING sign made the other kids on his floor feel, or his roommate, who switched dorms at semester he was so embarrassed.

According to notes made by a school therapist Tyler was forced to see, he was combative about the sign. The counselor was concerned about some of the books Tyler quoted during sessions—Zinn, Chomsky, William T. Vollmann's *An Afghanistan Picture Show* (Tyler stole the library copy before he dropped out), the Bible, the Quran. This was all spring semester. There was no legitimate concern that Tyler was going to be expelled from Whitewater, though the chair of Military Sciences did her best to make it clear that certain core beliefs were requisite for cadets. If Tyler didn't share those beliefs, he should find another depart-ment to hang his shingle.

There were rumors on campus. Student complaints, red flags tripped by the therapist. Though unverified, it was common belief that Tyler Ahls converted to Islam at Whitewater. Technically, constitution-ally, this shouldn't matter one way or the other. But it was thought to be relevant, both by school officials at the time and, later, various func-tionaries in security apparatus, like Agent Schwaller. Tyler wrote a paper for PHIL 245 titled "Confessions of an Ex-Christian," which is about as unnuanced as it gets. And if he did lose his faith—coming from a family of true believers like he did—it was logical to assume something would fill the vacuum, and that's why he ended up in Central Asia.

But is it true that Tyler lost his faith? Didn't Agent Schwaller note from his time in Peshawar that Tyler attended All Saints Church? Didn't Tyler carry laminated sheets of scripture in his backpack? Maybe it isn't so cut-and-dry as all that, like the kids at Whitewater thought.

It's fair to say he struggled those years. He was provocative, what-ever conclusion you make about his faith, and he'd always had a way of putting his beliefs out in front of himself, even if he wasn't sure of the path those beliefs put him on.

For example: the Ahls family theme park wouldn't have existed if it wasn't for Tyler. He had a vision as a seven-year-old, in a dream: there should be a place for families on vacation to learn stories about Jesus and the Twelve Apostles. The folks who came up to those parts in the summer, to the Dells for boating and festivals and bratwurst, they would stop at a park that told stories about Jesus and his disciples. Annunciation, Nativity, Epiphany and the Magi; the Massacre of the Innocents by King Herod; Christ among the doctors at the temple on Passover; Palm Sunday and the triumph of Jesus in Jerusalem; Judas and his betrayal; Easter and Ascension; Pentecost and the descent of the Holy Spirit upon the apostles. Like roadside historical markers, that sort of thing, placards and cartoons to illustrate the text, and carved statues to embody the Twelve Apostles, Jesus and Joseph and Mary. Folks would walk around the figures and feel like they stood next to the apostles and Holy Family or witnessed Christ ascend to Heaven.

This is what came to Tyler in his dream, more or less. Maybe not the logistics or accounting, not the $13.50 for admission, but the vision of Apostle Crossing—the statues and cartoons and plaques. Over the next two years the Ahls transformed their property, based on what Tyler said—his revelation, as they saw it. Most locals around there were suspicious. Tyler's dream sounded like the fantasy of a kid who listened too closely at Sunday school—an occasion to say *oh, that's nice, dear,* then forget, instead of claiming it was a vision from God.

But that's not how the Ahls saw things. They ran with the idea, filled in the gaps between a dream and a business plan, carved Jesus and apostle statues in Gerry Ahls's woodshop, figured out how to arrange the carvings and gravel pathways in precise order so traffic wouldn't snarl at the most popular exhibits. They worked through insurance issues, hired a consultant experienced in advertising and monetization. Even if the Ahls were sincere in their faith—and by most accounts they were, they are—TV evangelists were the fashion at that time, if they'd been looking to pull off a scam. Tyler was well ahead of the "Heaven is real" craze, a curve set by Burpos and Malarkeys. At the center of Apostle Crossing was the Station of Tyler, with an inscription that read *and he just a boy of seven, pure of heart. Jesus said let the innocents come unto him and Tyler did. This is Tyler's dream,* and a picture of him at seven, the shabby bowl cut, the sweatpants and Packers jersey, Tyler posing by the chainsaws when a timber company came to clear a swath from the forest. How many times had he walked by that picture in his life? As a teenager? As a young man in his twenties? The Station of Tyler, as if he too were an apostle or a prophet. When Tyler swept out the park in later summers, there would always be some bumpkin in plaid shorts and a tank top saying *Hey there! Is'n it you?*

Maybe all boys are given a messiah complex. The peculiar kind of pressure parents put on boys to take care of things, that they're vital to the world and must be listened to, when really, no.

Many nights, as a boy, Tyler hid in the trees behind their house when Deb Ahls called him to dinner—before and after the vision of Apostle Crossing came to him. Gerry stood on the back stoop to beckon him, the porch light filtering through the wisps of oak and cottonwood and mulberry branches. Tyler waited for the chill after sunset, in Wisconsin, in autumn, huddled in the wet elbow of a maple where his dad couldn't see him. His skinny boy-legs in tight jeans, the rough bark rubbing through his sweatshirt. Gerry would go eat eventually, a tired look on his face as he returned inside. This was a recurring scene in their lives, a daily drama between a boy and his family. Tyler watched them through the window, Elisabeth scarfing her food, if Elisabeth was home for dinner and not at practice. Tyler pretended he was Slightly Fox in a Peter Pan adventure, the other Lost Boys with him, watching from the forest with dirty faces and grumbling tummies, even though his was the only grumbling tummy. A swoop of rust-orange hair over his forehead. He waited until the kitchen lights went out and for the blue strobe of the television coming from the family room. Sometimes he took the plate his mom left for him back to his room to wolf the cold meat and potatoes, still Slightly Fox. But other times he ate at the table in the dark with his head down and let his mother watch from around the corner.

Which is all to say, Tyler had a lonely childhood out there in the forest, in Apostle Crossing.

[23 Sep 03; Tyler returned from Tajikistan]

Tyler lost thirty pounds on his first trip to Asia. When his parents picked him up at Minneapolis–Saint Paul International, he hardly looked like the same boy who'd left six weeks earlier. Tyler so haggard—his cheeks hollow, his eyes sunken, even his clothes stiff and fragrant. He'd been inside an airplane cabin or airport for forty-six hours, miserably unwashed in the white lights and sanitized surfaces of airline terminals, and even when he emerged through the automatic doors from customs, the other arrivals kept their distance. Well, they probably hadn't spent the last few weeks struggling to keep their insides on the inside, like Tyler had. And he stuck out anyway—he was tall, over six feet, and had long copper hair and some tufts of a ginger beard, a pointed doppa-style skullcap he picked up in Tajikistan.

Deb Ahls too kept her distance, her arms crossed in a tee so her left hand covered her mouth. He could barely hear her mumble. "Oh, Tyler. Is that you?" Gerry Ahls stiff behind her, holding in a laugh. "She was going to offer to do your laundry," Gerry said, "but forget that. Be better to burn everything."

They would embrace him later. After he bathed and brushed his teeth.

At home, after his shower, after a good meal of chicken and noodles, after apple cobbler, Tyler emptied his backpack in the living room to show off the souvenirs he brought home. When he unzipped his bag, all his mementos and clothes carried a not-so-faint aroma of tobacco and spiced tea and limes. In fact, he lined the bottom of his pack in lime leaves so they might deodorize his socks. First he sent his mother out to the kitchen to start some water boiling, then presented her with a set of ceramic *chini* cups and two ounces of dried leaves wrapped in a plastic baggie. "What is it?" she asked, appalled. "Ma, it's green tea." Tyler had silk scarves for Mom (and Elisabeth, when he saw her again) in bright pinks, purples, and goldenrods—all of this noted by TSA—and, for Gerry, statuettes of a camel and its driver that were carved out of a dark wood that looked something like walnut in its grain and color.

"Well, thanks," his father said, smiling as he turned a figurine over in his palms. "I don't have one of these."

Somehow Tyler appeared even more different now that he was showered and dressed in his old sweatpants and a cavernous Brewers tee shirt that looked three sizes too big on his arms, billowing over his abdomen where he no longer had a gut. He left his gut in Tajikistan; now he showed bones in his elbows, in his jaw and throat. With the beard he was trying to grow, his jaw intrepid and mannish, his hair long and tangled. There was a look in his eyes, his eyes more gray than green now; he couldn't look straight at his parents, his stance slightly askance, like he watched over their shoulders.

"We were so worried," Deb told him, which Tyler knew. She told him this the six times he was able to call home from internet cafés, that she had nightmares he wouldn't come home.

"She worried you'd convert to Hindu over there," Gerry teased.

"Nah." Tyler shifted on his haunches to sit cross-legged and sip green tea from a *chini* cup. "I'm not that kind of backpacker. You go to India for that. Where I was, it's Islam."

He probably meant that as a joke, but who can be sure?

The Ahls hoped Tyler would have gotten out of his system whatever demon caused his rebellion at Whitewater, that he'd reconsider dropping out of college. Deb had even gone to the trouble of talking to an admissions official at Whitewater to see if they'd consider taking Tyler back, and the official sounded open to the idea, so long as he steered clear of Military Sciences. It's forgivable, when Tyler mentioned how he wanted *to go back ASAP*, that his mother thought he was talking about university.

"I'm not going to college. I'm going to Asia," Tyler clarified. How disappointed the Ahls must have been. How confused. "I'm never going back to college. Why would you think—"

"Are you going to move home permanently? I don't think that's—"

"Ma, I don't want to move home, not for good. Why would I want to keep the same room where I grew up? There are balloons on the fricking wallpaper!"

"But you have to work. If you're not in school."

"All I thought about on the trip home was going back to those mountains and how I can help those people. That's all I think about."

"Oh, Tyler. Don't obsess about this. You're always obsessing."

"Look at these," Tyler said.

He pulled from his pack a set of folded and wrinkled pamphlets. They showed a picture of Jesus (in sermon pose) but were covered in a foreign alphabet. Tyler straightened to his knees, jostled his *chini* of tea, to hold out the papers until his parents took a few each to look over. They didn't examine the papers like he wanted—they watched him instead, worry showing in their faces, fatigued, disappointed at how excited Tyler was to show them these pamphlets he brought home. Sure, he brought silk and tea and a pervasive odor of black pepper, those more traditional treasures, but the pamphlets are what excited their son.

"What are they?" Gerry finally asked.

"Religious tracts!"

They glanced to each other. "What do you mean?"

"The Gospels! Isn't that clear? There's Jesus. Criminy."

That first hike, Tyler came across leaflets like these in hostels and encampments, left by Mormon missionaries and Seventh Days, periodicals like *Adventist World* and *Signs of the Times* in Cyrillic script. The ones Tyler showed to his parents were Gospels, the Book of Mormon, translated into Tajiki Persian and Kyrgyz. Although he couldn't read Tajiki Persian or Kyrgyz (when he found them, he had to ask what language this was), he'd unfolded the pamphlets to stare at the lettering and turn them over, to look at glossy pictures of Jesus. On his last day, he slipped them in his pack to bring home. These were the only artifacts he kept for himself.

"Isn't that so cool? I wonder if they have whole Bibles like this."

"If there are Christians there, why wouldn't they have Bibles?"

"But God had to work through someone to do it, right? Translate them, print them. They don't just appear."

"Oh, sure," Deb said. She took the pamphlets Gerry held and ordered them with her own before she handed them back to Tyler. "These are very nice."

FILE 6

ELISABETH HOLLAND

13 Sep 08 to 24 Sep 08

18 Jan 05 to 08 Feb 05

[13 Sep 08; six days before the video aired]

If she wasn't scheduled, she let herself stay late in bed. Elisabeth couldn't help herself, which is why she despised days off work. Before long, curled in the blankets, she'd think about what life would have been like if Caleb had lived. If she was a mother for longer than two months. Before she and Nick conceived, Elisabeth imagined what it would be like if she had a child to watch out for and worry over. She wished for what she thought of as "toddler closeness"—a species of communication Elisabeth observed between moms and kids in dentist-office waiting rooms and grocery stores, when her guard was down. She imagined being so close to her child that his voice was like a second consciousness in her mind, one indistinguishable from her own. (She did remember Caleb's voice, his infant's bleat—she shot up in the middle of the night sometimes hearing him cry for her, when she would cry for him, it is noted—and his breathy sigh after he nursed, his big gummy grin, milk bubbling inside his fleshy cheeks.) Everything after that she had to imagine. The lying face to face at bedtime, his pulling at her hair; and once he was older, watching Saturday-morning cartoons on the couch until the drowsies evaporated and it was time for lunch, jelly sandwiches, and a nap, then maybe the park before dinner. If Elisabeth let her defenses slip, the dreams entranced her—like there existed a shadow realm where Caleb was alive and growing and three years old, and they visited preschools to see if he preferred the wooden works at one Montessori or another, and if she could stand to give him up full days, or if she could figure some way to make half days work so she'd get him to herself for lunch and thereafter. If she relaxed, if she stopped working, visions of this other place seeped in. Caleb's first day of kindergarten. Caleb kicking a soccer ball over the fence at recess. Caleb, the feel of his sticky face on hers, watching *Rudolph* on TV at Christmas, sharpening the end of a candy cane with his tongue. Caleb playing with her stethoscope when she came home from work, putting it to his bare chest so he could hear his heart beat, then in through the armpit of her shirt to hear hers underneath her laughing. Some mornings she heard his heartbeat, a sound she'd listened to thousands of times before, the raspy persistence of the lives of others. Caleb's was strong and clear, without a trace of arrhythmia or murmur, in this other place, when toddler Caleb rushed to the door to greet her and begged to listen to her insides. Caleb would have been three and a half years old. He would have been able to talk to her, a real kid at that age: singing; telling hackneyed jokes; whispering softly, ashamed, chin to his chest, after he knocked his blue cup full of milk to the carpet. Sometimes Elisabeth heard his voice—the sound of his shadow. She knew it when she heard it: what Caleb would have sounded like at one, two, three. His voice grew within her, in that other place.

Early that September, Elisabeth cleaned her apartment the mornings she had off work. She lived alone, there wasn't much to clean, but she liked to tidy—how the sink stayed free of dishes and its porcelain was scrubbed white and how when she wiped down the shower her sponge never caught on a blotch of scum, how her hand moved smooth across the surface of tub and tile, because she was cleaning something that was clean. She still had some of Caleb's stuff—she'd sold a lot of it when she left Chicago—and she kept most of it in the guest room where there was a daybed and a desk and a dresser she could cover in stuffed animals. Velveteen rabbit, penguin, polar bear, lamb. He had so many, really too many for an infant, but they'd been gifts and she didn't have time to cycle them out to Goodwill by the time Caleb died. By one or two years old she would have given most all of them away. Now she could never throw them out. She kept a box in her closet that contained the most devastating of mementos, clippings, and certificates. On her mornings off, when she cleaned, she moved all the stuffed animals to her bed so she could dust the dresser, then returned most of them, except for the few she wanted for later. Those she left to guard her pillow.

This was sixteen days before Agent Schwaller came to visit—when he'd notice the growing mess in her dining room—but even the dining room was spotless at midmonth. (This was seen through the eyes and ears of her cell phone, the video stored in servers, in the mind of God. The whole Ahls family was under close watch, not just as collateral objects in a Venn diagram of other surveils, but subject to their own FISA warrants by this point, as the video of Tyler in an Afghani cave was in hand but not yet public.) Elisabeth held herself together still. Her magazines in a caddy, wineglasses aligned atop a hutch, table wiped and clean. Only a few newspapers on the table—no stacks and binders and maps, no articles traced in rectangles of red Sharpie. By this point, she'd read about the first safe haven adoption cases: Philip Phelps, Emory Butler, Willa Hall, Adam Cherry. She kept newspapers with stories about safe haven kids on the table. No child had been left at Saint Wenceslaus yet.

She heard on the news, read it in the paper, was told by admins from HHS, how Nebraska was the last state government to enact a safe haven law—which allowed parents to release custody of their children to a state-appointed guardian, no questions asked, in the emergency room of a hospital. But Nebraska differed in the parameters of their law. Most states put a limit on the age of a qualifying child, which was the point, more or less, to stop distressed teens from leaving infants in a trash can at their high school prom, or worse things people did when they couldn't cope. In Nebraska, any child up to *eighteen* could be dropped off at a hospital. That's how the legislature wrote it into law, so that's how it was.

Later this month, nine kids would be left at the hospital where Elisabeth worked, but Emory Butler tops the list in the official safe haven record. Sure, there were other children abandoned earlier that year: left at Grandma's or dropped at a neighbor's or never picked up from school. But by statute, Emory's was the first case. Emory Butler, eleven years old, left by his grandmother at Immanuel Medical Center during the late afternoon of September 13. Emory had a small build and a bald-fade haircut that made his ears look big. He wore Minnesota Vikings gear because he liked the colors purple and gold; his shoes were purple with gold laces. Though Emory was identical to his twin brother, only Emory punched holes in the walls of his grandmother's house. While no honor student, Emmitt was a good boy, one you could see a future for, who didn't trash the house, who wore white sneakers with white laces, who didn't set fire to a boys restroom at Druid Hill Elementary, like Emory did. The grandmother checked Emory into Immanuel for psychiatric evaluation, then invoked the safe haven law after Emory was piloted by orderlies to another room.

The article caught Elisabeth's eye. She was curious what it would be like if somebody invoked the safe haven law while she was at work—though she wasn't an ER nurse. But this kind of thing, you never know.

Elisabeth had seen bad things at Saint Wenceslaus before, during the year she worked post-op and documented surgical mishaps for the malpractice-insurance carrier: catheters, sponges, latex gloves forgotten on the inside; inadvertent incisions; botched deliveries when forceps crushed an infant's shoulder, an infant's cranium; a surprise mastectomy; gastric perforations; rectovaginal fistulae, which had to be the worst imaginable outcome for any procedure. Having to type these incidents into the web portal made her queasy. Usually her hospital was quiet, unlike the university med centers that took all cases—those places were like city-states unto themselves, massive complexes with their own bureaucratic and security arms. Nurses there had to deal with fights in their waiting rooms when the victims of drive-by shootings were in emergency, stabbings in their parking lots, aggravated assaults in elevators. Saint Wenceslaus was different. There was order. What was sacred was kept sacred, in the way they cared for the injured and ill, in how they let family members set up camp in the rooms, and how Elisabeth performed her duty because, frankly, she saw it as duty.

She was on the floor the night Cary Junger brought his nine kids to the hospital. She wasn't in emergency when it happened, but word spread fast. Sandy, who was charge nurse on the third floor, said a couple of them who had their charting done should go see if the staff down there needed help with all those kids, nine of them, so that's what they did.

Emergency looked more or less normal when they got off the elevator. A little eerie, because it was so quiet except for the printer spitting out paper at intake. The hallway empty until a social worker came sprinting to answer the ringing phone in her office. Sandy stopped a scribe nurse to see what was going on.

"Where is everybody?"

She looked so young, the nurse, like a teenager, with her stringy blond hair loose on her shoulders, her green scrubs, a laptop stand she wheeled down the hall with the laptop clam open. "The kids? They're in the rooms," she said.

"The parents still here?"

"Not parents," the scribe nurse said. "Only dad."

"Stop a second," Sandy told her, matronly, hand on her bicep, Sandy's voice gruff in comparison to the girl's pastel cant. "How many kids? We heard nine."

"That's right. Eighteen months to eighteen years."

The scribe nurse explained how it happened. How they walked in through the metal detector, the ten members of the Junger family. The older kids carrying the youngers. Their image doubled on security monitors, how the dad was last through the metal detector then sifted through his kids to straggle up to the intake desk. *I already told them why it has to be this way,* he explained to the registrar.

Why what has to be what way? Which one is hurt?

The whole pack of them silent as the registrar looked them over, a couple RNs too by that point, to see what was what. How the kids cast their faces down, how they couldn't look the registrar in the eye when she tried to connect; one teen girl holding the baby to her shoulder, the baby cradling a bottle filled with apple juice; everyone in the waiting room studying their bodies, their appearance, to see what was wrong with these kids, these lumpens in hand-me-down jeans, in tee shirts that showed cartoon Skoal Bandits and Joe Camels, the like. Maybe one a little sclerotic, another jaundiced, another with thinning hair. But no broken bones, no lacerations, nothing acute. The registrar must have figured it out by then, all those kids and one squirrely, shamefaced father.

Tell me what you're here for, she said.

The dad twisted away at the hips. Rubbed the stubble on his jaw with his palm.

I told them in the car. I got to use the safe haven thing on them.

Tell me again, the registrar said, polite and insistent. *We can't do nothing if you don't state exactly that you want to invoke the safe haven law to give up your kids.*

I want to use that law to give up my kids, he said.

Bays were found immediately for the nine. Nurses summoned to usher them away two or three at a time. Emergency at Saint Wenceslaus was small, a suburban hospital like that, without much space: a few triage and low-acuity rooms, one high-acuity room that could masquerade as a trauma center in a pinch. All staff in the department were paged. Each kid had to be admitted to the hospital and given a medical exam. The father was escorted to a separate room to glean all known family and medical information; he was given coffee and a snack bag of chips, urged to sit and think about what he was about to do. The staff called 911, meanwhile, for the police to come enroll the kids in protective services. This all adhered to statute. For the next month, the next year, Elisabeth and nurses she knew would rehash the details in meetings, at happy hours, so everyone knew how she'd seen it go down.

They split the kids into pairs, got chocolate-chip cookies, juice boxes, formula for the baby. Sandy and me jumped in to see how we could help. None of the kids were injured, that was checked first. Some dehydration, pink eye, lice, malnutrition. We went to a bay and pulled the curtain to find two boys alone, so we went over these two again, Sandy and me, put them up on the bed and checked for broken bones. Checked their eyes and ears and throats. We had no idea what we were doing—just keep a patient busy so he doesn't have to think about his situation. Tell a dumb joke. That's it, right? What else could we do? (Elisabeth Holland, Mobile Audio, 27 Sep 08, Omaha 68124. Saint Wenceslaus Hospital.)

Sandy pulled Elisabeth to the hall and said she was going back to the third floor. "We got our own shit to worry about, right?" Sure, Elisabeth agreed, but Elisabeth wanted to stay.

She wandered the hall like a ghost after Sandy left. There were police by then, spinning lights from their cruisers refracting through the automatic doors onto the walls. Everything was so quiet. The echoes of heels. The sound of the elevator. The squelch of the EMT scanner. Most of the staff stood around. They'd never had a safe haven kid, now nine at once.

If Elisabeth hadn't thought about Caleb earlier that day, she surely would have then. All this hullabaloo, the news, caused her to daydream about Caleb even more often, more deeply—what he'd be like if she still had him. She went to registration and found the manifest of the nine who were brought in. To herself, aloud, she read their names. "Colton, Chase, Emma, Elsie, Jefferson, Melody, Kyle, David, Belle." And once more she read them, her lips murmuring.

"Hello again." It was the scribe nurse. She wheeled her laptop stand to the desk. "I'm Amanda," she said, tenting her smock as she pulled to show her name tag.

"God," Elisabeth said. "Nine? What guy has nine kids to take care of all by himself? How does that even happen?"

"Can't keep it in his pants, I guess. What about the mom? Who keeps having kid after kid. And with that guy. Did you see him?"

"I didn't. What's the story with the mom?"

"Deceased. Eclampsia with the last one."

"That's too bad."

The registrar looked over her shoulder to glare at Elisabeth and Amanda, phone cord hanging from her head; she said, "Professionalism, ladies," then turned back to her call. "That's right, J-u-n-g-e-r."

Amanda leaned in, her stand colliding with the desk as she leaned. "Do you have kids?"

"I don't."

"Good for you. I don't want them either. It gets under my skin when everybody acts like a woman's self-worth is tied to her desire to procreate. Do you get that from people too?"

"Sometimes."

"You know what I'm saying. Give me a break. I'm not ever going to end up like these people," Amanda said, thumbing over her shoulder. "Nine brats. And with a guy like that."

She played with the ends of her long hair, the trimline of her bangs coming uneven as she leaned in close to conspire. "Do you want to see him?"

"See who?"

"The dad," she whispered. "He's just down the hall."

"No. I don't think so."

"This is going to be a big deal, you know that, right? This is going to be on TV." Amanda mouthed the words *nine kids* without making a sound, then *wow*. "Come on, take a peek. Then you can tell people you saw this dad the night he abandoned his kids." Again, *nine, wow*.

Elisabeth said okay. "Just for a second."

The dad was older than Elisabeth thought he'd be, which made sense, given how his oldest kid was eighteen. He sat at the desk holding a cup of coffee, stared at the paperwork and the duplicates. Cary Junger hardly moved as Elisabeth watched his profile from over his shoulder, the leathery skin on the back of his neck, how it looked like he usually shaved his head to hide how he was bald on top but hadn't shaved in a while and the hair on the back of his head, his neck, grew in thistles. He was small. He didn't carry them, of course, but, Elisabeth wondered, how did nine kids come from him? The muscles in his neck twitched. He turned and saw them peeking, Amanda at one side of the doorframe and Elisabeth at the other. Amanda spun and flattened against the wall, but Elisabeth froze, like his bloodshot eyes locked her in space. Ashamed, caught like that, she looked like she might weep. Her muscles seized, heart in her stomach, staring at Cary Junger, who still sat there debating whether to give up his kids or to reconsider. Elisabeth couldn't see if he'd signed the forms yet or not, this man with small shoulders and dark eyes and burned skin the crimson and ocher of a sunset. Elisabeth stared until Amanda pulled her halfway down the hall.

"What do you think?" Amanda asked, her hands on Elisabeth's shoulders. "You think he signed? The kids are still here. Maybe he got cold feet and they'll all go home together."

"Could be."

"I hope not," Amanda said. "They're better off in foster homes."

Elisabeth felt like she should say something, but the words didn't come out. Maybe there were no words to combat what the scribe nurse claimed.

"There's nothing we can do," Elisabeth said, freeing herself. "I should go back to third." And she turned, said *see you around*, and headed to the elevators, but the image of that guy stuck in her head. Cary Junger in his jeans and orange tee shirt. He was going to be a celebrity, of sorts, if he signed the papers to give his kids away to the state. Elisabeth stood at the elevator without pressing the button. She pictured Junger sitting at the desk and those kids in the bays waiting for the police to place them in protective custody. She couldn't hit the button. She leaned against the wall and looked to the social worker's office where Cary Junger sat at a desk with a pen in his hand, a bag of Fritos open in front of him as he deliberated. Elisabeth watched to see if he'd pop out the door to take his kids home. That was a possibility, then, at any second; if he stood and said he changed his mind, then all would be forgiven, legally, and his kids would still be his kids. They would pack into the van and stop for burgers on the way home and each of them would sleep in their own beds. But if he signed, that was that.

Sandy could page Elisabeth if she was needed on three. There were thirty minutes until shift change, but it had been slow all night up there. She peeked in a bay again to see if any of the kids needed help. One had pink eye crusted at his lashes; a nurse tried to get him to lie flat so she could put in drops. One had eczema on her arm; her arm was slathered with Aquaphor. In another, a nurse entertained four older ones by showing off equipment—trays of syringes, oxygen masks, defibrillator paddles—baby Belle bouncing on a sister's hip. Elisabeth didn't know why she loitered. They didn't need her. She was supposed to be checking fluids and vitals and saying *you'll feel better soon.* She turned to the elevators again, rounded the corner, and then she saw one of the little ones alone in the hall.

"What are you doing there, buddy?" she asked.

He didn't answer. His hair long and greasy, sticking up in the back. He let his eyes fall so he stared at the floor. "Where's my sissy?"

"Let's go," she said. "Come with me until they're ready for you."

He pulled back when she took his arm, one of the younger ones. Elisabeth couldn't say exactly how old, but guessed he was about seven. His pajamas half-undone, hanging off him. Hand-me-downs stretched out by the four siblings who wore them first. "What's your name?" Elisabeth asked. "Kyle," he said. She felt her hands shake when he looked at her. "Is there anything you need, little man?" she asked, a reflex, her nurse voice kicking in. He said, "I'm fine."

The dad signed the papers and social workers began splitting up the Junger kids. Foster homes had to be secured right away, nine spots at one throw. They'd be lucky to see each other again. "Are you sure you don't want nothing, buddy? There might be some pizza." Elisabeth didn't want to pester the boy, but she asked a third time. "What can I get you?"

The boy looked past security to the automatic doors. Sometimes paramedics rushed in screaming with a chest case on a gurney, but that night a dad brought in nine kids and handed them over to the state. Two of the girls walked out with a woman and got in the back of a car.

He was shaking. I didn't know what to do. I picked him up and took him back to the room he wandered out from. I held him. Sat in the chair and hugged him and patted his shoulders. He squeezed back and put his arms around my ribs and clutched a fistful of smock and buried his face in my armpit. "It's going to be okay," I told him. "I promise. Everything will end up fine." I don't know why I said that, but he looked at me and he calmed down a little. He stopped shaking. (Elisabeth Holland, Mobile Audio, 27 Sep 08, Omaha 68124. Saint Wenceslaus Hospital.)

"Your name is Kyle?" she asked, and he nodded and buried his face again in her smock.

She let him play with her stethoscope. She didn't know what else to do. "Here," she said. She put the eartips in his ears and took his hand

and placed the diaphragm to the inside of his elbow. "Do you hear anything?" He shook his head. "Try this." She held out the bell and he took it with his little fingers, his nails black with dirt and jam, and "Put it over your heart," she said, then guided his hand up the front of his pajama shirt. "Now?" The boy said nothing, but Elisabeth could see it in his eyes, how he heard the lub-dub, lub-dub. "That's your heart."

"Can I listen to you?"

Elisabeth hesitated. The boy sat still, slightly ridiculous with his stringy hair, his hand up his shirt and the binaural hanging from his head, the scared look in his eyes still doing battle with a look of wonder, still listening. "My heart?" she asked. Well, sure. She took the bell and leaned close to put the diaphragm over her smock at the spot where her fourth and sixth ribs met. She whispered, so she wouldn't hurt his ears, "Is it there? You hear it?" He shook his head. So she moved closer, close enough their elbows touched, that she heard his breath pass over his lips, that she smelled the fast food in his skin, the smell of cats in his pajamas, and she put the stethoscope up her own shirt to her bare skin. Then he nodded yes, it worked. Her blood rushing in her ears, so they both heard lub-dub, lub-dub.

The social worker was looking for Kyle. "We're in here," Elisabeth said. There were three social workers now. They'd been looking all over, they said. They needed a head count of who was left. Elisabeth replaced her stethoscope around her neck. She didn't move. She didn't hand over the boy, not right away. "He's right here where you left him."

Elisabeth watched as Kyle and the last of his siblings were escorted out the automatic doors and put in the back of a police SUV. It was unpleasant to see little kids climb into the back of a cop car, like Kyle, his short spindly legs rushing back and forth to keep up with the big cop, then the big cop lifting him to the back of the Tahoe, then closing the door. The kids would be shuttled to a shelter for the night. Still, it was the kids who rode away in a cop car and the father who walked out the door a free man—if a little confused when he left, later, glancing behind himself in the parking lot to make sure there wasn't a little one in his shadow, and again behind the wheel, when he lit a cigarette and checked the mirror because it hardly seemed possible that the rest of the seats in his van were empty.

Elisabeth stood a long time watching the automatic doors. Nobody disturbed her. She was in uniform. If she wanted to lean against a wall and process what happened, that was her business. For all the staff who belonged in emergency—the orderlies putting the bays back together, the interns trying to catch the attention of the resident physician, the social workers pacing, arms full of paperwork in quadruplicate, in overstuffed D-ring binders—they were too busy to care what Elisabeth had on her mind or why she didn't go back up to three where she belonged.

She went to the chapel that night. There was a priest sometimes and almost always a nun—sometimes one in a black habit, sometimes one in blue, the Vietnamese nun. Elisabeth didn't care who was there. She didn't want to talk to anyone. The chapel was small, a few pews upholstered in scratchy green fabric, the lights turned askew so they shined down the drywall and left a murky aisle in the middle where the light couldn't reach. Elisabeth sat in the front pew and flipped the kneeler, went to her knees and put her hands together. She tried to think about what to pray for. It had been a long time, over a decade, since she'd prayed with any sincerity. What did she want to ask God now? She wished she was Catholic, ready with an incantation she'd memorized as a girl, a Hail Mary. Some bargain she could strike that was pre-weighed by a council of priests and could be presented as penance to the immortal. She thought *Lord Lord Lord Lord Lord Lord* because she didn't know what else. *Watch over Kyle Junger,* she said to herself, or she said to God. *Give him a chance.*

Elisabeth had never prayed about Caleb, she realized. Had never prayed for God to watch over her own son's soul, though she'd apologized over and over, in her grief, that she never had her boy baptized. Praying felt like such a useless thing when Caleb died. She never asked that events be changed so they happened differently, or demanded to know why everything she treasured and depended on had been taken from her.

It was melodramatic, this praying. It had been a long time since she'd even pretended she could speak to God.

The nun at the back came and sat next to Elisabeth; Elisabeth stood. She didn't want to talk about anything with a nun. But she didn't rush out either, didn't want to make it seem like she was in great distress. She smiled at the nun. A middle-aged woman in puffy blouse and blue habit.

"What do you think is going to happen to those kids?"

"I don't know," the nun said. "That's what I was going to ask you."

Once Nick was gone—when he left Chicago and abandoned Elisabeth with the baby—was he gone forever? Yes. And Caleb was fine when Nick left, he was breathing? It's the truth.

Elisabeth didn't know what to do. She didn't call the police, didn't call her parents for help. She called Nick's dad, the sugar-beet farmer. *Nick you say? No. Haven't heard from Nick since the baby was born. Is something wrong?*

She realized how little a surprise it was that Nick took off. His whole life pointed to disappointment, didn't it?

She spent every moment with Caleb, twinned to each other in the chair asleep, in half dreams. A gale off Lake Michigan battering the window, Caleb's fingers wrapped inside the collar of her sweatshirt. His tiny body clenched into hers, his grasping little hands, his eyes that scanned left and right without seeing, until he saw her. Then he smiled and buried his face into her chest.

These were things Elisabeth was prompted to talk about, a month later, by a psychiatrist, in the three free sessions she received with her insurance.

We did smile practice first thing in the morning. Well, first I changed his diaper and put him on the breast. But after that, if I didn't have to change his diaper a second time, then I left him on his back in his crib and we smiled at each other. We laughed. My mom said he was mimicking me and it didn't mean Caleb was happy to see me or being silly or anything. I don't believe that. My mom was wrong. That big toothless smile. The way his body shook when he laughed and he tried to roll over because it was too silly a thing to look at his mommy's funny face. (Elisabeth Holland, VoIP, 30 Mar 05, Chicago 60640. Edgewater View Building.)

They watched food shows. Elisabeth couldn't explain it, but Caleb was engrossed by Bobby Flay. If they watched anything else, *The View*, *Big Brother*, not so much. She watched *CSI* when he slept, or *SVU*, but it was only Flay if Caleb was awake, or else he'd cry.

Caleb was ten weeks old. He could hold his head up on his own, a bit wobbly. If she left him on his tummy long enough, he'd push with his legs. Not crawling, but a start.

They only left the house to refill her medications—antibiotics, ibuprofen, vitamins—and for Caleb's well visits. Everything was fine at Caleb's checkups, the two he had. He had jaundice, and they had to take blood out of his heel, but that cleared up after a few days under a blue phototherapy light. The doctor stretched his legs and felt Caleb's hips, listened to his lungs and heart, checked his circumcision wound and if his testicles had descended, asked if he latched without issue. All of it was fine, was normal. They had Elisabeth pumping breast milk and saving it in the freezer for when she would go back to work.

One day she visited the daycare where Caleb was supposed to go, to meet the girls who watched the babies, to make sure everything was fine with that.

It will sneak up on you, one of the girls said, the one who was holding Caleb, who was bouncing Caleb on her bent elbow.

What will?

The first time you have to leave this precious little man at daycare.

They'd walk around the block. Him against her chest, asleep, warm and swaddled tight in his package. It was a lot of work to get him wrapped up enough to actually go outside. Putting on a clean diaper, a onesie, maybe two onesies if it was really cold, a stocking cap, the coat that had built-in mittens and booties and three inches of down stuffing, then Mom bundling herself up so Mom didn't freeze and strapping him to her chest. Half the time Caleb would shit himself before they were out the door and it started all over with a fresh diaper. It would be nearly an hour later by then and he'd rather nurse, but out they'd go. She'd bundle him up again and nurse him, work a breast in among all those layers until he took a nipple. Then he'd sleep at least, Elisabeth blessed with an hour or so of peace to walk around the block and maybe stop at Dunkin' for coffee. She strolled and let the coffee burn her tongue while she tried to savor it.

Caleb slept through anything if he was strapped in and fed, so she stopped at a Walgreens for more Aquaphor, more diapers. But, really, this was just getting some air before the morning was over, the sun warming everything to barely freezing. The pavement frosted white like the surface of Pluto. Every twig iced on the locust trees. Where Elisabeth lived in Boystown was a funny place to walk with a baby. It wasn't like the pride parade was going through the streets, not in February. No drag queens. But she still felt funny being there, a teensy baby strapped to her chest, under all those layers, like she was hiding her baby, hiding that she was a breeder, and so young. Elisabeth always thought she'd move back home before having kids—or somewhere that was like home, rural or suburban—but this was very little like home.

A FISA warrant covered so much real estate. (This wasn't so long after 9/11; it still isn't; for an agent like Schwaller, it will always be in the back of his mind, the alert FBI felt, the shame. You can understand.) In a place like Chicago, any big city, that's millions of people inside the area a warrant covered, and nearly every minute of their lives was recorded, their phone calls, any digital activity, all metadata, their stories. Even someone like Elisabeth Holland, who was off the radar at that point. Even before her brother's activities made everyone in her family a person of interest, she still wandered in front of surveilling eyes hundreds of times. Her file built frame by frame, byte by byte.

Elisabeth put off getting Caleb baptized until the weather was better, when she could get up to Wisconsin, and she'd told no one how Nick ran away. Her mother was pretty upset about the delay and offered regular commentary on the baptism situation, in a not-so-conciliatory tone. *You're making a mistake, waiting like that,* Deb Ahls said on the phone. *Put me on the record. I oppose waiting. I told you to get it done ASAP.*

So it is noted.

When Caleb was born—when the Ahls came to visit for two days—Deb brought a baptismal gown with her, the same one Elisabeth and Tyler had been baptized in. (This was the day Elisabeth brought Caleb home from the hospital. Nick was still with them.) Deb spread the gown out over the top of the couch. All silk and nylon, bleached so white the fabric generated its own cherubic aura. Nick fingered the lace. He smirked and screwed his mouth back and forth, fighting to say nothing. Elisabeth knew what Nick wanted to say. He wanted to ask why the Ahls were going to put his boy in a dress.

"He won't wear the bonnet even if you try," Deb said. She tossed the bonnet on top of the gown anyway to keep the set together. "Get it done fast. You'll want the peace of mind, knowing he's been saved."

"We're not going this weekend. Is that what you expected when you drove down? We'd run over to a church and dunk a newborn in the water?"

"Who said anything about dunking? It's the tiniest splash."

"We can do it in Wisconsin, if that's what you want. Get a minister out to the park. When the weather's warm."

"That's too long to wait, Lis. God forbid something happens—"

"We're not Catholic, Mom. I'm not anything."

"Oh, don't say that."

Most nights Elisabeth ended up sleeping in a gray cushioned chair in the living room. There was a rocking chair too, a glider with blue fabric, but a screw had fallen out from inside the glider and now the thing screeched when Elisabeth rocked. It was easier to hold the baby while sitting in the gray cushioned chair, even though it didn't rock.

Elisabeth knew she wasn't supposed to fall asleep with the baby on her lap, but she couldn't help it. She was exhausted. It wasn't a big deal. She had a horseshoe cushion that held the baby to her breast, and that kept him from falling. Eventually she'd get cold, her shirt bunched up to her collarbones in the middle of the night, a raw tit hanging out, and she'd put Caleb in his crib and go back to bed. But Caleb wouldn't sleep if she wasn't in the same room. Maybe she'd get twenty minutes in bed before he cried for her, until she picked him up and rocked him in her arms, pacing the hallway, so long as she didn't put him in the crib.

The gray chair was a compromise. Elisabeth held Caleb; Caleb let Elisabeth sleep.

Wasn't she desperate to find where Nick was? Didn't she panic?

That would only be natural, but it wasn't how it happened.

Elisabeth was angry, she was confused, felt gullible and put over on and naive. But not so surprised, after all. Nick was a loser, wasn't he? Men like him, other losers, they walk out on their families. And she was too scared to file a missing persons, because what if the police called her in to look at some John Does they had in the cooler. She couldn't handle that.

Anyway, she thought Nick was still in Chicago, working at the warehouse, or out on a bender, that he needed a few days away or was ashamed of what was happening there in the apartment—the mother and child, the bonding, the tummy-time and smiling practice. Nick was like that. Elisabeth had seen it before. He felt shame if he received the blessings all people wanted. He felt profound guilt, for some reason, if the good in life didn't pass him by.

A week later, when Nick clearly wasn't sleeping on a friend's couch and wouldn't soon reappear, Elisabeth said *fuck him.* If he couldn't hack it, *fuck him.* She took pride in how she could get along alone. Maybe Nick had been weighing her down. She was so busy with the baby and making plans to go back to work in a few weeks, and she didn't have much time or energy or love to waste worrying about what Nick Holland was up to and whether maybe, possibly, he might come home. Fuck him. She was in the romance of first motherhood those days. She didn't want Nick's leaving to ruin that. She wanted to love her baby. That was all.

She sat in the chair all night, slept there, baby cradled on her lap in the horseshoe pillow so baby wouldn't fall to the floor. The lamplight reflecting in the window, the gurgling noise of the humidifier. She hadn't told a soul about Nick's leaving, just barricaded herself in that apartment and did her best to take care of her baby and herself. She had food and water and didn't need much from outside. Chinese could be delivered, and pizza. She'd stocked up on things like soap and toilet paper long before Caleb was born, packed the freezer with plastic-wrapped meals she'd premade: cheese-stuffed shells, beef stroganoff, chili, chicken and noodles, what froze well and could be nuked in a microwave. It was a little silly, a little sad, how much Elisabeth had prepared for the eventuality that she'd be alone with her newborn.

When her mom called to check on her, Elisabeth didn't let on that anything was wrong. Her mom shouldn't come visit. Not now. The weather was horrible. The whole city socked in with snow (an exaggeration) and the temperature at five below most nights. *The wind chills, Mom. It's bad.* Every few days Elisabeth uploaded photos of Caleb to Blogspot so her mom could see that Caleb was okay. Elisabeth liked doing things on her own, it was true. She was hardheaded. That was fine, except for the baptism. Her mother kept on her about that.

—*Don't put it off. I want to be there, but if you and Nick have to use sled dogs to get that baby to a church, then do it, for Pete's sake!*

—*Mom. I told you. When it's warm, we'll come up to Chippewa so you and Dad and Tyler can be there too.*

—*Oh, don't plan around Tyler. You'll never get that baby baptized.*

—*Spring, Mom. In spring.*

For some reason, when she held the baby overnight, when she inhaled the sweet stuffy smell of the baby's hair and felt the warm little body through the layers of swaddling, Elisabeth thought about her soccer days, all those years out on the green green fields of Wisconsin summer, the grassy scent of the wind in the down of her sunburned arms, and the traveling teams, the trip to Europe after her freshman year. She sunk into the back cushion of the chair, Caleb in her arms, and told him about it. How, in college, there was an assistant coach from Ireland who was very tough on the girls, who pulled the collar of his jacket over his face when he bad-mouthed them during games; how out on the field it was perfectly quiet except for the screaming; how she scored ten goals her first season at DePaul and was Freshman All-America at midfielder and All-Conference, and, on the strength of those decorations, she spent two weeks on a special traveling team, played goodwill matches against former Soviet-bloc nations in empty stadiums in Mannheim, Salzburg, Firenze, Trieste. Saying the stories out loud, Elisabeth was amazed at all the things she'd done, the places she'd been, and all because she was good at soccer. All that time, when she could still play, she never let herself dwell on the novelty of her experience, the stadia of Europe, or how tenuous her hold on that life really was. She thought of this later, holding Caleb, Caleb gurgling milk in the back of his throat. She thought how she hurt her knee sophomore year, and her life was disrupted.

When that midfielder from Dayton took her out—with permissible contact, by the way, no yellow card was raised—Elisabeth's ACL was torn, with a severe strain of the UCL. Rehab would take ten months after a surgeon reattached everything, a little less if she took it seriously. She saw the best surgeon Chicago had to offer. And sports psychiatrists, PT specialists. So long as she didn't flub the rehab, they told her, she'd be back on the field in time for junior year. She could be All-America again, could dream of the national team. These had been the ideals she held to tightly in her teen years, when she trained every day; when she had scholarship offers by senior year, half scholarships, quarter scholarships; when she met Brandi Chastain and Mia Hamm at a banquet in La Crosse. And then the postseason honors her freshman year at DePaul, her goodwill trip with the all-stars. She could dream of the national team then, all the free gear, appearances as the guest of honor at youth banquets, being a heroine to girls the same way that Brandi and Mia were to her. She worked astonishingly hard those years—and, at that point, sophomore year, she still had a chance to see it through. But she had to rehab first.

Rehab was the worst. All those exercises to regain strength and mobility and stability. The foam rollers, floor mats, leg-extension machines, the waking up at 5 a.m. to get bitched at by the PT staff. Being told to push harder, run faster, trust my knee won't give out again. Let the scar tissue break off, they told me, have faith. My knee didn't get much better. My range of motion improved, but not enough, same with strength and stability. I could still run fast, but not enough to be a college athlete. Not enough to satisfy Coach or the trainers or the doctors. They got mad, like my knee not getting better was something I was doing to them. (Elisabeth Ahls, Mobile Audio, 15 Apr 03, Chesterton 46304. Indiana Dunes State Park.)

She was breathless those days. Looking over her shoulder as she rushed from class to class to rehab to various meetings with functionaries in the athletic department to the assistant coach from Ireland who caught her in the hallway outside the locker room sometimes and asked when he could expect to see her back in the lineup. She'd explain to him, *I don't know.* There was so much left to do. She'd go over her schedule with the coach, her 4 a.m. to 12 p.m. daily, and try to sound like this was a rational way for a young woman to fill her days. But in her voice, her young woman's voice, she gave no clue if she thought returning to the pitch was a good thing or not. She protested that she did want to play again, and lamented missing road trips and being able to practice with the girls, but, from the face he made, the assistant coach must have heard the reticence in her voice. Elisabeth must have heard it too.

She went out with friends during rehab, was more of a regular kid. Hanging out late. Skipping PT sessions, spacing checkups with the surgeon because she was watching *Judge Judy* at a friend's off-campus apartment. It occurred to her (strolling the lakefront when she was supposed to be lifting weights with the team) that her favorite part of her trip to Europe wasn't the honors or ceremonies or even competing in the games. Her favorite part was standing outside train stations where sap from linden trees made the pavement sticky under her sneakers. Or sitting at street cafés to ogle men. There was a seed Europe left in her: the glory of having nothing special to do. The hours each day she and the other girls were left to be not-soccer-players. This wasn't losing focus, but looking elsewhere. Focusing on things other than her body, other than her properly stretched tendons. She wanted to sleep late, to style her hair in something other than a ponytail, in anything other than a style named for a pack animal. So Elisabeth stayed up reading instead of getting to bed early. She skipped team meetings in favor of movie night in her dorm. She saw boys.

Her coach had a talk with her a month before the end of her junior year. He'd met with the doctors and trainers—got it straight from them, he said. Elisabeth's knee should be better; it looked improved from the MRI, as a matter of fact, as is noted. But Elisabeth kept saying her knee was tight, that she couldn't put all her weight on that leg, that she couldn't really burn it up when she ran, because she was afraid the ligaments would tear. Elisabeth had to push harder, the trainers told her, the specialists, the psychiatrists.

If you're not ready to play, the coach said, *we can't give you a scholarship anymore.*

She'd already missed two seasons, basically. They'd been more than fair with her.

I can't do this, Elisabeth told them, her voice barely a whisper she was so overcome by what she was saying. *Even if I lose my scholarship.*

There was a lot of crying about that, arguing with her parents, having to tell them she didn't want to play sports anymore. Deb and Gerry lectured her about all the sacrifices they suffered in the name of her playing soccer—it was Gerry who taught her how to play when she was a toddler, who signed her up for regional select teams and drove her to neighboring states, who spent his winter months dubbing her highlights onto VHS tapes and mailing them to at least fifty coaches—but she convinced them in the end. What choice did they have? DePaul took away the scholarship, which was only a quarter scholarship her junior year anyway. The school had been generous to her, really, compared to what other girls had to put up with to keep playing. Most girls got nothing. Deb and Gerry said they'd pay for her last year of school. She didn't have to transfer to a state school in Wisconsin—they let her stay at DePaul, a private school—so long as she understood it was their decision. Elisabeth went along with what they said (however they wanted to perceive reality) because it meant she got to stay in Chicago. One more year and then she'd be free. That was all she wanted.

In the end, the end of her soccer life, Elisabeth was glad how things worked out. Wasn't that why she flubbed the rehab, why she let the ligaments in her knee wither and tighten, so she could move on? Her feet wouldn't be crucified by blisters anymore, her shins no longer blotchy with bruises when she wore a bikini or flip-flops and sundresses. She wouldn't have to dedicate her life to sports—even though she still liked soccer, which was the odd thing to her. She liked the game itself. She hadn't been so fond of waking up at four thirty for training and medical treatment and weight lifting, then tutoring and classes and practice and film and more treatment, training, tutoring. The same twenty-hour schedule every day. And the grind was even worse during the season. But if her knee didn't get better, if she couldn't play at a high-enough level to warrant a scholarship to an American university, then she could do something else. Be someone else.

She could meet someone, she started thinking, those long early mornings on the training table. She could have a job, she could sleep in, she could, one day, have a baby.

And she had a baby. That's why she sat there crying in the chair, Caleb fitful in his sleep, his eyes shocking open now and again for no reason. Elisabeth cried because this was the unknown she'd wanted, the unknown she'd traded soccer for. She cried because the enormity of that. She cried because she didn't know where Nick was and she couldn't tell anyone Nick was gone, because she was afraid they'd find him. She cried because she was holding a baby, her baby, and that's what one does sometimes, rocking in a nursery in the middle of the night, holding her baby, she cried because it was her baby. Caleb. His name was Caleb.

I don't remember what I dreamed the last night I held him while we slept in the chair. Nothing at all probably. Most of the time I didn't sleep long

140 .

enough to really dream, just dreamy versions of the sleepy-time music I played for Caleb when I needed him to sleep. "Twinkle, Twinkle, Little Star" and "Alouette" and "Hush, Little Baby." That kind of stuff. The songs repeated in my head, in my dreams, and when I woke up the CD had stopped but the lullabies stayed in my ears. (Elisabeth Holland, VoIP, 30 Mar 05, Chicago 60640. Edgewater View Building.)

Then it happened. A month, a few weeks, not long at all after Nick took off and left her alone with the baby and never asked how things were, and never turned back to help her.

I woke up in the chair. Caleb was on my lap, on the cushion I used to hold him the times we were sleeping. He was blue. He wasn't breathing. I said his name. I sat him up and patted him and said his name louder. He was blue. I shook him. I knew I wasn't supposed to do that, but he was blue and what else was I supposed to do? I laid him down in his crib and called an ambulance, then picked him up to look at him, he was blue, and I held him to my shoulder and cried on his little head, his swirl of black hair, the point to his skull, the furrows of skin on the top of his head, until the ambulance came and they took him away from me to try and save him, but not for long, before they decided I could hold him if I wanted, while they did paperwork and turned off the lights on the ambulance, and it wasn't very long, pinching two folds of his pajamas together where the paramedics ripped the fabric to get at his chest, his baby skin, his blue lips, his blue fingertips, holding him, until they had to take him to the hospital to finish; and yes I could hold him in the back as they drove the city streets and stopped at stoplights—with no sirens, no spinning lights—but at the hospital they put him in one room and me in another with a woman who promised to help me because I didn't have any family around.

And that was that.

FILE 7

TYLER AHLS

16 FEB 05 TO 08 MAY 05

15 JUN 07

[16 Feb 05; eight days after Caleb Holland died]

It was Tyler who stayed with Elisabeth. After the funeral in Chippewa (the disaster that was, the scene at the burial) Elisabeth refused to let her mother return with her to Chicago. Still, Deb Ahls knew it would be best to keep an eye on Elisabeth, and since Elisabeth wouldn't hear of moving back to Chippewa, Deb struck a deal with Tyler—if he kept tabs on his sister, his mother would buy him a plane ticket to Karachi. (This would be his first time in Pakistan, his second in Central Asia.) Elisabeth didn't have any support in Chicago. Her old roommate moved on to be a graduate fellow in economics at Carnegie Mellon; all connections to her teammates were severed when she quit the team. Sadly, as she learned after college, most friendships are bonds of convenience—to remove proximity is to sever the link. Her only human contact (in a tenuous way) were the folks she worked with at the direct-mail office. Nobody thought Elisabeth was the type to contemplate suicide; on the other hand, she was alone in a miserable basement apartment in the doldrums of Chicago winter, her husband had left her, her child had died. Who's to say, given all that, what type of person she was?

For his part, Tyler performed as his mother expected. He made sure Elisabeth had enough to eat. Tried to get her to talk about her situation—how she felt about what happened—though mostly that meant Tyler asking about Nick and where Elisabeth thought her husband might be. Her pain over Caleb was too raw; Tyler couldn't take hearing his sister in agony, couldn't handle seeing her cry. He was still mostly boyish, twenty years old, but he tried his best to comfort her. Made her oatmeal, got her takeout, offered to walk her to work, then (after she made clear this wasn't necessary) struggled to keep up with her to the El station. With Elisabeth out of the apartment, Tyler spoke with Deb Ahls to confirm that Elisabeth made it to work (or left for work anyway), that Elisabeth went to a movie one night (when she didn't come home until late and refused to explain herself), that she was eating (even if she wouldn't accept the oatmeal Tyler offered). It was clear Elisabeth wanted space. But in order to get his plane ticket to Pakistan, Tyler had to answer the phone ready with an update every weekday morning at 10:45 a.m., right before Deb Ahls was to make sandwiches and soup for her and Gerry's lunch.

Otherwise, Tyler was left to his own devices. In addition to sleeping on the couch, he spent most of his time in the apartment: reading, watching cable news, clicking on his laptop. He might have looked like he was wasting time, but, to the trained eyes watching, everything he did was about going back to Asia, and there were four big advantages to his sister's apartment. One, it was less time he had to spend living with his parents. Two, he could live spartan—eat only plain oatmeal or rice for most meals, or *kafta* from a Lebanese grill for a treat. Tyler never touched a drop of alcohol, to get used to its prohibition in Pakistan. Point three, the temperature stayed at or below freezing almost the entire three months Tyler was in Chicago. He made himself walk three hours after lunch for physical conditioning and reduced his layers of clothing by increments until he could tolerate down to negative twelve Celsius in a tee shirt and jeans. Point four, Lis had Wi-Fi.

Item two (preparing to go to Pakistan) was what caught the attention of NSA spiders, especially after his escapades at Whitewater. His web activity focused on making contacts in Pakistan. Reaching out to regional publishers about job opportunities, unsuccessfully. Connecting with education companies who arranged ESOL jobs in Central Asia. Curating an RSS feed of missionaries who blogged about the dangers they faced overseas. Other stuff, on message boards where Tyler made anonymous posts, ones he bookmarked, about how to cross borders without being detected, and whether it was worth it to go see *what remains of the real Afghanistan before Bush blows it to smithereens.* (His words.)

He found an online tutorial on how to pray like a Muslim, then attended an open house at a prayer center in Orland Park. In fact, he went to a few mosques during his three months in Chicago. Apparently he was learning about Islam. What better way was there than learning to pray? He was drawn to the decorum, the performance of *wudu*, which he'd thought was just the washing of hands and feet, but of course there's more to it than that. Cleansing his nostrils and ears, wetting his red hair, making his intention to pray known in his heart so there would be an opening to let in God. He covered his body in the gear he wore backpacking, his base layer and bug shirt and fleece and, of course, his rainbow-colored doppa cap. Memorized the positions as best he could: *ruku, sajdah, tasleem.* It was like yoga, he thought. The deep breathing, the opening of his chest, the smooth transition between positions, quads burning when he sat on his feet, hip muscles releasing, the bending and allowing his blood to circulate. He must have felt self-conscious, praying in Arabic, *"Subhana Rabbiyal Allah,"* even alone in Elisabeth's apartment—maybe Tyler felt he was doing something transgressive and that's why he kept going. If he'd only known NSA was watching through the webcam in his laptop, imagine the thrill he'd have felt about that.

Elisabeth caught him at it one morning. Tyler on the rug in front of the TV, straightening from prostrate *sajdah* to upright *tasleem,* sitting back on his feet with his eyes shut, in his flannel pajamas and doppa. She froze with an arm reaching into the closet for her coat, eyes narrowing.

"What are you doing?"

"Research," he said, opening his eyes like the lids were heavy, blood rushing to his head.

"For what?"

"So I understand people."

Elisabeth removed her coat from the coat closet, flipped closed the door, then turned to stare at Tyler once more. He'd begun again, bringing his forehead to the rug and moving his lips in Anglo-accented Arabic. "Little brothers are odd ducks," Elisabeth said. She zipped her coat, pulled on her stocking cap, and left him to finish. She let him be, like she did when he was a boy and he slipped into the forest to play out scenarios he dreamed up, usually something with Lazarus or John the Baptist or Peter Pan. He had always been sensitive, creative, gullible, which meant Elisabeth had to work extra hard to tolerate him, to protect him.

That evening, however, when she came home from work and saw Tyler sitting in the snow in only mesh shorts, she couldn't let that go. "Inside," she told him, keys and a grocery bag in hand, snowflakes frozen over her stocking cap and the lapel of her coat. She held the door until Tyler pulled himself up and tiptoed over the ice and salt, his toes beet red. She waved to the boys across the street who gawked at Tyler, his freckled back hoary it was so pale, his doughy middle, the way he breathed slow and deep. "Good night," Elisabeth shouted to the boys across the street, then, to herself, "Nothing to see here."

Tyler wrapped himself in a blanket and sat on the couch, shivering.

"Is that practice too?"

"Exactly."

"Get dressed," Elisabeth told him. "Then come eat. You're not having oatmeal tonight."

After he put on jeans and a wool sweater, he found her in the kitchen at the cutting board. "Sit down," she said, so he pulled a chair into the kitchen to watch as she julienned one red bell pepper and one green, an onion, and started oil in the pan. She unwrapped four sausages from butcher paper. All this she'd picked up from the store on her way home from work.

"I've been wanting to tell you that you're annoying," she said, setting water to boil, gas igniter clicking, "but it's nice to have you here. It's been a long time since we hung out together."

"If I'm annoying, why don't you make me leave?"

"You keep Mom away. At the funeral, she threatened to move in with me."

The sausage and peppers sizzled in the skillet, the two of them listening to the pops of grease, the way a sliced onion hissed its water when stirred to the hot spots of the pan, the splash when she poured dry rigatoni into boiling water. Even as the food heated (and quieted as it cooked, putting up less of a fight) Elisabeth didn't turn from the stove to speak. Both of them smelled the veggies, the fennel in the sausage. "I thought you might want to get out of Chippewa," Elisabeth said as she dished up their plates, her voice quiet now, out of the kitchen, as she spooned sausage and peppers on a bed of pasta. "And it's nice seeing you. I meant what I said. We were buds once, but it's been a long time since we had any time alone, just brother and sister. Not coworkers at Apostle Crossing, you know? I can't remember when."

"You always had soccer."

"Is everything okay?" She hadn't heard him. "Are *you* okay? With everything that happened?"

Tyler stirred his food together on the plate, fork held above as he blew on the steam. His eyes started to water, like they always did when his family talked about "the problem of Tyler."

"What do you mean?"

"I don't know. Like, emotionally, growing up how we did. Do you think the way we were raised messed us up? How else can I say it? Growing up in a theme park. Having to act super religious all the time. And for what?"

Tyler snorted at that, trying to laugh. He closed his eyes, blinking, and looked to the other room. He couldn't look at her, not with his eyes watering.

"There's nothing wrong with believing in God," he said. "It's something to be proud of, Apostle Crossing. Being a missionary is the highest calling for a Christian, the definition of *apostle*, even if it's just some dinky park in the woods."

"That's not what I asked."

"There's nothing wrong with God," Tyler said. "He doesn't mess up. God is perfect."

Tyler glanced up to see how he frustrated her, how it was now Elisabeth who sighed and rubbed the skin below her ear with one hand while she stabbed at pasta with the other, her fork hand. She must have wanted to press him, to ask since when did he still believe all that, to have him clarify what he didn't understand about her question. Elisabeth didn't ask if it was a good thing to build Apostle Crossing, if God had erred by sending Tyler a vision; she asked if they were damaged by having to live their faith so publicly.

Of course, if Tyler was damaged, if he'd gone crazy, how could he tell the difference?

Instead of pressing him, Elisabeth asked, "Did you get enough to eat?" She said, "There's more." And when he shook his head, "I forgot to make garlic toast, didn't I?"

Tyler tried to look her in the eye but couldn't. He could only glance to her, then back at his plate. Whether she meant to or not, she shamed him. Made him feel six years old—how it was when Elisabeth came to find him in the woods. Tyler up to a weird game in the trees. Usually he was Slightly Fox or John the Baptist, these his daydreams of choice. Hard to say if that's normal. Elisabeth listened, back then, as he explained the rules of the game he invented—how John wished to baptize Salome but wasn't going to get his wish, and he had to hide in those woods before Herod had his head on a platter. Elisabeth put her arm around Tyler, listening, and led him back home to the kitchen sink so he'd wash for dinner—still coaching him at the sink, to recite the alphabet while he washed his hands, to scrub between the fingers and not just rinse his palms, to wash his face, behind his ears, so he would be clean. Elisabeth had quite a lot of tenderness for him. He was her little brother, after all. It was never quite the same after Tyler had his dream about Apostle Crossing, and especially after the park was built. She lost him.

Still, she kept at this mothering of him that evening in her apartment, only weeks after her own child died, because she wanted him to be better, to be fine.

"Forget what I asked you. None of that matters. We're all just trying to get by, and it's hard. You're okay."

He told her then how he wanted to go to Pakistan. He hadn't yet been there, only to Tajikistan, where he'd found those Christian tracts written in Tajiki Persian and Kyrgyz. It was Karachi he had his sights set on next.

"That's what all this training is about," he explained. "See, it's not so bad. It's missionary work. I want to give away Bibles where it isn't easy to get one. That's the opportunity market, my best chance to do something special."

Elisabeth didn't say anything as he told her this. She ate her food before it got cold and listened patiently, as if they were walking out of the woods like they had years before.

"I've been doing research. There are Orthodox Christians in Tajikistan, Uzbekistan, Kyrgyzstan. I met some, and of course they have their own Bibles, in Russian mostly, but not so much in Pakistan, I don't think. Anyway, I haven't been there yet, but it sounds right. Wouldn't that be cool? The Good News in Urdu?"

He met her eyes and didn't shy away. There was something in him she saw, a hunger anyone would have seen—a glint, a pulse in his pupils.

"At Whitewater they thought I lost it. But what are those people doing with their lives that's so special? What acts of courage will they accomplish? The places I go, the sticky situations I wiggle out of— maybe I don't look it, but I'm brave, I'm capable. I can do this."

As Elisabeth stacked their plates and piled their napkins on top, she must have tried to smile at him, but her smile was upside down, like her grief was bubbling.

"I wouldn't do what you're doing," she told him, "but at least you're trying to make the world better. That's admirable."

They stood and she hugged him. Tyler was a half foot taller than her, so she pressed her ear against his chest when he pulled her in to squeeze. She was crying, he realized. "Promise you will be careful. Watch out who you talk to. Stay inside at night."

"It's going to be okay," he told her. And, "Okay," she agreed, and, "I love you."

When she took a step back and picked up the dishes, Elisabeth's cheeks were red, and her eyes darted around him so she didn't have to look at him. The words stuck in her throat when she said she loved him, because it was the only time she ever said so, and he didn't respond. Why did it have to be so embarrassing, she must have wondered, to say you loved your brother?

Tyler's whereabouts were known to agents during this time, so when Nick Holland placed a telephone call to Elisabeth's landline that March, it was no surprise that Tyler picked up. Nick phoned all the time in March and April, in 2005. He was only gone a couple weeks before he started working for Midland Pacific. The calls were traced back to a series of motels in Wyoming.

At first there was silence on the other end of the line.

—*Is anybody there?* Tyler asked, which made the caller hang up.

Tyler saw it happen with Elisabeth too, usually late at night, two in the morning, even later sometimes. Both of them asleep. Elisabeth in the bedroom and Tyler on the couch when the phone rang. Tyler didn't know what to do when his sister picked up the phone: Should he hide in the bathroom, or flee the apartment to give her some privacy? He pretended to be asleep and consequently heard everything—it was a small apartment, he was a few yards from the landline jack. It was strange how Elisabeth picked up the phone and didn't even whisper, not *hello*, not *who is it*, not *stop calling here*. Tyler pulled the blanket to his chin, eavesdropped on the nothing Elisabeth was saying and the nothing the caller said in return.

You didn't need to consult phone records to know it was Nick on the other end. Who else would call in the middle of the night and be too chickenshit to say a word? If it wasn't Tyler who picked up, Nick would stay on the line and listen to Elisabeth breathe until he fell asleep. And Tyler too, in the next room: he'd listen to the nothing, to her breath, until he fell asleep.

Tyler asked Elisabeth about the calls. "Was it Nick?"

"What do you mean?"

"I bet it's him. Or a pervert. How long has this been going on? Has he ever said a word?"

Elisabeth looked like she was going to cry, like she might lose her composure. "Shut up," she said. It was a mistake to ask about Nick's calls. The way she acted, it was as if the phone had been ringing nightly for quite a while, since before Caleb had died (which was true) and in her mind the calls were sacred.

One morning, home alone when the phone rang, Tyler said nothing when he picked up, like Elisabeth did. He knew it wasn't his mom calling—she certainly would speak when the line connected. This caller didn't. Tyler mimicked how Elisabeth kept the caller on the line. Didn't speak. Listened to the breathing on the other end. The heavy, half-awake breath, dry and raspy and hungover. He sat up on the couch, then kept as still as he could. To hear another's silence, their absences, was fascinating, how much you took that for granted, how with each breath there was noise, a disturbance of air, microscopic whistling, dust and mucus in your own throat—but you never heard it, mostly never. Its rhythm, its constancy, made the sound undetectable.

—*I can hear you, Tyler. I hear you breathing.* Tyler nearly dropped the phone when Nick said that. *You sound different than her.*

—*I am different,* Tyler said. Then, *Where are you?*

Tyler asked all sorts of things. *Don't you ever think of Lis and Caleb? Are you still in Chicago? Then where? Why do you call all the darn time if you have nothing to say? Are you coming back?* He thought Nick would hang up. But the reason Nick called was to explain himself. All the stuff Nick wanted to tell Elisabeth (but couldn't) he'd end up telling Tyler.

—*I got a job with a railroad. I'm not coming back anytime soon.*

—Why didn't you leave a note?

—I didn't plan on this. I was just going for a drive. If I'd wrote down everything I was thinking, then I wouldn't have left. I'd have talked myself out of going.

—Would that have been so bad?

—I don't know.

—Do you regret it?

—There's no crawling back. Nobody will ever forget.

Nick tried to explain himself. How he felt nauseous most of the time before he left. Panic attacks and that sort of thing. When they were alone, he'd put his hand on Caleb's chest and hyperventilate; he'd cry because of what was bubbling up in him. It felt like he needed a cigarette. (*I told Elisabeth I quit, but I couldn't breathe without at least one a day.*) That morning, he left, got in his car, and drove. He wanted to see the lake and not think about his wife and the baby and if they were missing him. He went exit to exit on the Dan Ryan, then doubled back to the Loop. Stopped at a convenience store to buy a pack of Camels, then headed west. It had been a decade since he was last in Nebraska, since the time he moved to Portland when he was in college, then hitchhiked to Seattle, before he ended up in Chicago. *I wanted to go to Nebraska,* Nick explained to Tyler. He talked and talked, gabbing—Tyler had never heard Nick like this before, he'd always come off as quiet—so it was clear that something was wrong inside Nick, whatever made him run.

How he was in a panic that morning when he convinced himself to do it. That's a six-hour drive to get across the Missouri River into Omaha, but he could go there and back and still make it home in time for work if he sped the whole way. Nick needed to do this stupid thing and didn't want to tell his wife what he was up to. But once he got there, he realized the town where he grew up was seven hours further on from Omaha.

—If I was going home, that wasn't it. I went in the direction of my dad's farm. But then I was afraid that Dad was going to ask questions if I showed up by myself, like, why was I alone? And where were Lis and the baby? I couldn't show up like that. What could I say to him? Dad hadn't even met the baby.

—Don't you know about Caleb?

—I don't know anything!

Nick was still rolling from his speech about leaving and the excuses he made to himself. He can be forgiven if he missed what Tyler tried to tell him, after he asked *how is Caleb doing?*

Neither said a word. Tyler shocked into disbelief, aware suddenly of the radiator clinking, of the way dust motes glide over sunshine. He hadn't really thought about this yet: that Nick had no idea what happened to his son, that Nick wasn't calling because Caleb died or to check to see if Elisabeth was okay. Nick was calling for himself. Because of his guilt. Because he missed them—his wife, his son—and still he wouldn't come home. Nick called only to hear her, to wait for Elisabeth to say she missed him, that she needed him, that she wanted him back.

Once Tyler realized what was going on, once it came over him how fucked up this was, something catalyzed inside him—an urge to protect his sister. If he staggered, if he was irate, that's understandable. If he wanted to hurt Nick, to fool him—after hearing Elisabeth cry herself to sleep, after bearing witness at Caleb Harrison Holland's funeral, when the boy's own father bore no witness—then, yes, you can understand what Tyler did next.

—Caleb is fine, Tyler said.

He astounded himself, those words coming from his mouth. How they slipped like gravel from a spade. How they stood because there was no one to set the record straight.

—Caleb is doing well.

—Oh, good. Is he sitting up? When do babies do that?

—Yes, he's sitting up. He's doing everything he's supposed to.

—Like what? Tell me.

—There's not a lot.

Tyler's laptop sat open next to him on the couch. He opened a new window and searched *3 month old*. It was that simple.

—Shakes objects in hands. Back muscles developing, so he can move his head around. Stuff like that.

Nick must have thought that over a moment—how the world kept spinning without him, allegedly, how if everyone was doing well, maybe running was for the best, after all.

—He looks just like me, or he did. Guys would say this to me, like creepy old men at Ace Hardware. "No denying he ain't yours, looks just like you." What a weird joke, like there's a chance Caleb isn't mine. It's true, anyway, he looks like me. In the eyes and cheekbones.

Nick went silent then, remembering, and Tyler waited. In the nothing being said, Tyler could hear Nick being overwhelmed again. Nick's breathing, Nick trying to swallow and not being able to swallow. The dry sound a mouth makes when it smacks open.

—Is Caleb there now?

—No. He isn't.

—He goes to daycare?

—Yes.

—Will you tell them that I think about them every day? And that I regret leaving.

—Yes.

—Tell Caleb I want to come home but I can't. Say my name when you tell him.

—Let me make a deal with you, Tyler said. *Every month I'll call to give you an all clear. Or email, whatever you want. If something happens, if you need to rush back, I'll call right away. You'll know everything is okay, so long as you stay away.*

—What do you mean?

—*It's all good. Everyone is okay, I told you. If that changes, you'll be the first to know. I promise. But don't come back. Do you understand? Lis, Caleb, they're better off. We're going to help them, my family and me. We're going to make sure she is taken care of, both of them.*

—*Lis said that? She's better off?*

—*Leave it to me. I'll send the all clear. I promise.*

[15 Jun 07; six months before Tyler Ahls disappeared]

By the time Tyler moved to Peshawar to teach ESOL, the files certainly contained evidence of the connection between Tyler and Nick. The two of them made quarterly calls, they emailed, but it wasn't terrorism or the US government they discussed—it was Caleb.

Over the course of these discussions, Tyler built a shadow life, one he escalated with details over time, stretching his lies: Caleb's first word (*dodo* for "dog"), and Caleb's first steps, and Caleb's first Christmas (*he got clothes, a Favre jersey*), and Caleb's first birthday party and the lemon cake Elisabeth baked and the face Caleb made when he tasted sour. How Caleb was tall for his age and was already learning how to swim, at two. How he liked to watch *Transformers* with his uncle when Tyler visited. How, the more Caleb grew, he didn't look anything like Nick, Tyler said, which Nick found surprising. But, no, Tyler said, *his hair is dark, straight, coarse like Lis, and his nose has a point to it, is narrow, like Lis.*

All this that Tyler made up. Does that show how desperate he was when he went to Peshawar?

Does it show a connection to Nick Holland? It's hard to say how this reflects on Nick's character, that he played along.

In the spring, Elisabeth grew restless in Chicago. Whether it was from genuine healing, if her heart thawed with the Lincoln Park snowpack, if only slightly, or whether it was because living with her brother in that apartment was utterly unbearable, who's to say?

For weeks she put the seed in Tyler's mind that his presence in Chicago wasn't necessary, certainly not in her apartment. He should go back to school or learn a trade or return home to Chippewa. When Tyler shook off these suggestions, she told him in a terse midwestern rage (the intensity of her voice rising all the way to medium) that he should go back to Asia.

That's exactly what he intended to do—once he fulfilled the terms laid out by his mother, in regard to the surveillance of his sister. Still, Tyler acted like he found the suggestion objectionable.

Don't you like having me here?

You're my little brother. What do you think?

She must have realized her only hope was to get out. Chicago hadn't been far enough to run, not far enough to keep an Ahls from following.

Whatever the reason, she made a sharp turn in April. Nick still caught her on the phone, albeit rarely, late at night, though that was a much less frequent occurrence than before. (Nick called drunk and couldn't help himself—when he needed to hear her breathe—but there was no real threat of his speaking. He made that bargain with Tyler.) A few weeks passed, then Elisabeth didn't even answer when the phone rang in the middle of the night.

She wearied of the routine, Deb's phone calls, Tyler's insinuations, his slobbish ways—unwashed clothes cast everywhere, red hairs curled on her soap, his spilled oatmeal turned to cement on the linoleum. There's more, but why go on? What bothered Elisabeth most was that Tyler obsessed over Nick. He asked all the time why she didn't divorce him, or suggested she should track him down and set the score straight.

Dad hired a PI to find him, she'd say. *What do you expect me to do?*
He doesn't know about Caleb, Tyler would say. *Somebody should tell him.*
Of course, Tyler wouldn't be the one to tell Nick about that.

Elisabeth would have done anything for change. She started looking into nursing programs when she stayed late at work, the light from her cubicle the only one that bled into the lukewarm darkness of the direct-mail office. Twenty tabs open in Firefox so she could browse every nursing program in North America that looked halfway doable. Her main criteria was that the school have flexible academic terms and rolling admissions with exceptions made for those who applied on short notice, and that the program would require her to move at least six hours away. That's how she found the school at Saint Wenceslaus in Omaha. In general terms, it fit the criteria she set. As she flipped through the tabs one of those nights cloistered in the office, the idea of moving to Omaha stuck in her mind so bizarrely and persistently. She returned twice, then three times to the tab for Saint Wenceslaus and its accelerated program, then decided to complete the online application that night and save herself the trouble of worrying later. Maybe she sold herself short by attending a school that would admit her two weeks before the term began, but she didn't care. She was getting out. The very minute she received an email from admissions, she forwarded the message to her mother. *I'm doing this,* she wrote. *If Tyler wants my apartment until June, the place is all his.*

Deb Ahls knew enough to not fight Elisabeth on this. She knew enough to avoid even asking if this is what Elisabeth truly wanted. *I'm coming to help you pack* is what Deb Ahls replied. She would arrive in Chicago within thirty-six hours.

Tyler didn't take the news as well: *Isn't that where Nick's from? Doesn't his dad live out there on a bean farm or something?*

It's sugar beets. And, no. Their farm is halfway to Canada from where Omaha is.

The three of them stayed together in the basement apartment for Elisabeth's last ten days in Chicago. Tyler on the couch, Deb and Elisabeth together in the double bed. Elisabeth worked at the advertising office until the day before she left. It was up to Deb and Tyler to box her stuff. The two of them packing what Elisabeth would need in her new life and tossing in the dumpster what they felt was superfluous, mostly what Nick had left behind. The rest of it was sold on Craigslist or to a secondhand furniture store, the larger items like their bed, their sofa. (Tyler then had to sleep on the floor, which he claimed to prefer, and Elisabeth and her mother shared an inflatable mattress brought along from Chippewa.) Somehow it was her bike basket that made Elisabeth break down, the one Nick had bought for her on their first date. The bike basket was sold still attached to Elisabeth's Schwinn; the bicycle hawked at a steep discount to a sophomore from Northwestern who couldn't believe anyone would sell a ride like that for cheap—not even when Elisabeth explained how she was moving to Omaha to go to nursing school and the Schwinn didn't fit in her car. Elisabeth cried after the sophomore's boyfriend tied the bike into the trunk of a yellow cab and they drove away—because of the look of profound pity the girl had given her. Pity because Elisabeth was not a college sophomore bike-hunting with her boyfriend, like the girl was. Elisabeth cried thinking about that girl and her pity—locked herself in the bathroom hoping her mother might leave her alone, rested her head on the sink to cry—not because she wanted the bike anymore, or to be a pretty sophomore or to have a meathead boyfriend. No. Elisabeth cried because she wanted the opposite of those things. That is, the end result of those things, in the natural course of human life. A husband, a child, a home that wasn't cluttered with her college junk.

All the packing and selling and the unending spats about what Elisabeth would actually need in Nebraska and the passive-aggressive undermining of her ability to make a decision. You might think Deb Ahls would take it easy on her daughter, given the circumstances, but you'd be wrong. Deb had only a few dwindling hours to impart wisdom before Elisabeth left.

On the last day, they loaded Elisabeth's Pontiac to the gills and had coffee and doughnuts together at the curb before she drove off. Deb waving with the apartment keys in hand. Deb would return to Chippewa in the afternoon, but Tyler stayed behind for a month. He'd hand the keys over to the super. He had it set up to return to Central Asia, to Pakistan this time, first to Karachi, then north. His mom had already bought him the ticket.

FILE 8

ELISABETH HOLLAND

01 OCT 08

[01 Oct 08; two days after Agt Schwaller arrived in Omaha]

Agent Schwaller still hassled Elisabeth. She met him three times, told everything she knew about her brother, and a lot that had nothing to do with Tyler, personal things, about Caleb, about Nick, her parents. The agent was all the more interested when she opened up about her private life. When she stopped for dinner in the evening, she'd spot him in the parking lot watching through the window. When she jogged around the park, there he'd be, down the block by the tennis courts, scribbling in a notebook—about what? The color of her jogging shorts? How she wore aviator sunglasses when she ran? How she wiped her forehead with a fluffy red wristband? *I told you everything,* she said when he called her at work. *What the fuck more do you want to know? What can I say to make you leave me alone?*

Elisabeth thought the agent was trying to drive her crazy, and, sometimes, late at night, she wondered if she had in fact lost her mind, if Agent Schwaller was an aberration, a paranoia she dreamed up, and if Tyler had not, in fact, disappeared from a mountain canyon in Pakistan, after all, and there was no ransom—maybe she'd dreamed that too, Tyler's absurd ranting in that video. Elisabeth breathed deep when unhealthy thoughts threatened to spill over the levee one after another, ones that might hurt her if she let them loose. She got back to brushing her teeth. She had work in the morning. (Sandy switched her to first shift after the Junger kids came in, at Elisabeth's request.) Elisabeth didn't have time to waste deciphering if she'd lost her mind or not—and for that reason she was grateful she had to go to work.

Growing up in Wisconsin, she never once doubted the government was on her side. Not until all the stuff her family went through trying to find Tyler when he disappeared. The State Department worked against them—sandbagging FOIA requests, redacting documents, severing the family's contact with overseas leads like the Pakistani PI Khan Khalili. It seemed like State knew something about Tyler's whereabouts, but State wouldn't say. State didn't help track him down or give the Ahls peace of mind, if indeed, like Khalili claimed, Tyler died falling into a canyon. Of course, all this changed when the video surfaced of Tyler in a Haqqani bunker. All sorts of government and extragovernmental agencies were suddenly interested in tracking down Tyler Ahls.

Elisabeth didn't mention this fear (State deliberately undermining her family) when Agent Schwaller asked again and again for her to go through the story of what the Ahls had done to track down Tyler in Asia. What contacts they made. What groups they talked to and if they made any deals, or traded information. *What was your opinion of the US government before and after the ordeal? What do you think about Iraq and Afghanistan? Do you consider yourself a patriot? Do you ever empathize with terrorists? Even a little? Even an iota? Do you ever, even for a moment, think America had it coming on 9/11?* Ridiculous questions. Pointless questions.

She threw the agent for a loop after a while. Switched up her schedule at work, started going to a different part of town for dinner, was out late driving the north side of the city. She wasn't sleeping much, it is noted. If she was home, she left the lights on.

Elisabeth spent so much time tracking the news in the weeks after the video of her brother aired, as you might expect. A lot of bad things happened, and perhaps that exacerbated her mental condition—how even that morning there was a suicide bombing at an Eid celebration in Peshawar that killed four people. She couldn't help but be reminded that Tyler might be executed by his captors—it was possible there could have been another video released, at any time, that showed this in terrifying detail. (It was easier to grieve for her brother when she believed he drowned in a mountain stream.) She felt even more alone, more isolated, when something reminded her of the innumerable acts of barbarity that could befall her brother—and that if something monstrous did fall on his head, the world would be watching, they would expect to see her reaction. That part—being observed in her isolation, her grief—that was the worst part.

So she read about the Junger family in the newspaper after the nine kids were processed at Saint Wenceslaus. Nebraska's safe haven snafu was national news by then, on every evening talk show. This dad's photo (some strange Glamour Shots–style portrait, him wearing a black leather do-rag, its tails swung around to his bare chest) was plastered in every paper across the country after it hit the wire. Cable correspondents congregated at the hospital, around the ER, the lobby, posing questions to anyone in a hospital uniform who'd stop to talk.

A father dropped nine kids at a hospital and gave them over to the state. He was overwhelmed, he said. His wife died, he lost his job, and he didn't know what to do. It was better to give up his kids, he said, than to let them struggle and fail and starve, which is what was happening under his watch. Now those kids were celebrities of a sick sort. Still without much going for them, but celebrities nonetheless. Maybe they were better off, like the father hoped.

Elisabeth needed to know they were safe in their foster homes—Kyle at least, the one she let listen to her heart and told that everything was going to be okay. But she didn't know where any of the Junger kids had been placed, of course. She asked a social worker at the hospital, but giving out that information was verboten. *Is that a HIPAA thing?*

The social worker shook her head. *I can't deal with this shit right now. You understand what's going on here? I got Brian Williams on hold.*

Elisabeth drove around the neighborhood where the kids came from. She'd never been to that part of the city before. Up around Ames Avenue, in North Omaha. She crossed Dodge Street and went up Thirtieth. Hugged along the North Freeway on side streets. This was dinnertime, the sun still out. To Lake and Bedford, to steer clear of city parks. Elisabeth didn't know why she was scared. She'd lived in Chicago—in Boystown, before that in dorms, but still. On the north side of Omaha she sat low in her car to hide behind the seat-belt strap and not make eye contact with teenage boys who bumped rap music. She felt very much like a girl from a place named Chippewa, like a woodsy Wisconsin girl, white and comfortable, embarrassed that she listened so rapt to *All Things Considered*, how a little thrill rippled through her chest when Robert Siegel mentioned Omaha—all the pundits so disappointed in the failings of Nebraskans, talking Saint Wenceslaus specifically and those poor Junger kids. Elisabeth wanted to hear what new information the reporters dug up, but she struggled to hear. She couldn't listen to NPR at a stoplight with neighborhood boys next to her clowning.

She took Creighton Boulevard to Paxton to Fontenelle—nearly caused a collision when she failed to properly navigate a series of Y-shaped intersections—then she hopped on Sorensen Parkway and got out of there. Kept up with the evening rush until she was at the airport (comforted) then headed north again, hugged to the river, passed trailer parks, a water plant, Mormon Bridge, until the road twisted into the trees and the nice houses on North River Drive. There was a place up there she'd been to before, the Surfside Club on North River. They served catfish and corn fritters and lemonade, and she could eat outside at a picnic table by the river. It wasn't a place a person went to eat alone, but Elisabeth wanted to see speedboats fool around on the river. The Missouri moves fast, it's polluted and murky. A few people drowned each summer along this stretch. Elisabeth threw corn fritters to the water and catfish gasped at the surface to eat.

She spent ninety minutes on the patio before she went back to her car. Why would she have a leisurely dinner alone if she was in such a rush before? She had looked lost driving earlier that evening, slowing at intersections to read street signs, then accelerating without warning to rejoin traffic. She'd been lost. This time she took the freeway, which was easy to navigate, more comforting with its high fences and barrier trees, how, when it was built, they dug into the natural landscape to lay pavement so you didn't have to look at a neighborhood when you drove past. It was just freeway. A comfort in its blandness, its same-as-anywhere quality. Maybe Elisabeth felt better driving at high speeds, no stoplights to slow her. An American in her natural state, on the freeway, nothing ahead or behind except lined pavement.

On September 21, a Sunday, Lincoln Hamilton's mother, aunt, and grandmother started driving from Detroit. They took turns at the wheel to make better time and arrived at Creighton University Medical Center at 1:30 a.m. on a Monday. They had no family here; the boy was in no immediate danger, was not a threat to himself or others. Rather, the mother, aunt, and grandmother crossed four state lines for the sole purpose of transferring custody of Lincoln Hamilton to the great state of Nebraska. This was a tricky situation, as Nebraska had no intention of taking responsibility for every problem child dragged across the Missouri River. The mother in this case saw about Nebraska's unique safe haven phenomenon on TV. She told this to the nurses at CUMC—how there was a lot of stress in her life and she couldn't deal with her son anymore. Lincoln Hamilton carried his own luggage—a suitcase and a backpack—through ER security. He packed five days' of clothes in the suitcase; the backpack held only a basketball, regulation orange. When the women left him, the aunt handed Lincoln a ten-dollar bill.

When Elisabeth got off the freeway, she drove aimlessly—still in North Omaha. She was unsure where she was but wasn't worried, food in her stomach. Elisabeth was getting used to what she saw—boarded-up businesses on some corners, boarded up for so long that they still advertised lemon-lime Slice and RC Cola in faded paint on the side of buildings; auto shops in spaces that used to be restaurants, the windows bricked in, rusted tanks on the lots that held spent oil; a burnt house every now and again, charred and blackened, alone on a block, one window gaped open where the plywood was ripped away so squatters could get in— and she saw new things too, things her eyes couldn't see when she sped through the first time. Plastic castles and slides behind chain-link in daycare backyards; the deep front yards of houses along the boulevards that crisscrossed the big grassy parks, with massive bur oak, sycamore, cottonwood trees that made the old stone houses underneath look like toys; bare-chested boys ambling home from the park; lanky men in jeans and sweat-through tees getting home from work, the men smiling as they walked up the driveway. Then the main drags. Little kids dancing raunchy on the sidewalk outside a house. Little boys humping air in Elisabeth's direction.

She was going about this the wrong way, she realized. She went home and got on her computer, went to the Douglas County assessor's website. Accessed the records, refined her search, and found what she was looking for. It was all there. A photograph of Junger's house, the address, what he'd paid for it, who'd owned it before, the layout of the house, the square footage, what taxes were paid in what year, what taxes were still owed, the actual worth in case you were maybe looking for an investment property, to pick up a bargain off a guy who couldn't pay his taxes. All the info was there, all the intel, in those electronic files.

Elisabeth felt like a creep looking this up. But there it was. Like medical histories she studied at Saint Wenceslaus, there in the valuation history: the declining tax base, the blighting of property. And maybe within the figures, within the layout of spreadsheet grid and the values listed in each field, maybe you see some of why nine kids were dropped off at a hospital.

Hunk Boyd's parents took him to BryanLGH West in Lincoln because he didn't obey the rules at home and they couldn't afford the programs he needed. They worked at a plastic-components plant, but their insurance didn't cover youth behavioral rehab. His stepfather told a social worker that Hunk put the family in danger, but wouldn't elaborate as to what that meant. Hunk was previously a ward of the state, two years before, after he was charged with misdemeanor theft and disturbing the peace for stealing beer from a grocery store. He'd been a runaway. He didn't last long in the group home, however, because he didn't follow the rules. *I'll be good, I'll be good,* Hunk cried in the ER at BryanLGH West as a nurse and security officer escorted him to an examination bay. *Don't leave me. I promise I'll be good.*

Elisabeth waited in her car outside the Junger house. It looked the same, more or less, as it did in the photo she found online: same color trim, the scraggly maple in the front yard, if a little more scraggly, as a limb from the top half had snapped and hung so the rotted heartwood of the tree showed. Elisabeth referred to layout and property-line diagrams she printed off at home and articles she clipped from the newspaper, to cross-reference with what she saw in person, to understand what it was like inside those walls. But, really, these consultations, Elisabeth made them because she didn't know what else to do now that she'd found the house.

Should she knock on the front door? Ring the bell? Then what? Did she want to talk to the man, if he was there, the father of those nine kids who'd been dropped off during her shift at Saint Wenceslaus? Did she want to ask him why? Did she want to slap him, chastise him for not being a better father? Did she want to ask if he regretted what he did? If he'd slept a single restful hour, or if he paced the floor to stare into their bedrooms at all the backpacks, toys, their clothes, their video games, the baby's diapers? Did she want to ask if he would take his kids back if he had the chance?

She turned off the car and pulled the key from the ignition and put it in her purse so she couldn't drive off the moment she got scared. If the car was running, it would have been easy to get a glimpse of the house for a second, then go, like a tourist. Elisabeth didn't want to be a tourist. She wanted to feel something about the house those kids came from. Senseless things happened all the time, and there was nothing anyone could do about it. Elisabeth knew this. God erases for no reason. But was she supposed to accept that? That God takes love away and there's no reason for any of it except for God's reason? That the flock doesn't get to understand?

She had that day's *World-Herald* with her. There were several articles on the Junger case. Quotes from Governor Heineman and Attorney General Bruning, from experts at far-flung universities with insight into such cases, allegedly. Elisabeth sat in her car and read the newspaper, here and there because she'd read the articles twice already, all the pertinent details at least. There was a photo of Cary Junger. He was tired. Kind of wilted. This man fathered nine kids. That seemed unlikely, looking at his photo. When she pictured men with big families, with a whole crew of kids, Elisabeth saw brawny guys. The big families she knew in Wisconsin had factory-worker dads, lumberyard dads; an ample-hipped wife somewhere in the middle of their portraits, all the children straining to get a hand on her, an arm around her, for the photograph. Elisabeth thought of Mormon families she knew, industrious and clean cut, scrupulously blond. She didn't think of a scrawny dud from high school siring nine kids. Not the twerp in remedial classes. The kind of person Elisabeth—she'd been focused, driven, always tried to do the right thing, a high achiever, and also self-involved, she had to be—the kind of person Elisabeth forgot about in high school, until one day the dud was next to her at graduation, looking as ridiculous in robe and mortarboard as everybody else, and she supposed a twerp like that had been there all along too.

It was in the *World-Herald* how Cary Junger married young. Eighteen, right after high school. Cary and Glory—his wife's name was Glory, so perfect a name for the article, so perfect a name for Anderson Cooper to recite with glee on cable news. Cary and Glory. Married young, had nine kids together.

I pray they're better off without me, Cary Junger told reporters. *I was married seventeen years. She's gone. What was I supposed to do alone? We had the kids together. I couldn't give nothing to those kids without her.*

Cary Junger was thirty-four. A widower. A laborer, but unemployed since July.

The article mentioned how Douglas County took his kids away before because his house was in poor repair. Broken septic tank. No gas, no water, but plenty of pets. Three dogs, four cats, two rabbits, twelve caged mice (and a number of, presumably, uncaged mice), two salamanders, and one lizard, as is noted in the files. HHS officials found jars of human waste inside the house. This was 2004. Glory was still alive. They weren't done having kids, yet the state took the seven they had then and put them in protective custody for nine months, until the house was habitable again, then they had two more kids over the next three years. Cary and Glory. Neither had steady work. HHS paid their rent and utility bills, once the kids returned.

That case from 2004 was scrupulously notated in the files: how Cary *lacked common sense* and Glory was *prone to expressing distorted thinking* and both resisted the idea of employment and ignored foreclosure threats and wouldn't help the kids with cooking and cleaning—and still Glory wanted more children.

For what purpose did she want more children? The file is cloudy on this matter. She was demented, more or less, the file makes this clear, and there's no law against having kids.

Elisabeth went to the door. Stood there a moment. Looked in the windows. She recalled the names of the children—Colton, Chase, Emma, Elsie, Jefferson, Melody, Kyle, David, Belle. Through the window, Elisabeth saw how somebody had left a light on. A bare bulb burned weakly yellow in the kitchen, though no noise came from inside. It smelled like the sewer backed up frequently, as was the case. The grass wild to her thighs, maple branches decomposing in the yard. The door itself, the paint peeled off, the wood splintered near the dead bolt, like someone had tried to kick their way in, a while ago, but the lock was intact. Elisabeth was going to knock, but the lady next door came outside and asked what Elisabeth was doing.

"You with the news? I already told the papers and the TV. Cary left. Him and his girlfriend. The next morning after he got rid of his kids. Walked out with a big blue suitcase."

"Where did he go?"

"To live with his girlfriend."

"He has a girlfriend?"

"The girlfriend has four kids, did you know that? None live with her, they're all in foster care, which is for the best, you know."

"I didn't know that."

"It's the truth." The woman leaned out her door. She wore a floral-print flannel dress, except it wasn't exactly a dress, more like pajamas, her hair in small gray curls. "Do you need my name for the article? Or want to take a picture?"

"I'm not with the news," Elisabeth said.

"I wish people'd quit talking about Cary. Makes the whole neighborhood look bad."

"I suppose it does."

"I used to buy those kids popsicles, whenever my grandkids were here. They're not bad kids. I hope all this hubbub turns out good for them in the end. Do you think that's possible?"

"I don't know."

Elisabeth followed the cases in the news. She couldn't help herself. Each morning a child was given to the state, she held back tears as she read about the drop-off in the newspaper, then clipped the article and pasted it into its own page in the binder she kept, in her files about the safe haven kids. Tommie Hayes, who was twelve, left by his grandma at BryanLGH West in Lincoln because his mother was trying to regain legal custody and his mother was a meth addict. Adam Cherry, who'd lived with his grandfather as a toddler, until his grandfather died. Then he moved to Omaha to be with his father, who had a string of DUI convictions. He was sixteen when his dad drove him to Children's Hospital and left him there, a little before noon on a Sunday.

Elisabeth had tried hard to give Caleb a good start in life. All the required visits to her obstetrician, the tours of delivery rooms, the reading of manuals and attending birthing classes, the watching of her diet to avoid gestational diabetes, the buying of supplies and toys, and reading of consumer reports; even letting Nick go without a fuss, because letting go of Nick seemed like it would be best for the baby. When she read about safe haven kids, it was so sad, the way most of them were torpedoed from the start. The situations into which these kids were born: fetal alcohol syndrome, drug abuse, poverty, one of them born in a prison infirmary. Most all these kids would still grow up into something, into adults. Maybe they'd be imprisoned too and give birth to FAS babies, or they'd end up like that loser who shot up the Von Maur in Omaha the December before. Elisabeth wondered how many messed-up kids there are who slip into adulthood for each who doesn't. It was devastating to think about how random the world could be, how fateful, how black, chaotic, blue.

Maybe Elisabeth was unstable. How she spent her free time in her dining room, flipping through newspapers with a red Sharpie, then going back through with the scissors to extract articles for her blue vinyl binder. How she had both city and state maps and marked locations for each hospital where safe haven was invoked. How she kept old editions of newspapers, ones with holes cut in their front pages. She looked through the old ones sometimes, to make sure she didn't miss something she wanted and to see what else was newsworthy the same day as a safe haven day. There was a presidential election. Obama. The economy going to shit, the biggest crash in eighty years; Congress holding bailout votes and finally electing to rescue Freddie, Fannie, and Merrill Lynch, but not Lehman Brothers. This was monumental news, the kind that people—those who took heart when they witnessed history in the making—used to keep front pages from as collectibles. And these people, when they looked back later in life, would see that not only did a black man excel in a presidential debate and take a commanding lead for the office, not only had the stock market crashed, but in a small city on the plains, parents were giving up possession of their children with shocking frequency and walking away like it was nothing. Further, they might remember a Wisconsinite named Tyler Ahls who appeared in media spots that were filmed by a terrorist network.

It wasn't normal, what Elisabeth was going through. Maybe it occurred to her that somehow she had dreamed all this. That she wasn't a nurse. That she'd only read in the newspaper about the Junger kids being left by their father and had delusions that she was present when it happened. And that this Tyler Ahls in the news also happened to be her brother? Another paranoid delusion. On the other hand, she wasn't hysterical, the room didn't spin round her. Who are we to say how she should react? If she wanted to assemble binders, then flip page by page through them nightly, as she bit her lip and brushed hair off her face to read; if tears snuck down her cheeks while she read the newspaper, the memories of her baby echoing through her; if she had to stop herself from remembering, breathe deep for a while, go brush her teeth with her head in the bathroom sink until she calmed down—who are we to say what's normal and what's not?

FILE 9

TYLER AHLS

12 SEP 07 TO 15 DEC 07

[12 Sep 07; three months before Tyler Ahls disappeared]

That Ramzan began a month after Tyler Ahls arrived in Peshawar was a stroke of luck. From all accounts he would come to alienate his colleagues at the English school where he taught, for a variety of reasons, but Tyler was still new when the crescent moon was sighted that month (Ramzan, the ninth of the lunar calendar; coincidentally, it was September that year, the ninth of the Gregorian) and as an American with a curly beard, block-shaped head, gray eyes that were almost always squinting into the glare of sunlight reflected off windshields, long coppery hair at his shoulders, Tyler was a rare object—a big *firangi*. And as his Urdu and Pashto were elementary, his colleagues practiced their English to hear his American drawl, not exactly like a movie cowboy but not entirely unlike a movie cowboy, as far as anyone could tell.

Though he'd been to Pakistan twice before (trips paid for by Deb Ahls) the Modern Language Spoken School handled Tyler's living arrangements in Peshawar. Greased the wheels for a work visa after his application for a missionary visa was denied. Set him up in an apartment not far from the whitewashed building where classes were held. Remunerated him via bank transfer to his account at Chippewa State Bank. Drove him to the supermarket to ensure he bought food, his first two weeks, which was no small ordeal for new arrivals. To be fair,

Tyler got along better than his colleagues presumed he would, but they looked out for him nonetheless.

The first night of Ramzan, before fasting, a fellow teacher at Modern Language named Bilal Afridi drove to Tyler's apartment in University Town. This had been arranged that afternoon in the teachers lounge. How Tyler would recognize Bilal's Chevette once he heard it honking. It seemed to Tyler that Bilal was late, already an hour after the call to prayer—when Tyler had run to the roof of his building to hear *adhān* echoing over the city, off the buildings; the muezzin timing his breaths so each wave of "Allahu Akbar" was not quite absorbed into the hillside before the next began; how there were fireworks over the mosque as soon as the minaret went silent. It was dark by the time Bilal laid on the horn outside Tyler's apartment. Tyler ran down the stairs and jumped in the car and asked, "Don't we need to hurry?"

"Not at all," Bilal told him.

Tyler understood so little—as true in Peshawar as it had been in Chippewa.

Traffic went slow. Tables were erected the whole length of the avenue, one block over from Tyler's place, so all those stuck out-of-doors could feast—the fatherless, homeless, nationless, who slept under clear sheets of plastic along roads. Two bowls were given: one a red stew and the other long-grain rice. One block further there was a military parade, a small ceremonial militia manned by gibbous pensioners, most of whom squeezed bagpipes along their limping march. If you loved all things of the Muslim world like Tyler Ahls claimed to love all things, an idling tour of Ramzan in Peshawar was an endless dream. Roman candles popping above buildings. Twinkling lights draped from balconies, from the fronds of palm trees. In all his travels, Tyler had never experienced a legitimate Ramzan—always an outsider, backpacking through—but he was in the thick of it then, off the line at two miles per hour in a lime-green Chevette, Bilal revving the engine so the Chevette didn't stall in traffic. Packed buses—adorned like peacocks in colorful paint and papier-mâché brocade—stuck next to them in traffic, motor rickshaws darting into every gap between bumpers. To spite a Taliban prohibition of music, endless Nusrat Fateh Ali Khan came from car windows and courtyard barbecues, its eddying ululation and tribal gypsy music, Afrobeat and accordion and tambourine. Did Tyler weary of pan flutes? Did the smell of scooter smog, the constant steeping of tea fatigue him?

Are you kidding?

The street Bilal lived on was filled with the smell of kebab and tikka and curry. Once his door opened, Tyler heard the sizzling of meat. Bilal's whole family was in the apartment, spilling into the back courtyard. His grandfather, cousins—even seconds and thirds—many of them from the capital. Along the length of the apartment to the sliding patio door, where a long wool blanket stretched over the aluminum precipice. The others—Bilal's family, his neighbors, his friends—had not waited. Men foraged wrist-deep in nuts, raisins, dates, apples, and tea with rose syrup. From outside, the meat was passed from hand to hand through the patio door and sagged to the breaking point the Chinet where it was piled.

"Do they all live here?" Tyler asked, Bilal escorting him, introducing him.

"Of course not. Only my sister and her husband, our parents, and my grandfather. What are you thinking?"

Bilal maybe had second thoughts about inviting Tyler—that it would have sufficed to wish him "*Ramzan Mubarak*" in the hallway and left it at that, rather than insisting Tyler come to his home. Maybe Bilal extended an invitation solely because of custom. Peshawaris in general are extraordinarily hospitable, with further amplification on high religious observance. Tyler was invited to take his shoes off before he entered the room, he was given a seat along the rug and urged to eat his fill with other men before the meat was passed to children, then to women last. Bilal's family wasn't so traditional, wasn't so strict, but, still, order is order. Throughout dinner Bilal asked Tyler if he was satisfied with the food, with the apartment where he lived, with the school. More than once Bilal told him they were friends. An oppressive hospitality to some. From where Tyler came from (his family, the restrained sensibilities of the locals in Chippewa) you can forgive him if he thought his presence was a special honor for Bilal and his family, as opposed to any guest they indulged. You can forgive him if he let it go to his head.

Tyler took extra care to compliment Bilal on the rose syrup and the tikka and the dates. "Some of the best dates I've had yet," he said. "I'm something of a date connoisseur."

"Feel no obligation," Bilal told him. "You will like Peshawar."

Tyler thought Bilal and his family were so sweet. All the cousins smiling. Every man shook his hand and bade a warm welcome. Most of all it was exhilarating to commune with who he saw as candid people. Not like at home when Deb laid on a guilt trip every time he opened his mouth and Gerry somehow managed to slip out to the woodshop before anyone noticed he was gone, like he'd built a trapdoor under the head of the kitchen table. But Pakistanis were happy to discourse. Tyler kept his mouth shut as much as he could out of respect for the holiday, but he had to ask what it was like for minorities here, if Bilal knew any Christians. There was a Christian church in Peshawar. Tyler wanted to know if Bilal had been there, so he asked.

"I have never been to All Saints," Bilal told him, the two of them alone on the carpet, the other men crouching along the fence to smoke. "Why would I go to your church?"

"You're never curious about it? I've been to all sorts of mosques and temples to see what's inside. Don't you wonder about Jesus?"

"I know about Jesus. Īsā ibn Maryam, yes, I know."

The two of them whispering in English.

"But you don't think he's divine, do you? That's the difference with Muslims."

Bilal stared with his hazel eyes—he was very slim, with a narrow jaw that made his head an inverted ovate shape—his lips quivering. "My friend. Why do you say this to me?"

"Don't you dream about doing something monumental with your life?" Tyler moved close, their foreheads nearly touching. "Like the prophets. Like Īsā ibn Maryam."

"You believe *you* are a prophet, *al-Masīḥ*?"

Tyler turned red at being called *al-Masīḥ*, which was a common name for Christians in Pakistan, not just for Tyler Ahls. That Tyler Ahls had a messiah complex was a coincidence.

"Have you ever seen something like this?" Tyler pulled a squared piece of glossy paper from his pocket and unfolded it to show Bilal a section of the Gospel according to John that had been translated into Pashto.

"Where did you get that?"

"I want to make whole books like this, if I can get help with the translation. Don't you think it's something people need to see? The faith will spread here in the next hundred years, and this," Tyler said, holding up his bit of scripture, "this will be the start of something important."

"No, no, no." When Bilal shook his head, his curly hair spread across the back of his neck. "That is a very bad idea."

"I know, by the letter, it's blasphemy to preach anything other than Islam. But this is Īsā ibn Maryam. That's Islam, right?"

"They will kill you."

"Don't get upset. Pakistan wouldn't execute an American."

"I didn't say Pakistan government. If I were you, I wouldn't mention this Jesus business."

Tyler popped another date in his mouth, leaned back on his hands to grin. "I've seen it before. These Jehovah Witnesses in Karachi had Bibles in Arabic, they spread the Good News. I know there's interest here for the Gospels in Pashto."

"Forget that, my friend. You honor your family by doing this, yes, but it is unwise. Your parents will understand if you come home without delay."

"They don't want me in Pakistan," Tyler explained. "If they didn't think I was working with a Christian missionary group, they never would have paid for my ticket. If I came home, they'd be thrilled."

"Then I don't understand. What are you doing here?"

Agent Schwaller often wondered if Tyler had lost his mind by this point. It's hard to say exactly. He taught English six days a week at Modern Language Spoken School. He fasted for Ramzan. Every evening at sunset he went to the avenue to find pakora and pan-roasted nuts and 7UP. He went to All Saints Church, which looked more like a mosque with its white stone minarets and *qubba* dome. Every week he sat on a dusty red cushion in the pews, stage right, on the side for men; found a spot under a ceiling fan, as close to a breeze and the open shutters as possible; listened to the music, what sounded like "Auld Lang Syne" played on a rabāb; had his offer to teach Sunday school rebuffed; had his offer to deliver a layman's sermon on Christianity in America declined. Even on the dirt-covered bricks outside All Saints, after services, the parishioners weren't sure they wanted to stand next to Tyler as he tried to distribute his leaflets.

That sounds like normal behavior, or normal enough given the circumstances. But on long weekends Tyler hiked into tribal areas to see if he could drum up curiosity in his Bible translations.

Even when he wasn't hiking in tribal sectors, Tyler spent a lot of his free time walking the city. He'd go after morning sessions at the school if there was no monsoon. The rains hardly hit that part of Pakistan, which meant it was still hot, but walking gave him time to think, and he liked seeing other parts of Peshawar, he liked being seen—a white man like him, an American with an orange beard, his face sunburned red, the effervescence of his rainbow doppa cap. That he stood out made him important, made him singular. He felt this often as a boy, when Apostle Crossing was being built, then as patrons filed past the Station of Tyler every summer day to read about his vision, his dream, and believe what was written on the placard. What was it? . . . *a boy of seven, pure of heart. Jesus said let the innocents come unto him* . . . Yes, that's it.

In his last email to Nick, one he sent from Peshawar, Tyler confessed how his childhood sometimes weighed on him, how, in so many words, he couldn't escape certain conclusions he'd come to as a boy, or certain conclusions that had been made for him.

I think a lot about David Koresh. It's a bad omen, right, I know. I was seven when Branch Davidian burned and even now I remember seeing its tower in flames on the front page of the Chippewa Zeitung. *I saw Satan in the flames. The outlines of a face that resembled Koresh's face and I knew it was Satan. Whether Koresh was evil or divine I had no idea. He had Jesus hair and looked like Jesus was supposed to look, tall with a bony chin and that gaze in his eyes. He got all those folks to follow him. And then there was me. My sad chubby body, my freckles, a ginger. It felt impossible that God cared what happened to my life. That was the same year I had my dream about Apostle Crossing, a month or two after Branch Davidian burned. For a long time I worried that God had no plan for me, then, poof, God had a plan for me. If there had been a David Koresh why couldn't there be a Tyler Ahls? It's not like I was obsessed (don't worry about me) everybody thought about the Branch Davidians, didn't they, and how the standoff was baffling. They were Christians! Why would the ATF murder American Christians? I didn't understand, I had nightmares about the government knocking down walls and starting fires. As a teenager I was terrified something like that would happen at Apostle Crossing if the FBI got the wrong idea about my dream and what God had planned for my family. It's not crazy. We weren't bigamists, we didn't have many guns. We're Lutherans! But if the feds can attack one group of Christians, doesn't that constitute a slippery slope? . . . I pray a lot to figure out why my folks jumped in on AC with both feet.*

Was it pure faith in God or faith in prosperity or out of fear to keep the family together? Lis was hardly home because of soccer. My parents knew what I saw in the picture of Branch Davidian burning. We talked about that even before I had the dream about Apostle Crossing. There were probably a thousand pressures I didn't know about. Was Mom in love with the president of the bank where she was a loan officer? Did Dad have an affair with the receptionist at his insurance agency? I don't know. There had to be something, right? How different everything would have been if they didn't build AC, if I didn't have that dream. Would Dad still have his insurance agency? Could they save up and retire early to Florida? What about me? I could have had a girlfriend at some point and gone to youth group and made friends instead of getting tortured at school. Even the teachers were so darn suspicious of what we were up to out at AC. Like it couldn't just be what the sign said it was. Like you can't just love Jesus and not have it be a scam. I don't have regrets. I don't allow them. But sometimes I'm weak and can't help speculate that I would have been happier selling home and auto policies like Dad used to do. Instead of my life being about getting to Pakistan and sharing the Good News, I could have been sitting on a couch with my kids (ones I'll never have) and watch some dumb TV show. Maybe save up to buy a boat and a wakeboard. Tyler Ahls: normal dude. I wouldn't have been spit on or threatened or told I was a fanatic, a lunatic, and I deserved to have my head chopped off. That kind of stuff. Whatever. I yam what I yam and that's what I yam. (Tyler Ahls, Email, 06 Nov 07, Peshawar 25000. Modern Language Spoken School.)

Poor Tyler. Didn't anyone from home recognize how much he was in trouble?

By then he'd even blocked out his mother and communicated mostly with Nick Holland. But even with Nick, he'd pushed things past the breaking point.

More and more, those days, it's obvious in the files, Tyler's deception of Nick was played out. Both were clueless as to the median development of a white, male, midwestern-American toddler. Tyler had Caleb walking by eight months and engaging in full conversations by sixteen. At the rate Tyler had him going, shadow-Caleb would have been driving at five years and holding down a junior-exec position before puberty. If Nick was aware of the abnormality of the stories Tyler told, he didn't let on. Some people, religious or not, worked hard to believe a good many things on faith.

Still, Tyler pushed things too far. His lies were bound to unravel. He claimed Caleb was an acolyte at church one Sunday, and Nick called him on that. *Isn't that the kids who light the candles? Why would they let a two-year-old do that?* And if that was a lie, as it obviously was, then why should Nick believe at all?

Tyler should have told Nick the truth at that point. What did he owe Nick? Nothing. He was only keeping Nick away from his sister. But by then, Elisabeth wouldn't have wanted to see Nick; there was no risk of her taking him back.

Call Caleb yourself. You don't need me to speak for him, Tyler wrote that summer. *If you wanted to track them down, you would have by now. You moved on. Admit it. Stop bothering me.*

What did Nick say to that?

He was concerned. *You worry me. I won't ever understand why you have to go to Pakistan. You're a different person there. I try to respect that and hope you respect what I have had to do in my life. Write when you can.*

They stopped communicating altogether not long after Tyler went to Peshawar, one last time, on a ticket paid for by his mother because he told her he was going to be a missionary. Once Tyler disappeared, once it made the news, Nick went to Chippewa to see what was going on, to find out the truth about his family. This is in the files.

At the restaurant in University Town, Tikka, Tyler spent many evenings talking to patrons (somewhat) and waiters (mostly) about his dream of publishing the Gospels in Pashto. How surprising it is that he ended up a proselytizer, after all. He was an uncommon breed, regardless of the continent he roamed. Tyler tried to be slick when he talked about his translations. Made sure he knew his mark before he jumped in talking Jesus. This was his fourth trip to Central Asia. Nobody was going to throw stones, he didn't think. Sometimes he played snooker with students or talked to a young waiter. The old-timers were easier to get going. Tyler only had to mention *the old days*, then wait while they sucked the grease off chicken bones before they ranted about how different everything was when Pakistan was a secular state. It was no matter if they thought life was better or worse—they said it had been worse without Sharia; you never know who might be listening—the point was to get them going about how change is possible, even in Peshawar; then Tyler could show them the papers he carried everywhere, hidden in the lining of his backpack in case he was searched by police or militia when he wandered around town or headed out to the hills or came to Tikka to show off a leaflet. The Beatitudes in Matthew 5 was a popular one. ("Blessed are you when people revile you and persecute you and utter all kinds of evil against you falsely on my account. Rejoice and be glad, for your reward is great in Heaven, for so they persecuted the prophets who were before you.") Then he'd ask, *Do you have a place in your heart for Īsā al-Masīḥ?*

It took only a week before Khan Khalili, the Pakistani PI, heard about this American who was trying to convert the waiters at Tikka to Christianity. As it happened, Tikka was owned by one of his uncles. This uncle got in touch with him and asked for help, as the uncle knew Khalili worked as a private investigator, that he was an informant for Americans, as CIA sometimes came to the restaurant looking for Khan Khalili, men in sunglasses and gray tweed jackets, who ate rice with forks, who requested a cup of the Johnnie Walker that was kept in a teapot in the back, who denied they were CIA when the junior waiter asked if they were CIA. The uncle hoped Khalili could put his skills to work and dissuade this American boy from exhibiting his Bible translations inside the grease-speckled walls of Tikka. They didn't dislike Tyler Ahls. They were hospitable, they welcomed all, but such stupidity could get them all in trouble if he wasn't more careful. It was up to Khan Khalili to protect Tikka.

How appropriate that Deb and Gerry Ahls would pay this same man, months later, to track down their son on the Khyber Pass. It was Khan Khalili, out of anyone in Peshawar, who knew the most about Tyler Ahls, so this made sense. In all his reports, however, Khalili never once mentioned the restaurant Tikka.

Khalili had not shaved the evening he met Tyler Ahls. His jaw was black with stubble because it was a busy week for him, working as a fixer for a group of six Chinese investors, and he didn't have time to stop at home. At dinner, he held his cell phone almost the whole time, in case the investors required him. His gray linen suit was wrinkled and spotted with sweat as he walked in from outside. It was evening and still thirty degrees (nearly ninety degrees Fahrenheit). There was a trick to selecting a table in a place like this. You, of course, couldn't sit too near the kitchen and its tandoori ovens, but an outside wall could also bake through from the heat, the sun. It was best to sit as close to the ell as possible in Tikka—where young men lounged in front of oscillating fans that hung from the ceiling—so long as you didn't mind leaning away now and then to avoid a boy's elbow as he shot snooker behind you.

Khalili sat in the empty chair across from Tyler Ahls. "This is okay?"

Tyler was more than pleased to have a partner for dinner. One who folded his suit jacket over the back of his chair with unhurried elegance, whose hair was turning white, who appeared perfectly dignified except for his big ears and a chipped front tooth.

"Would you honor me by letting me pick the menu?" Khalili asked.

Well, of course. Khalili would know best. He looked vaguely amphibian in profile, when he turned in his seat to dissect the menu, then told in Pashto the tall young waiter what to bring. Shinwari tikka, bhindi okra, *doday* naan, Mountain Dew—all Khalili's favorites. Tyler ate rice with his fingers, which might have been endearing if the American odors that came from his body weren't so nauseating. Even then, when Tyler sweat, his skin radiated dairy and unseasoned beef.

"You like Pakistan?" Khalili asked, nodding along before Tyler answered. "You're going to stay in Peshawar? A long time?"

"That's the plan. I'll stay as long as possible to explore the mountains. I want to see Khyber Pass."

"And you work?"

"I teach English."

"Say something to me in Urdu."

Tyler complimented the food.

"Ah, yes. Not bad. Now say something in Pashto."

"I don't know much Pashto. I'm trying to learn."

With all the questions, it should have been obvious to Tyler he was being played. But he liked the attention, especially from a suave man like Khan Khalili. Khalili rolled up his sleeves as he ate. He unlatched his gold wristwatch and set it on the table next to the bhindi.

"You are the Christian? Yes?"

"That's right."

"They call you *al-Masīḥ*?"

"I don't know. Lots of Christians are called that in Pakistan."

"Yes. But most do not desire to martyr himself, my friend. That's what that means, you know. *Al-Masīḥ*, 'the martyr.'"

"No. It's messiah."

"Yes, sometimes. There can be two meanings to *al-Masīḥ*."

Tyler was really sweating, wracking his brain to think of something to prove Khalili incorrect about this martyr business, but of course Tyler came up empty. It wasn't his language. He sat straighter in his chair, tee shirt soaked through, striped Adidas pants stuck to his legs.

"I did some checking," Khalili told him. "You show off Christian scripture. You carry it in your backpack. I don't want to see. Just listen. When you are hiking, you talk to people about Jesus and ask if they believe. I don't see why a man would do that, unless you want to get killed. Do all Americans have a death wish? Or just ones like you?"

Tyler, speechless, reached for his backpack and unzipped before Khalili stopped him: "Don't show me." Tyler with his nervous dark eyes, with his teeth that spent so long aligning in wires that even in adulthood he looked like he had braces, like then, when his mouth froze in rictus and he didn't know what to say.

"I won't go with you."

"Of course not. I'm not here to take you. I'm not police."

"I'm safe because it's my calling to be here," Tyler said. "I'm speaking the Good News, and that protects me."

Khan Khalili didn't look up from the plate where he pinched the last cubes of meat between his fingertips, one by one, and put them in his mouth.

"If you desire to martyr yourself, that is okay. Don't get these men hurt in the process. They are my family. I entreat you." He stood up, slipped on his gold wristwatch and secured the clasp, seized his cell phone with his left hand. "That is all I have to say."

A few weeks later, when classes were adjourned, Tyler found a guide who would take him up Khyber Pass. This was his main attraction to Peshawar. He mentioned this to Nick, in emails, that there was something mystical, magical about a place at the crossroads of nearly every conqueror civilization imagined in both Asia and Europe.

The guide—a taxi driver—arrived outside Tyler's apartment building in a bright-yellow Suzuki wagon with steel panels and boxy frame.

A sturdy car. It might not go more than thirty miles per hour, less than that on an incline, but it wouldn't fall apart. Tyler didn't vet the driver. He asked around a lot before this, when he got tea in a café near his place, when he rode in a taxi to All Saints. *It's not trouble I'm looking for,* Tyler would say in mangled Urdu, or something close to that. *Will you take me on Khyber Road? As far as Torkhum?* A driver usually had enough sense to shake his head vigorously after peeking at Tyler in the rearview mirror. Tyler Ahls in his army-green jacket and blue reflective sunglasses, with his long red hair, his Western accent marbling his mouth as he asked to be taken along the road to the border with Afghanistan. *No no no. Only town,* the driver shouting, turned fully in his seat to wag a finger in Tyler's face.

The driver who would take him to Torkhum actually sought out Tyler. Tyler should have understood that was trouble. Tyler had never seen the driver before, but he looked normal enough. He had green eyes and long black hair and full beard. He wore a linen shirt to his knees. He smiled when he saw Tyler come into Tikka. *You are looking for a guide?*

Yes. Do you know the way to Torkhum?

There was only one road.

They traveled west of the city through the Jamrud bazaar; past the high earthen walls of the Sikh fort and the white bricks of what looked like an ancient gate at Bab-e-Khyber that marked the entrance to the Khyber Pass; out onto the loess-dusted, two-lane Torkhum Highway to the wide-open plains and big sky of tribal lands, to verdant valleys higher up, where shacks leaned so close to the highway that the exhaust and dust clouds, the scattered pebbles and insects, must have suffused the shacks like fog. Tyler had come this far before, west of Jamrud. He hiked often in the foothills, camped alone, wandered paths up to where there were dugouts along the valley, hills pocked with hollows that, from afar, weren't unlike ground-squirrel dens in Wisconsin. Tyler approached the hollows, the doorways—doppa on his head, his blue sunglass lenses glinting—so he could talk with who he found there. Afridis, Mullagoris, Shinwaris. Villages like this were his favorite; he'd wandered into so many on his hiking trips, and they were peopled by such kindness, like when a Pamiri woman took care of him on his first trip to Asia and tried to cure his spinning stomach with the chalky purgative she made. From its edge, a village often felt deserted, like a spaghetti western, cyclones of dust twisting across the road between buildings, a solitary plume of smoke rising from an adobe rooftop. Tyler stopped at doorways when he came across them, in ancient villages, even before he had scripture to peddle. He'd pause at a door where there were two knockers that each made a distinct racket—one for women to use and one for men, so the woman inside would know if she was allowed to open—and Tyler, ignorant, could only guess which he was supposed to knock.

He was euphoric when he passed into the fissured red mountains, with dust puffing through a gap in the windshield in the left front, where he sat. Boys selling bottles of water at a checkpoint while soldiers glanced under the car with mirrors on sticks. Then up the edges of mountains, where the road balanced ridge after ridge. He'd glance down the valley and see tents of white canvas huddled around a bit of water, a crick, with goats and some linen hanging from lines. The traffic heavy with shipping trucks and massive, roaring NATO vehicles. Tyler leaned his face against the window and let his eyes close. The car rocking as it muscled the incline. The looking out on dusty hills and military forts once British but now manned by Khyber Rifles militiamen.

Tyler knew, he must have known, that it was a bad idea to fall asleep. He was alone in the car with the guide, the driver. He'd never met this man before the other day. But he felt so hot, even though it was cool in the mountains, in December, his mouth was sticky even after he swallowed his water in only three gulps. Even as he sat up and took a deep breath of thin mountain air, before long Tyler slumped against the door again and felt in his stomach the car weaving through traffic as his eyes closed.

He slept so deeply on the ride, he must have dreamed of some green, cool valley. Of a lakeside beach lush with oak trees. A tire swing hung from an oak branch.

When Tyler woke, they were nearly to Torkhum, the car engine whining to go yet more vertical. Maybe he was still half-asleep, Tyler, when he started giving his pitch. "There should be more Christians in Pakistan," he said to the driver. "People might like it here more if they had the choice to make on their own." Tyler delirious, his tongue sticking to the roof of his mouth as he spoke. "Would you let me baptize you?" he asked the driver. In what Urdu he had, Tyler asked the driver if he would pull over to a river at the top of the mountain.

"*Shayad,*" the driver said. *Maybe.* He pulled the taxi off the highway when they reached what felt like an apex of the mountain they were climbing—what turned out to be a ridge four miles short of Torkhum. Tyler couldn't keep his eyes open. He blinked and blinked and blinked but couldn't see. Dust in his eyes gunked with his sleep. He tried to drink more from his water bottle, but it was empty.

The car stopped and the driver helped Tyler from his seat. Up on his feet, walking, Tyler must have noticed how the air was damp here in the trees as he was led along a winding trail amid parasol pine trees and Himalayan cedars and junipers and yews. Through the tree trunks he saw the rocky valley with streams here and there. "It will take only a minute," Tyler said. And, "I've never baptized anyone before. You'll be my first."

There were eight of them waiting for Tyler. Around a bend on the trail. Combatants from the Haqqani network, a small cell who heard about him. They would tie him up, put him in the back of their van, and drive across the border. They had Kalashnikovs.

"Look there," Tyler said dumbly as the men surrounded him, pointing west. "That's Afghanistan."

The guide returned to Peshawar alone. He ate at Tikka that evening and sat at his table chewing fennel seeds a long time after he finished. Drank a liter of orange Fanta while he waited, until Khan Khalili arrived. The guide waved Khalili over to his table.

"Your friend said to tell you," the driver said. "The American. He's going on a journey in the direction of Tirich Mir. He will be gone a long time. He has abandoned his teaching position."

Khan Khalili understood what the guide was telling him. That there was no use going to look for Tyler Ahls. He was going hiking, a long journey into the Hindu Kush, along the border with Afghanistan. If Tyler were to disappear—and it would soon be known that he had disappeared—then he must have been lost hiking. He must have drowned in one of the many streams that cut into the rocky valleys and threaded among tree trunks.

"I wish him well," Khan Khalili said to the guide, his face void of emotion, no sadness in his deep hazel eyes except the sadness he carried with him everywhere, as he said, *"Allah hafiz."*

FILE 10

SANDY LAIKA

03 Oct 08

[03 Oct 08; two days before Agt Schwaller left Omaha]

She was seeing Agent Schwaller on the regular.

He dragged his face along her thighs and hips to feel the small hairs of her stomach hook with the sandpaper of his muzzle. He called the hairs on her stomach her Russian hairs and she had to tell him *I'm not Russian!* Her whole life Sandy was ashamed of the hairs on her body. She wasn't so comfortable with how Agent Schwaller played, up in his hotel room on the starched bedding, with his suits hung on the closet door near the brushes he used to groom them. But it was good to indulge the agent when he got happy and weird like that. He'd close his eyes to feel her hairs on his lashes and his lids and break out laughing. The hairs on her arms. The hairs on her navel and below there, the black ones. He nibbled at them with his front teeth. The agent scraped his jaw against her mons to hear the crunch of hair and called that her rose garden. He begged her to grow it long. She asked if there was time for that. *That takes more than a day for that kind of hair, and a little long is long enough.*

Against his better judgment, one morning Schwaller agreed to dinner at Sandy's house. "Oh, absolutely not," he said at first. "I've been in town four days and now you want me to meet your mother?"

"Don't flatter yourself. Can't dinner just be dinner? I'm not trying to marry you."

They lay on the couch in his hotel room—facing each other, him on the inside, her on the outside with her long black hair spilling to the carpet. Usually Sandy hated being on the outside edge of the cushions if she shared a couch with someone, because she felt like she was going to fall, but they were naked with their hips flush. He wasn't going to push her away.

"I'm an honest woman—"

"Now who's flattering?"

"—so I won't pretend like there isn't something I want from you."

"Well, that's actually refreshing. Tell me."

"My mom has a moderate immigration problem—"

"That doesn't sound so bad."

"—that stems from her minor support of some guys who turned out to be Chechen terrorists."

The agent was amused by this. He couldn't help snickering, so he hid his face in her neck, put his hand on the small of her back and tickled with the tips of his fingers. "That's why you asked me out for a drink when I came up to the hospital?"

"I asked if you wanted to get coffee."

"Sure, you did," Schwaller said. "I'm not eating dinner at your mother's house. Unless one of those terrorists happens to be named Tyler Ahls, seriously, I don't care."

Of course Sandy perked up when she noticed Agent Schwaller at the nurses station that day—when he held up his government badge in the plastic ID sleeve and asked where he could find Elisabeth Holland—particularly when she heard what detail the agent worked. When Schwaller removed his dark sunglasses and slicked back his hair and barged in to show off his ego, a surge of hope snuck through Sandy that maybe this agent could do something for her. She must have been desperate to think Agent Schwaller could help her just like that, even if her mother's troubles were mostly under the radar. Her mother came from the Soviet Union many years before; she'd lived in Lithuania then Chechnya then South Omaha after that, for decades. She was sort of an odd bird. But what else would you expect? All the things she'd been through as a migrant. Who cares if Peggy Laika drinks iced Manischewitz or gets in arguments with the mailman, with her priest, with the teenagers stocking shelves at the grocery store? Normally, no one cared. But Peggy Laika had a big mouth, in particular about Chechen rebels, and she accidentally donated funds to Islamic terrorists. That was something a lot of folks would care about.

Sandy griped a lot about the trouble her mother was in that summer, especially to heavily medicated patients at Saint Wenceslaus as she changed their bedding, when she thought nobody was listening.

There's such a thing as free speech here in America, I tell her, but you never know. Sometimes it's better to keep your mouth shut. Let go what happened to all those schoolkids in Beslan, admit the rebels had something to do with the massacre too. Russia isn't always to blame! What you shouldn't do, you shouldn't get in an argument with the ladies at church over Putin and end up in a tizzy about Chechnya. You shouldn't take the bait when Connie says, "If you care so much, put your money where your mouth is." Everyone knows we lived in Grozny. Who cares? You don't go to the library and find some rebel group to give a little bit a money—just to prove a point!—and then send them $22.50. Really. Who does that? (Sandy Laika, Desktop Audio, 15 Aug 08, Omaha 68124. Saint Wenceslaus Hospital.)

This is all true. Peggy Laika browsed online for Chechen charities on a dare, for what she thought was an aid group but turned out to be one focused on spreading international jihad, one tied to notorious thugs in the Caucasus Emirate. She sent an electronic payment for $22.50, which somehow slipped through and went overseas. These things happen. A few months later Peggy gets a letter from the US Department of State to notify her that they were aware of her illegal donation, her giving aid and comfort to a known terrorist organization, and they let Homeland Security know what she did too. The term *deportation* was in the letter, among the possible repercussions. It's hard to believe a little old lady from South Omaha was connected to international jihad, but once she was flagged in the system that takes a lot to undo.

Peggy Laika's transfer was intercepted by the Russian government, who complained to State about the aid of illegal groups. (Not just Peggy's, but a whole bulk of intercepted donations; Peggy wasn't the only American to wire money to jihadi groups inside Russia's border.) Not such a huge deal, really, twenty bucks, but you can imagine how anxious a State Department letter made Peggy, who already fled once around the globe. She had most of the day, every day, to brood over what this could mean. You can imagine how this made Sandy feel too. Sandy, who worried constantly that her mother was going batty, and then her mother tells about the time she tried to set straight a lady at church by tendering support to Chechen jihad.

"It's complicated, it's ridiculous," Sandy said to Schwaller, her brown eyes big and round, the sandalwood aroma of her shampoo in an aura around her head. "Mom keeps running her mouth, she's going to get herself deported."

"She's not a citizen?"

"For God's sake, she's been here most of her life. We came here on a plane. They welcomed us at the airport."

Sandy wasn't ashamed to tell these things to Schwaller. Her mother wasn't a criminal. This was an honest misunderstanding that needed clearing up, that's all, a brief lapse in judgment. For over thirty years nobody says anything about how Mrs. Laika never actually took the citizenship test—how Sandy finished the paperwork and performed the ceremony, but her mother hadn't. Now it could be a big deal just because of $22.50.

"What can I do about it?" he asked.

"Just come to dinner. Scare her a little. Tell her you're an investigator. Tell her to let it drop about Chechnya and that she absolutely must take her citizenship exam. That's all I'm asking."

"I don't like the sound of this. You know, my official duties—"

Sandy tucked her arms under his so he felt how she was a woman—a woman, naked, who was asking for help. "Just come to dinner. That will be enough. Don't make me beg."

"Fine," he said. "When you put it like that, maybe I would like to meet your mother. She sounds like a wildcard."

Sandy and her mother lived together in South Omaha, not far from meatpacking plants and the old stock exchange. She didn't bring men home very often. It was embarrassing. Her mom always hanging around, for one thing, and Sandy thirty-nine years old. This was the house she grew up in. Not much had changed in thirty years. All the bronze and brassy colors, the ornamental plates with religious scenes painted in fine rustic detail lined up on a pine board around the ceiling of the kitchen. Redecoration was out of the question as far as Peggy Laika was concerned. Peggy spent most of her life putting the house how she liked it, so why replace anything? Why rearrange the furniture? The colossal microwave in the kitchen that somehow still worked even though it shook when on. *It leaks radiation it's so old,* Sandy told her mother. *Eh. You're crazy,* Peggy said. *Don't believe what you see on TV.*

Peggy Laika made tacos for dinner. Doughy flour tortillas fried in a skillet, ground beef she turned with a spoon in a Crock-Pot, lettuce she sliced with a butcher's knife from a head of iceberg, sharp cheddar from a bag. Agent Schwaller had no idea what all this was about. He expected sauerkraut and baked fish in heavy white sauce, rhubarb-tinted wine served in an unlabeled brown bottle that was fetched from under the stairs.

"Mom likes tacos," Sandy explained. "It's her best American food."

The tacos weren't half-bad. A little greasy, but Schwaller was hungry and ate five of them. For a second course Peggy nuked a can of chili in the microwave and served it with more cheddar and Tostitos. Again, not bad. Schwaller nearly ate the whole bowl himself.

"Super Bowl food," Mrs. Laika said. "It's good."

With his hunger battened down, Schwaller asked questions about how they ended up in Omaha, the Laikas. Polite conversation, for him, with a tinge of menace, like Sandy wanted.

"Sandy said you come from Chechnya. Why did you leave there? Was there trouble, like now, with the terrorists?"

"It wasn't good," Peggy said. Sandy nodded in agreement.

"Why Omaha, of all the places in the world?"

"We knew people. Lots of Lithuanians in Omaha."

"Her sisters," Sandy explained. "They came here after World War II to get away from the Nazis, but Mom was too young for a trip like that, so she stayed in Kupiškis with her *čiutė*. It took a while to track them down later when we came to get away from the Communists. Her sisters all lived in this neighborhood. We didn't speak English very well, so it was easier to find jobs, to find places to live. You understand."

"Mine is an immigrant family too," Schwaller said, "like all Americans. My father's family was German, you can tell by my name. The Schwallers are a tribe of Bavaria. My mother's family came from Canada to work in the great Detroit auto factories. I don't know what that means, exactly, if she's Canadian. She always claimed she was equal parts Dutch, Austrian, and Scotch. Take from that what you will."

Schwaller must have thought he was getting on well with Peggy. He thought older women always liked him, so this was no surprise. They were getting comfortable, getting to know each other in a casual sort of way. "Did your husband die in Chechnya?" he asked. "Was he a Russian soldier? KGB or something."

"No! He had a heart attack at work. He made molds."

Plastic molds, Sandy explained. For manufacturing. A line job his cousin got him once they moved to Omaha.

Peggy cleared the table, took the empty chili bowl away, rolled up the bag of tortilla chips and tossed it on top of the fridge, mumbling in Lithuanian, "Who's this asshole? What's with all the questions?"

"Maybe cool it with the questions," Sandy said, winking to urge him on. "She thinks this is an interrogation."

Schwaller didn't think he was interrogating the woman, but maybe he was, benignly. He shouldn't have worn a suit here—although he wanted to impress her, like Sandy asked, and he'd only brought work clothes to Omaha. Was he supposed to carry around khakis like a slob?

"She talked to a lot of inspectors when we left the Soviet Union."

"I'm not an inspector or an interrogator," Schwaller pointed out. "I'm a special agent of the Federal Bureau of Investigation. A detective, more like it."

"Call it what you want. You're making her nervous, Herr Inspektor." Sandy laughed to herself a moment and then said it again. "Herr Inspektor." This time pointing at Schwaller, speaking so only her mother could understand. "Yes? Like a German inspector."

Peggy and Schwaller shared a long look at each other, one as uncomfortable as the other about Sandy's laughter. Peggy's face sour, her mouth turned upside down. She didn't care for this alliance, as brief as it was, coupled with the agent by being the butt of Sandy's joke.

"Who cares? If he wants to take me to the gulag, let him." Peggy walked away from the kitchen sink, where she was leaning, and stomped into the living room to turn on the television.

Schwaller wiped his mouth in an elongated circular motion to make sure he got any chili that might stain his lips, then sat back and drank a Corona until Mrs. Laika was out of the room.

"What's all this about 'Herr Inspektor'?" he asked. "You're making me curious about your mother now. What is her immigration status?"

"She's a legal resident, but not a citizen."

"And you?"

"I'm a citizen. I told you that."

"Except you were born in Chechnya, yes?"

Schwaller sat back and smiled at Sandy. She was hard to figure out. How she did her hair for the occasion, puffed a round bouffant in a bun with strands curling past her ears to her neck, to her mouth; how she smiled back at him playfully, with a foxy look in her eyes, a glint of deceit; how she wore a sundress patterned with tiger lilies to bring out the orange in her tan. Why was Sandy telling the agent all this about her mother? Did she really think he would help them? Sandy made it seem like Mother Laika was quite an unruly character, and she was, but he was beginning to suspect that Daughter Laika might have her beat.

"Is your mother Chechen or Russian?"

"Agent Schwaller, Chechnya is *in* Russia."

"I know that. But why does she refuse to go back?"

"Why would she go back? There's no family there. The only reason she and Dad went to the Soviet Union is because of jobs in the Grozny oil fields. Then they didn't like it. They wanted out of USSR and we moved here."

"So you're Russian?"

"We are *not* Russian," Sandy insisted. "We're Lithuanian. It just worked out that my parents went to Volgograd when they were married and later to Grozny."

"And that's where you were born?"

"Yeah, but I'm not Russian. I was only born in Chechnya. I'm really Lithuanian. And we moved here when I was two, so I've lived my whole life in America, as far as I can remember."

Schwaller took another swipe at his mouth with the crumpled napkin. "I'm confused then. Are you asking me for my help in getting her citizenship? Because I can't change what's written on the form. If the form says Peggy Laika is Chechen, that's not good. And it certainly doesn't help if she sent aid and comfort to terrorists. She shouldn't have done that."

The smile fell from Sandy's face. She swept the spirals she'd so carefully curled behind her ears to get them out of the way.

"I don't know what to tell you," Schwaller said, trying to make peace. "Can't she just go to Lithuania? If she's a Lithuanian citizen, or was at some point, that seems easiest. It's better than Chechnya. What's the problem?"

Sandy sighed and dropped her head into her hands. "I'm trying to keep her from being deported, not talk her into leaving. That's the problem."

Maybe dinner wasn't going so well, but that didn't worry Agent Schwaller. He wasn't there to score points with anyone—that was clear enough. He had a right to be annoyed. All the questions Sandy peppered him with. What was his time in Omaha moving toward? What was he still even doing in Omaha? How much longer might he stay? These were questions he couldn't answer. Did he have phone numbers of friends in high places she could call? Would he vouch for Sandy's importance to the Ahls investigation? The case was a matter of great national importance, as far Schwaller saw it, but what did Sandy's contribution amount to? What could it get her mother? If the federal government wanted to deport Peggy over a little aid and comfort to the enemy, could Schwaller do anything to help?

"There isn't a single thing I can do to help," he admitted.

"Yeah, great," Sandy said. "In the meantime Mom is afraid to leave the house, afraid to drive, because she might get a speeding ticket and off she'd go to Kupiškis. It takes more than a ticket to get deported, I tell her, but she don't believe me. 'Watch out they will change the rules on ya,' she says all the time. 'There are rights in America, human rights,' I say. No, no. She's not buying it. 'If they can change the rules whenever they feel like it, then there are no rules.'"

The whole time Sandy raved, her mother didn't move a muscle except a slight twitch in her ear at the mention of Kupiškis. In the other room it was only her eyes, her whole body, glued to *American Idol*, except the twitch of an ear.

"I think you're overreacting," Schwaller said.

"Sure. Tell me—"

"There's a thing called mandate—"

"—tell me all about how I feel. Go on."

"—how sometimes you think what the government really cares about is not at all what's important. The federal government is a leviathan. Take what I'm doing with the Bureau, looking into this Tyler Ahls problem. Not long ago, it was impossible to collect and collate all the details so quickly. Sure, the information exists, but it's locked in files in a dozen different agencies, his doctor's office, his high school whatever up in Chippewa. That takes time to put together, cooperation with local judges and administrators and guidance counselors. Your classic police-work bullshit. But things change! Now, it's good the Ahls case is counterterrorism. That loosens the rules of what we can do. There's FISA, you know what that is? There's mandate. Before, if I wasn't sure it was okay to access a file here or there, I had to get permission from a prosecutor, then they talk to a judge. Each time! Now there's no prosecutor involved. There's hardly a judge, just a signature to request and then I get carte blanche for ninety days. It's Heaven. If I'm not sure what I'm doing is kosher, sure, go ahead—that's what FISA means—check the email accounts of his family, his doctor, his attorney, their SMS. Worst case, I'm caught poking where I'm not supposed to: throw the Patriot Act in their face, ask if they want to be the guy who lets the next Mohammed Atta slip by. I didn't think so!"

"What in the world are you talking about?"

The agent realized he got carried away. He froze with his mouth open a moment, let his lips fix into a smile, swept his hair back with the blade of his palm. *What all had he told her?* he must have wondered, sitting around Peggy Laika's kitchen table in South Omaha. Sometimes he said too much, a bad habit for an agent, and maybe this was the reason he was out in Nebraska interviewing these nice people in the first place instead of interrogating insurgents at an Egyptian black site. That wasn't for him to say.

"I'm saying, stay calm. Maybe that letter from State is not such a big deal. State doesn't arrest people. It will be okay. You'll see."

Something about Agent Schwaller wasn't convincing. Sandy didn't know what it was exactly, but she had to figure out if he was on the level. (This was the day after she first stayed with him at his hotel, when she returned home early that morning.) She checked to see if he really was an FBI agent from Chicago like he said he was. She found an article about Frank Schwaller on Google, a profile in the University of Michigan alumni magazine.

It was a fluff piece. Nothing special: a photo of clean-cut Schwaller in his black suit, sans his usual wayfarer shades to show off his stone-gray eyes; a few columns about how his first detail with the FBI was investigating the Unabomber. He worked three months on the case in 1996, the spring when the Bureau's twenty-year hunt for Ted Kaczynski came to an end. Despite a reputation to the contrary, Schwaller swore he didn't personally have much to do with capturing the Unabomber—he was only learning the ropes—though corroborated rumors said Schwaller made the connection between a private investigator who was looking into Unabomber leads and David Kaczynski, whose suspicion ultimately led to the capture of his brother. It was a connection any agent could have stumbled over, but Schwaller was the one who saw how the stars aligned. Whether the rumor about him taking down Kaczynski was true or not, his career surely benefited from having a reputation as a savant. This was in the San Francisco field office, where Schwaller worked three years before he was transferred upon his own request to Chicago, to be closer to home. Along the way he had a goal of visiting all fifty-six field offices over the course of his career, in either an official or personal capacity, and he'd made it to thirty-eight by the time the alumni glossy went to press. As an agent he contributed to numerous high-profile cases—LA skinheads, white-nationalist militias in Texas, spent a few months in the Bureau attaché in Baghdad to chase terrorists, played an uncredited role in assembling the infamous "Terrorism for Dummies" seminar. The *Michigan Alumnus* article noted that Schwaller returned to campus for two Wolverine home games every autumn, was still an avid fan, and claimed to have refused a promotion once because the new position required he move to Columbus, Ohio.

The sad thing to Sandy was that there wasn't a ton to find out about Schwaller. She thought he surely had secrets—illegitimate kids in three different states, tax fraud, a failed dry-cleaning business he tried to set up on the side. Who knows? He's an FBI agent—he should be good at keeping secrets. But from what Sandy could find, there wasn't much to the man.

Schwaller had no children, for the record, legitimate or otherwise, no business on the side. He never cheated on his taxes, as his file shows. He grew up in Detroit, the only son of a homemaker and a GM accountant. He was the baby, with two older sisters; he played small forward on Detroit Jesuit's varsity basketball team but appeared sparingly and recorded little in the way of stats. Twelve rebounds. Two fouls. Seven points, all on free throws, his senior year.

This isn't meant to deride the man. Frank Schwaller made varsity based on skill and hard work. It takes talent to stay in the room. The same as with the Bureau—he wasn't there for decoration, he was a contributor. He just wasn't an ace.

"Can she hear us?" Schwaller gestured to where Peggy Laika watched TV ten feet away in the other room. Peggy gazed intently at the screen, but something about the way she sat, the way her frumpy little body was angled, Schwaller thought her ear was aimed directly at him.

"Of course she's listening. She's making mental notes to argue about later. That's why she agreed to make dinner, in case you couldn't deduce the underlying facts."

He didn't understand why Sandy was pissed off. He came to dinner, didn't he? Pressed her mom a little about keeping her distance from Chechen rebels? Just like he promised her he would. And now she was upset.

"I think dinner went well," he said, stacking the plates and carrying them to the sink. She laughed in an unfamiliar cant when he said that, like she was trying to be cruel to him. "Should we do the dishes?"

"Fuck you, Herr Inspektor."

He waited until the water steamed from the faucet before he stoppered the drain and squeezed Palmolive into the stainless-steel basin. "Didn't I keep my promise?" he asked. "Or do you actually think something more serious is going on between the two of us?"

"Jesus Christ, Frank! Why are you such an asshole?"

"Well, I disagree." He let the noise of the filling sink muffle his voice. "What do you expect? There was no quid pro quo. There was no romance, was there? I mean, you came to my hotel. When I set my key on the bar, you took it."

Strictly speaking, the agent was in the right. Sandy consented.

"I know you made a deal with Lis," Sandy said. "You promised to track down her husband."

"Did she tell you that?"

Sandy laughed, her snort still sarcastic, cutting, which surprised Schwaller. "Was it Lis?" she asked. "Or did you tell me, Herr Inspektor Loose Lips? I don't remember, but I think you're the one who divulged that secret."

His mouth hung open as he turned at the sink to look at her, wrinkles in his forehead, confused. These people, they couldn't just answer his questions, they always wanted to take something from him instead. Schwaller turned back to the sink and shut off the faucet. He scoured the pan.

"Do you know where he is?" Sandy asked.

"Who?"

"Nick! The guy you told Elisabeth you'd track down, that's who!"

The agent couldn't divulge that he'd stopped the tail on Nick—the direct surveil ended because Schwaller would return to Chicago soon. Following them around, watching them, it wasn't proving fruitful. Only the metadata connected Elisabeth and Nick at this point, which was beyond the agent's awareness.

"I can't say," he told her. In the sink he arranged the skillet, gummy with hamburger grease, under the bowl with its streaks of beans hardened in the microwave. "What I know, what we can talk about, is this: You said you'd help me with the case. You said you knew all about Elisabeth and the Ahls family. But you haven't provided a single useful lead."

He turned to face her, held a plate in front of himself as he scrubbed, let clomps of suds fall to the floor and hit with a sucking sound as he spoke. "If you don't know anything, that's fine," he said. "But, for fuck's sake, quit leading me on. You know Nick Holland, don't you? The truth this time. You've met him."

The way he looked at her. He had a way of threatening with his eyes, like most cops. Sandy clammed up with the agent looking at her like that. She must have told a dozen times that she didn't know Nick Holland, but she told again. "I don't know the man. Never met him."

"There's only so much I can do for you and your friend. Is that what you're worked up about? You're trying to protect Elisabeth from me poking around in her life? Trying to protect her privacy by distracting me? Well, let me tell you, there's no magic spell. I'll get what I want."

Sandy sat back, her eyes wide; they brightened, as if she was greatly amused. Her hands lifted, palms opened, begging Schwaller to go on.

"If you want up to my room tonight, Sandy, come because you want to come, not because you think I'm trying to trick you. I like going to bed with you, that's all."

To his surprise, to Peggy Laika's surprise, Sandy followed Schwaller out the front door as he made his escape. He drove her slowly, deliberately, back to his hotel, where they would amuse each other for the rest of the night.

FILE 11

ELISABETH HOLLAND / NICHOLAS HOLLAND

04 SEP 08 TO 05 OCT 08

[05 Oct 08; one day after Nicholas Holland fell in the river]

—*Did you see?*

—*I don't know anything about what happened. What am I supposed to know? He tripped or something. Slipped. He didn't wear the safety equipment. That's what they told me. Who's to blame for that?*

—*Oh, honey. That's not why I called. Don't you want me to come there? Don't you need me to help you through this?*

—*No, Mom. It's okay. A phone call is enough. What's there to help with anyway? The railroad will take care of everything. The coroner is keeping the body, I don't know what for. If there's no one to blame, what do they need with the body?*

—*It isn't your fault. I don't want to hear you say that.*

—*He came to Omaha to see me. If he didn't come to Omaha . . .*

—*I want you to say this isn't your fault. Sometimes tragedies happen for reasons we can't understand.*

—*Don't say it's God's plan. I'll hang up if you say that.*

—*Things happen. It doesn't always have something to do with us.*

—*Yes, that's true. But if he doesn't come to Omaha, he doesn't fall in the river.*

[04 Sep 08; the day Nicholas Holland arrived in Omaha]

Nick did go to see Elisabeth first thing when he came to Omaha—
something Schwaller was wrong about, an error that wasn't corrected
in the agent's contribution to the files. After he returned from visiting
the Ahls in Chippewa, Nick asked Midland Pacific for a transfer. He
told his bosses he wanted to be a little more stationary, that he wanted,
specifically, to be near Omaha. They were fine with that, there was
plenty of work in the area. Nick had lived out of a suitcase a long time,
from motel to motel, job to job, bridge to bridge, all across the western
plains. Maybe a man wanted to put down roots. Nebraska was where
Nick grew up. If he wanted a place to call his own, he'd earned that
much. He worked hard, knew what he was doing on the job, on the
bridges.

He arrived in summer. Found a cheap room downtown and went to
the hospital to find Elisabeth. Gerry Ahls told Nick where she worked
and what department. When Nick arrived, he went to the visitor's desk
and asked what floor the department was on. He was smart enough to
not ask right away if Elisabeth Holland was working that day, knew it
would be suspicious, and he couldn't stand the thought of having to
explain that he was her husband. And possibly: *Yes, she's married. She
never mentioned that?*

He went to the nurses station right outside the elevator and asked if Elisabeth was around.

"She's with a patient. You have to wait." It was Sandy Laika at the nurses station, purling strands of her long black hair around a finger, Sandy who said, "And who are you? I haven't seen you around before."

He shifted his feet, considered coming back later or leaving altogether without a word, driving away and never coming back. Nobody would notice if Nick left this time, if he got himself transferred again, this time west of the Continental Divide. But he came all this way and Elisabeth was close. If he left without seeing her, he would never take a chance like this again.

"Tell her Nick wants to see her," he said. Then, "If you'll point in the direction of the waiting room, I'll stay there until she's free a minute."

Sandy showed where the vending machines were, the television and sofa and armchairs, then returned to the desk to digest what happened—the way the guy, Nick, was shaking he was so nervous. A kind of rough character, shaggy sun-bleached hair, his hands all beat up and swollen, his face red because he'd just shaved from the look of it and wasn't used to shaving.

That's Nick? Sandy must have speculated. *Elisabeth's Nick? The long-lost-bastard Nick?*

Who else could it be?

She walked down the hall and peeked around the corner to get another look. His Carhartt pants, his plain white tee, how he stood in the corner and flipped through the pages of a magazine and shuffled his feet as he waited. He was a flight risk. He couldn't sit still a second.

Elisabeth wasn't with a patient, like Sandy had told him. Elisabeth was out at lunch and wouldn't be back for forty-five minutes or so. Sandy felt the energy of the moment, and that she should save Elisabeth, for some reason.

"You're Nick Holland?" she asked. "Lis's husband. That Nick Holland?"

He flushed, and the look in his eyes, like he was surprised to be caught so easily. But then his face unknotted, he smiled at Sandy, put the magazine back in the rack.

"She mentioned me?" he asked. "What did she say?"

"I shouldn't have to tell you this, but you can't see Lis. This is her place of employment. People depend on her. She can't drop what she's doing."

"Sure."

"I understand it's a sticky situation. You have a lot to talk about. That's important." Sandy grabbed Nick's arm and sat him on the sofa. "Let me help. Tomorrow morning. Meet me for breakfast and we'll talk."

"Nah," Nick said. "When does her shift end? I'll wait. I got nothing to do."

"I can't tell you that. I'd get fired." Sandy wouldn't let him pass. "Tomorrow. Where are you staying? Okay. You know where Elevenworth Café is? Fine. Meet me there at eight."

So this is how it happened that Nick and Elisabeth didn't see each other for so long when he came to Omaha? This Sandy Laika? She came between them, the same as she did when Agent Schwaller came asking questions later that month?

Not exactly. She was trying to help, in a way. Elisabeth had told Sandy that Nick probably didn't know what happened to Caleb after he left. Elisabeth and Nick never talked about it (they hadn't talked at all since he bolted from Chicago in the middle of the night) and maybe that was better. Elisabeth couldn't stand the thought of telling Nick what happened with the baby; she couldn't stand the thought of *admitting* what happened, that's how she put it.

It didn't make a whole lot of sense to Nick how he ended up meeting Sandy. One of Elisabeth's friends, he guessed. When Nick thought it through, he saw where she was coming from. You can't let a guy waltz in where a woman works, not with how the world is. It doesn't matter if the guy claims to be the husband—that could be worse. He ate breakfast with Sandy and told his story. How he met Elisabeth outside a bar, where they lived in Chicago, their trip to the dunes. Sandy was pushy, but Nick didn't mind. She already knew most of what Nick said. Elisabeth had told her these stories.

She asked Nick why he ran off. He told the gist of it. Driving one morning, not knowing where he was headed. Panicking. Ending up in Wyoming and not wanting to sit and feel bad for himself, so he got a job. "Once you get a job," he told her, "three years can get behind you pretty quick."

"And you didn't think of calling that whole time?"

"I did call. I called a lot." He waited as the waitress refilled their coffees before going on. "I couldn't say a word on the phone. She didn't either. It was stupid. The whole time I'm dying to say 'Hi' or 'How you holding up?' or anything. Instead it's like junior high. A month later, the line's disconnected. She moved or something. I had no idea she came to Nebraska, of all places."

"That's sad."

"I know it is."

Nick figured it wouldn't be long before he saw Elisabeth. He fantasized about it more or less constantly while he was at work, in the truck on the highway between jobs. Where would they go to dinner? What would he say, and how would she respond? Was there some special landmark she liked there in Omaha, and could he take her there?

On the days he thought about Elisabeth he stood a little taller, anticipating how he'd see her again soon. There was extra bounce in his step. He stuck around late in the repair yard after work to hear the foreman's jokes. They were bad jokes, bigoted and smutty, you can imagine, but Nick laughed. The prospect of seeing her must have been a light shining into a dark room. He didn't feel like such a misfit all the time. And in the evening, every few days, he met Sandy to discuss how it was going to be.

A month went by like this.

Sandy convinced him to lay low awhile. That it wasn't a good time to burst back into Elisabeth's life, and Caleb's life too, she said. She added that part because she had no idea if Nick knew what had happened to the boy. (People are so strange. How can they communicate at all with such weighty disconnect?)

Nick didn't know how to react. It would have been best to stop Sandy and tell her he knew Caleb died as a baby—of course he knew, Gerry Ahls told him, had showed him Caleb's grave. That Nick played along says a lot. That he was ashamed. That he was afraid he might cry in front of Sandy and he didn't want to do that. That he was a bit impish, that he wanted a little bit of power over Sandy, knowing something she didn't, letting her go on with the lie.

"What's he like?" Nick asked her.

"Who?"

"Caleb."

"He's a good boy" was all she said. If Nick pressed for more—was he good at sports? did he need glasses? what was his favorite food? what size clothes did he wear?—Sandy shook her head and tried to change the subject and said there would be time for all that later.

"I don't want to get between you and your family. There's a lot for you and Lis to talk about. Once the time comes."

Nick already had one shadow life for Caleb. Why was he so eager to start another?

He got used to this routine. Comfortable with the fantasy of seeing Elisabeth, so Nick could ignore how near he actually was to his wife, in the same city, on the other side of the freeway, and he could have stopped by any time he wanted. Work picked up with Midland Pacific and Nick accepted his assignments, drove to the sites and did his job. What else was he supposed to do? He'd spent three years going to work each day, never speaking to any of his so-called loved ones. What would another week hurt?

Did things change when Agent Schwaller arrived in Omaha?

Yes, certainly. After the agent tracked down Nick and started asking all those questions, after he followed Nick out to the jobsite, out on the bridge. The agent seemed like a maniac to Nick. The way he combed his hair and how he talked, the way the agent made his voice go high when questioning, a needling in his pitch and pronunciation. But Nick still went about his day. Maybe the agent was a maniac, but it couldn't make much difference in the grand scheme of things, or Nick's life, what he saw as the next fifty years of his life. Maybe Nick figured not much was changed in America after 9/11, the country still the same, day to day, still essentially decent in the way people went about their business. But there could have been a little doubt in there too. The Patriot Act, extraordinary rendition, black sites, those sorts of things. Nobody knew what was going on exactly, or how much the government was listening. And, really, the government, its functionaries, they didn't wholly know either.

It isn't hard to understand why Nick Holland was wary of approaching his wife out of the blue—why he might think it a good idea to involve an intermediary like Sandy. Nick wasn't the most considerate guy, surely, but even a stunted mind can see he was wracked by the shame of what he'd done. You might hope anyone in his situation would feel the same.

But what in the world was Sandy Laika thinking?

She liked Nick. He was an attractive guy, even if he was too serious. Given the circumstances, who would blame him for being a little dull? *Dull* isn't the right word. He was brooding. Wouldn't talk about the election, wouldn't say how he felt about Sarah Palin, didn't even seem to know who Sandy was talking about when she aped Tina Fey's Palin routine. *I can see Russia from my house!* When Sandy mentioned Obama, there was no recognition. There was only one thing in the world Nick was interested in: the life he'd pissed away. It was kind of sick. And Sandy was pretty sure Elisabeth still loved him.

Does that explain how Sandy got stuck in the middle?

It started because Sandy thought Nick might want to hurt Elisabeth. She saw that stuff all the time on the news, at Saint Wenceslaus. Murder-suicide, that kind of thing. The way Sandy saw it, she had a duty to protect her friend, one of her nurses. She vetted Nick, tried to decode his intentions, see if he was a threat.

It's no secret Sandy was under a lot of stress. The hospital admins made everyone miserable over those safe haven cases, after Cary Junger left his nine kids in emergency. Sandy's boss called her every day to bitch her out for some unrelated issue, like tripping hazards or the tone of voice nurses used visiting with patients. Sandy understood all this hostility began amid the fact that TV trucks were transmitting from the parking lot and cameras were aimed at staff. Admin was concerned that even a tiny mistake like spilling a bedpan might end up on the nightly news.

In a perverse way—or maybe a beautiful way, depending how you look at it—Sandy distracted herself by bringing Elisabeth and Nick back together. She just wanted to know, if Nick was so desperate to be with his family, why did he leave in the first place?

"Couldn't you take having a baby around? Did you regret getting married? Were you not attracted to Lis anymore?"

"No. That wasn't it at all."

He tried to explain. They were just married. He was a new father and hadn't conceded anything yet, not like most married people do over long stretches of time. They had sex until her seventh month, he went out with friends, still drank, etc., etc.

"If I settled," Nick said, "my whole life would have been nothing but settling after that. Every decision would be about the safety of institutions and what was best for other people."

"What do you mean *institutions*?"

"Family. The nuclear family. I didn't want to shoot for the safe middle. Every move I made was about choosing risk over safety, avoiding mediocrity, as a determinant of who I was and how I saw myself. I don't feel that way now. But, at that time, I did."

"That's the reason you left?" Sandy asked him. "For real?"

It was such bullshit. He probably turned that around in his head for the last three years, all day, every day. Of course he did. But hearing a man say that, in those words, like it was a philosophical choice he made. It isn't like he ran off to track down bin Laden or feed starving kids or build homeless shelters or whatever. He left to get drunk in motel bars and meet women, to repair railroad bridges in exchange for a decent wage. There was nothing mysterious or noble about Nick Holland. Sandy didn't think there was, not in the way Elisabeth talked about him sometimes.

Sandy pushed Nick to go see his wife, even threatened him. "I'll tell her where to find you, if you don't go. Then what if she sends a divorce lawyer and you still never get to talk to her?" She even conspired to occupy Agent Schwaller so their reunion could be private. No agents watching, no photographs. She invited Schwaller over to dinner that night, to meet her mother. She insisted the agent come, wouldn't take no for an answer, so Schwaller would be occupied.

"Do you know he's following you?" she asked Nick.

"Who?"

"Frank Schwaller."

Nick shrugged. "You know that spook? I could care less about him, but, yeah. He peeks through windows, that kind of creep. Comes out to where I work, so the other guys are starting to wonder. I stay at a different hotel than them, then this dandy-looking fellow pulls up in his car to proposition me. Either I'm a gigolo or running a narcotics ring, the guys haven't decided yet."

"He's got a real interest in you," Sandy said. "I don't know why. I haven't told Schwaller anything, but he asks about you every time I see him."

Nick glanced her over. They huddled close at a tabletop, in an intense conversation, and Sandy couldn't keep quiet enough, because she knew someone might be listening: she turned off her phone before she even went into the diner to meet Nick, though Nick didn't turn off his. Sandy made it sound like she was an informant. Nick looked a little disturbed about that, how he sat back and held up his hand to stop Sandy, to shush her. He couldn't imagine what Sandy would tell the agent—Nick didn't believe he had any secrets that were of interest to national intelligence. He did some bad things over the years, but nothing illegal, nothing seditious.

"What do I care if a cop is watching through binoculars? I want to see my wife. It's not going to change a thing if somebody is listening."

"You don't understand. The stuff he talks about. Using computers to watch people use the toilet or jerk off. It's sick. And it's not just him. That's what I mean. Lis deserves some respect, a little privacy. She has something important to tell you."

Sandy told Nick a date and time when he could visit Elisabeth without Schwaller following. She couldn't keep a straight face, telling Nick. She'd conspired for days, ciphering who was on whose side and how she could make a difference for the side of good.

"He's coming to my mom's house for dinner," Sandy said, laughing. "At six thirty. That gives you a few hours. That's all I can promise. Schwaller will have no idea what he's missing."

These were Nick Holland's last days.

Of course, nobody knew that. Certainly not Elisabeth.

Sandy explained to Elisabeth how everything was supposed to happen. This was after work as they walked out through emergency to the parking lot, Sandy grabbing her arm and saying there was somebody she was going to want to meet. She thought Sandy meant Kyle Junger at first, because that's what was on her mind. Elisabeth struggled to concentrate on anything besides that night, those kids. Elisabeth was planning on going back to the Junger house after work, but first Sandy tossed her purse on the driver's seat of Elisabeth's car and closed the door.

"Nick is in Omaha. I don't know for how long. He works for Midland Pacific and has a room downtown on Harney Street. He wants to see you."

"Nick?"

Sandy reached for Elisabeth's hands, like Elisabeth swayed with the news, like she might fall. Elisabeth didn't sway. She slapped away Sandy's hands, said, "Give me a minute," but she didn't need a minute. "How long has he been here? Why didn't he come to me first?"

"That was a mishap. He came up to the floor to see you—"

"Here?"

"You were out to lunch and I was at the desk when he got off the elevator. I intercepted him once it dawned on me he was your husband. Or, some guy claiming to be your husband. There's guidelines on that—I can't tell strangers your personal information."

"I'm not mad."

"You trust me, don't you? I'd never lie to you."

Elisabeth snorted at that, she laughed, to show she wasn't dumb. "I don't know," she said. "I don't want to see him," she said. "This is too much."

Elisabeth reached for the door handle, but Sandy held the car door shut.

"Don't you want to know why he left? What he's been up to all this time and—"

"If he's still alive."

Elisabeth didn't understand why it was Sandy telling her all this and not Nick himself. What was she supposed to say?

"Okay," Elisabeth said. "But he has to call me first. I want to hear his voice before he shows up at my door. Is that clear? If some guy stops by my place without me saying it's okay, I'll call the police."

[03 Oct 08; the day before Nicholas Holland fell in the river]

If Elisabeth thought it would be easier to talk to Nick on the phone, she was wrong. Had she forgotten their history? Those first months after Nick left her and Caleb? When Caleb was still in the apartment with her, and a few calls, six or seven or eight, even after Caleb. Nick called late at night and neither said anything. Her brother lived with her by then in the one-bedroom ground-floor in Boystown, in Chicago. If Tyler answered, Nick would hang up. If it was Elisabeth who answered, he waited. It was so stupid how he'd done it. Calling in the middle of the night. A selfish thing, Elisabeth thought later, after the calls stopped, a year later in Omaha—Nick calling so she'd know he was alive, to let her hear his silence, to know he could come home if he wanted to, but he wouldn't.

—*Don't be a kid about this, please. Say something. You called me, so talk.*

—*Sandy said it was okay to call. Thanks for letting me.*

Elisabeth didn't recognize his voice, it had been so long. Fear rushed through her. What if the man on the phone wasn't Nick? What if it was a weirdo? *Say something else,* she demanded, a little desperation in her voice, because it felt like a mistake, agreeing to this, for them to speak when they could remain silent like before and change nothing.

—Tell me . . . Tell me where we went on our first date.

—We went lots of places, I guess. Is that what you mean? I don't know if that's a date. Mostly we just walked up and down Milwaukee.

—What did we buy?

—Junk. We went junkshopping in Wicker Park. You got a DARE shirt, right? And a basket for your Schwinn. We went in a few places. DAV, Salvation Army, whatever that Mexican Catholic place was called that sold prayer candles and used shoes. They had a bin of old panties and I tried to get you to pull on a pair.

—Where were we when I asked you to move in with me?

—The dunes, in Indiana.

—Yes. Why did you get embarrassed and blush on the beach?

—I blushed?

—Yes.

—Oh. I remember. You took your top off. I thought some guy might see, but we hid behind one of the dunes.

It wasn't about the facts he named, was it? To see if this man on the phone knew the details only Nick Holland could know. Hearing him talk about these days, their first date, Nick sounded like himself. Elisabeth recognized his shy, out-the-side-of-his-mouth laughter when he talked about the bin of women's undergarments. If she asked him about his life now—where he worked, why he was in Omaha—she wouldn't have recognized his voice. He would have sounded like someone else, and rightly so.

—Do you want to come over?

—Yeah.

—You can come over, if you bring something to eat.

Not even an hour passed before he arrived. The timing was perfect, according to Sandy's plan. Agent Schwaller was just then sitting to dinner at the Laika house, building his first taco, using his vast intellectual powers to deduce why an old Lithuanian peasant woman served chili con queso for dinner and why she called it her specialty. At that same instant, Nick parked his Buick outside Mount Vernon Apartments. Elisabeth watched from a window, from where she lived on the third floor. How Nick stood from the car and walked to the security door; how he wore jeans and an orange shirt from work; how he froze, switched the plastic bag that held dinner from one hand to the other. He looked lost, holding the food behind his back, inelegant, as though he was going to wait all night. It was amusing to watch, a man biding time outside a three-story brick building, checking the address, checking the rattly old windows to see if somebody noticed he'd arrived.

He looked different, Elisabeth realized. Of course, he should. It had been three years. He was thicker in his chest and back, his skin darker. He didn't let his hair fall in his eyes like he used to, but it was buzzed tight so he could see when he walked from tie to tie over a rail bridge. Elisabeth saw, three stories up, that his hairline was advancing rapidly, he was balding. But he still stood with a western posture—one foot offset from the other, a slight bow to his legs, his back straight as he pulled a pack of cigarettes from the pocket of his jeans and lit up.

It was surprising that Nick smoked. He'd quit when Elisabeth was pregnant, and she hadn't thought he might someday stop quitting, that this would be one of the first things he reclaimed when he ran—and it was, he bought a pack of Camels before he even crossed the Chicago city limits, that early morning he left. The smell of his smoke, the nicotine acidity, surprised Elisabeth as it scaled the bricks to where she sat on the sill of her bedroom window, one of five in the room, a room that jut out from the building so an H-shape formed where the front door was set between her apartment and the apartment mirrored across the way. His smoke crawling up the H along invisible vines.

"You want me to buzz you in or not?" she called down to him. The way he spun to scan up the bricks and locate her, how he tossed the cigarette into the grass without sneaking a last breath, she must have scared him. She didn't want the smell in her apartment. It was enough having smoke come through the window, that's why she spoke up. If she didn't speak then, Elisabeth might have sat a long time and watched Nick. The amused look on his face, the instant they made eye contact. He looked like he'd been living hard—how he walked a little sore in his hips—and that made her feel better for some reason. When he came up, Nick said she looked just as he remembered, which felt right, even if it was a clueless thing for Nick to say. At least he didn't try to touch her. There was no hug. Just, *hello.* And *it's you.* And *it's me.* Nick was getting old, but it was him.

He brought dinner and went right to the dining room, peeked from side to side down the hallway until he spotted the table. Didn't even bother to clear that day's newspapers, the updates on the safe haven kids, just put out what he brought on top of the splayed broadsheets. He lined up the bundles, presented them to Elisabeth. Some of her favorites from Chicago. Piña Jarritos, churros, burritos, from a taco truck parked at a laundromat a couple blocks east. "Seemed legit," Nick said, handing over a wrapped *adobada*, keeping a *barbacoa* for himself. "That's what you like, isn't it? I can't find a place here that sells pierogi."

She didn't speak, only allowed a little smile at the crack about pierogi. The word made her smile, the little bit of Polish, and that Nick was trying to make this go smooth, whatever this was they were doing. She didn't laugh, she smiled a little. She sat and they unwrapped dinner. If they were eating, they didn't have to speak. Just: "Do you like living here?" It was okay. Sometimes the neighbors across the street were loud. The plumbing worked. And "You're a nurse? How long have you done that?" So she explained.

Every time Nick opened his mouth, she wondered if he was going to ask if she'd tried to divorce him, or if she wanted a divorce. For her part: What was Nick doing in Omaha? What did he want from her? Was he dying? Did he need money? Had he talked to her brother and had some secret about what Tyler was up to in Afghanistan?

They didn't ask these questions. They made small talk.

Nick got up after he finished eating, threw away his garbage. He was always polite like that. He asked where the toilet was and walked in that direction when Elisabeth pointed.

He didn't come back after she heard a flush and a wash and the shunt of the lock bolt reversing into the bathroom door, then the hinge squeaking open. Elisabeth went to see Nick snooping in the office, in the guest room, whatever she called it, where a velveteen rabbit with long, droopy ears was propped up on the antique dresser. A stuffed animal that had lost some stuffing, with button eyes skewed loose from the spot where they were meant to hold tight.

"I'm sorry," he said. Not looking at her, looking at the rabbit. "I don't know what you thought about me the last few years, but I never wanted anything bad to happen. I mean, with Cal. It's only been a couple months since I found out. If I'd known"—reaching a hand to the rabbit—"I'd of come right away to help, and for the funeral. Your dad showed me where he's buried."

Nick turned to Elisabeth and startled, seeing her. She wasn't crying, she wasn't angry. She nodded along with what he said. Maybe Nick thought she'd break down if he apologized, or scream. But here was Nurse Holland, a new woman to him. Stern, patronizing in manner. "All right," she said. "Apology accepted."

Did they go to the living room then? Did they go back to sit at the table, eat the churros? No. She asked him right then and there as she blocked the doorway. She asked why he found her.

"Tell me you didn't come all this way just to say you're sorry."

"Well, no. That's not all."

Nick took a step toward the door, but Elisabeth didn't budge. Didn't she want to go sit on the sectional so they could talk about things like people? No, she didn't.

"I wanted to check on you," Nick said. He stepped back, spun the swivel chair so he could sit down. "I came to see if you're okay."

"I'm okay," Nurse Holland told him. Nurse Holland was fine with standing, arms crossed over her chest. She hardly even blinked she was so fine, looking Nick in the eye to make sure he was listening. "You don't have to worry about me."

"Before I found out what happened, I wanted to see Cal and spend some time with him. I've been saving money, a college fund, and to put Cal's name on the account I needed his Social Security number."

"His name was Caleb."

"I was going to call him Cal when he was older."

"But you didn't call him that. You never will."

Nick shrunk in the chair. It's difficult to imagine how he thought all this would go, coming to find her, but this surely wasn't it. He looked like he was going to cry. Swallowing hard, his eyes watering. He turned half away in the chair so he didn't have to look at her. Both Nick and Tyler did this; it got on Elisabeth's nerves how much of a struggle it was for them to look her in the eyes when they were talking to her. Nick hunched in her swivel chair and was about to have a breakdown, and she really didn't want that to happen. If Nick cried and she had to say something nice to make him feel better, she would have died.

"What are you going to do with the money?" she asked.

"What money?"

"What you were saving for the 529. That's what they call them. College funds."

"I haven't thought about that. It's still his money."

"You should give it to charity. There are a lot of kids who could use a couple hundred bucks way more than you."

"Sure, I know. And there's more than a couple hundred bucks."

"Here in Omaha. That's what I mean. Boys and Girls Club, or Lutheran Family Services. Places that help keep the heat on in people's homes, and get them dinner, the kind of stuff that keeps families together."

He sucked his lips, squinted, tried to figure if she meant to sound like that. She meant it. Nurse Holland did not misspeak.

"Sure," Nick agreed. "That's a good idea."

"There's these kids," she started saying. Elisabeth was going to tell him, even if the thought of the kids, of Kyle Junger, made her heart rate elevate, even if the words stuck in her throat. "Don't you watch the news? Or read the newspaper?"

Nick shook his head. She was already explaining anyway, about the safe haven kids, motioned for him to stand and led him back to the dining room, picked up her wrappers and threw out the leftovers. "Here. Look at this, if you want to do some good with that money."

Nick glanced at the articles without really looking, then back to Elisabeth. "Is that what all this is?" he asked her, motioning with his eyes to the stacks of newspapers in the corner. "It's like a detective show in here, with all the maps."

She made a face at him, crimped her lips and wrinkled her nose, because she thought he was teasing her. He wasn't. Nick looked at her, maybe worried she wasn't all right. Not that she didn't have money, or that she was alone, but that she'd gone eccentric. That all the stuff with Tyler, with Caleb, all of it, had taken too much of a toll on her sanity. There's only so much a person can take, he said with his eyes, with his being there.

But she was bigger than that, stronger.

Elisabeth saw all of a sudden how things must look. Her research on those kids was the only thing out of place in the apartment— everything else was spic and span, except the kitchen table. The stacks of newspapers along the back wall, the blue vinyl binder where she kept articles about the Junger kids. There were a few others she'd cut out but hadn't yet added. The scissors still there, blades open in an ex because she dropped them to the table to use again. What did it matter to leave scissors out on the table, the blades exposed? Who could it hurt to leave them lying there? There was no child to come pick up and run with the scissors.

"Look," she told him again. She lifted the binder from the floor and opened to the first page. "There's no reason you should care about any of this. But I want you to look."

She told him about the night the Junger kids came in. Just the basics. Names and ages. Seeing those kids in ER, the sadness in Kyle's eyes, when Elisabeth sat with him, when Kyle saw his older sisters led out and driven away to who knows where.

A shudder went through his body. They were all confused and so beaten down by things. But that look in Kyle's eyes, that was too much.

"And you were there? With the nine?"

"It was my hospital. This little one I took charge of for a while. What could I tell him?"

"What did you say?"

"That everything would be fine."

Nick didn't understand. "What's so bad about that?"

"What if he gets forgotten, and I promised he'd be okay?"

"But everything should be fine, won't it? Now that he's with his aunt."

Elisabeth felt like crying but didn't let herself. "He's a little boy," she said, then she stood and turned away to signal the end of that.

The idea took over. She should take him to the house where those kids lived. Elisabeth grabbed her purse, snagged his arm. Pulled him to the door, left the lights on, left the binder open on the dining room table because she wouldn't need the binder if she could show him.

She raced down the stairs and out to the church parking lot. "Get in," she told him. He asked, "Don't you want me to drive?" "No, I don't. Get in." There was little talk in the car, over the ten-minute trip north.

Elisabeth knew the way. Followed Saddle Creek to where it turned into NW Radial Highway, then veered onto Fontenelle Boulevard. The way she breezed through yellow lights, it would have been clear to anybody she knew where she was going. She'd been to the Junger house twice by then, it has been noted. Agent Schwaller wasn't aware of this, but her license plate was picked up by traffic cameras and the moment logged when her vehicle cut through Fontenelle Park, then across Ames Avenue to the environs thereabout. A male passenger was in the car—the record shows this too.

"There it is," she said, a little winded, like she'd held her breath driving. Everything the same as before. Nobody had cleared wind-felled branches or mowed thigh-high grasses or painted the rotting eaves of the tattered bungalow. No bank had yet foreclosed on the property; it held no strategic value for any investor and would slump on its plat a long time, until the windows were knocked in, until squatters came along and the city would have to board up all points of entry until budget materialized for demolition. No tragedy was embossed over the front door, no crime tape. Maybe you would never live in a place like this, not if you had a choice. But people did, they do. What did Elisabeth want Nick to see? Life here was inelegant but not invalid.

The way they were situated in her car, at the curb, Nick had to turn in his seat to look at Elisabeth, to look in her face for some indication of what he was supposed to say. He acted so sad, in his bearing, the wrinkling of his forehead, in his concern for Elisabeth and what she was feeling. His face tanned so the lines ran deep. Coming here made him nervous; his body contorted, like being in the car with Elisabeth hurt his back.

"Are you sure you don't want me to drive?" is what he said. He didn't say he was worried or scared. He wanted to protect her; he'd be happy to drive if she needed to look out the window, if she needed a few minutes to pull herself together.

"No," she answered. "I'm okay."

She didn't understand why this place was so bewildering, except that this was ground zero. She wanted someone to see that. If nothing else, even if she couldn't explain what she felt, at least Nick could look at the house where those kids lived. "Don't you ever think about it?" she asked him. "Some families fall apart and some stay together, and it doesn't always make sense why one is one and another the other."

"I think about that a lot."

"There's nothing anyone can do about it. God takes for no reason."

"It's sad what's happening to those kids," Nick said. "Nobody can say any different."

Elisabeth recognized him for a moment. His voice, the rhythm in the way he spoke. She remembered what it was like to trust Nick, when he took her for a walk in Wicker Park, when he drove to the dunes and she ended up confessing what she wanted out of life during the ride back. This time, Nick slumped in the seat of her Pontiac, in blue jeans, in a hazard-orange tee shirt that was pricked with dots of tar all along its front. The birthmark on his neck, what he called his strawberries, because of their globbish shape and pinkish color. How she'd talked to him in those early days, and how amazing it was—that he merely wanted to know her, merely but deeply, without keeping score, without forethought for future manipulation. And they could talk for hours in the car because they didn't have to look each other in the eyes; she could let go of what she'd been holding too close to her heart, those days.

"I've been praying," she said, "for the first time since I was a kid, twelve or thirteen. I don't remember when I stopped."

Nick looked at her and, reflexively, absentmindedly, she reached to turn the key and start the car. She cried and gripped the steering wheel and faced straight ahead.

"My mom said, when I was growing up and anything bad happened, she said it was God's plan and that we don't get the privilege to know how everything fits in the big picture. She called that eternity. It's bigger than life, bigger than history. I never liked the sound of that."

"Where's the grace?" Nick asked.

"What do you mean?"

"That's what you're asking, right? Where, in all this mess and suffering, is God's grace?"

He turned to look at her, so she looked at him. That sly, almost involuntary smile taking over his face, like it did when he joked around or thought he said something smart. He couldn't help how he bunched his shoulders and his back bowed to hide his chest. Even this Nick with muscles and dark tan and short hair, he still wanted to hide like he was a little boy. The affectation disgusted Elisabeth, Nick acting like he was damaged. She breathed deep, then let the air from her lungs escape slow. Combed back hair from her forehead with her fingers and felt her own body, her back straight, her chin up, as Nick watched, as he waited; how she felt short in her seat, arms stretched to reach the steering wheel; how her face, her lips felt dry; her knee a little sore that day beneath her scar, as it sometimes was, a little grab at the back of her thigh, fatigue along her shins. Elisabeth wanted to stand, to move, so she could feel her muscles stretch.

"I'm not talking about grace," she said.

"Yes, you are."

"I'm saying responsibility. Not grace. Not forgiveness—don't even start. It's fairness I want." She was exasperated, surprised, like it shouldn't be so hard to talk to someone you once or still loved. That person should be able to listen, shouldn't they?

"Nick, you don't even believe in God. Why would you say the word *grace* to me?"

She was speechless, fighting herself, trying to not kick him to the curb and speed off. But then a man parked across the street from them. Nick didn't recognize him, but Elisabeth did. It was Cary Junger who parked across the street and went up the walk to his front door.

He was such a little guy. His skinny legs and balding head. His patchy beard because he shaved maybe weekly. Even the way he stood at the door, how he drooped and sagged because his bones bowed. There on the stoop, digging in his jean shorts to find the right key, to pull the key out and see if it still turned the lock, like he wasn't sure it would.

Elisabeth was out of the car and behind Cary Junger as he tried a key in the front door. The key didn't work. He tried one in the dead bolt and then the other, the only two on his key ring. Nobody had come to trim the yard, but somebody changed the locks. A bank, maybe an investor who would soon own the house and recognized the name on the title. *Well, fuck that guy,* somebody said, then they changed his locks. That, or Cary brought the wrong keys. He pounded where the wood was splintered around the dead bolt. "Fuck me!" he shouted into eternity.

"Are you Cary?" Elisabeth asked. "It's you, right?"

"I already talked to everybody." He turned to Elisabeth, looked her in the eyes. That she was one woman (Nick at the curb) and wasn't holding a TV camera or microphone or even a notepad to record his every tic must have surprised Cary Junger. He flinched, confused, let his dark eyes show he was pissed off and suspicious. He screwed his head at her and flared his nostrils, like he saw himself as a cornered animal.

"I met your kids when you left them at the hospital," Elisabeth said, then, "Do you remember me?"

"What do you want to know that hasn't been asked already?"

Elisabeth didn't move. She didn't need to say anything to him. The twerp. She was there to look at him, to observe and record, like she was a reporter, her eyes cameras. She recalled the names of the children again—Colton, Chase, Emma, Elsie, Jefferson, Melody, Kyle, David, Belle—but she didn't say their names aloud. She ground her teeth and thought of those kids that night at the hospital, thought the incantation of their names.

"There's nothing you got to say, is there?" Cary Junger's ears burned red. "Who are you? Why you fucking with me?"

She wanted to jump to the stoop and punch him in the gut. To grab him by his jug ears and throw him in the grass. Her shoulders twitched, she didn't blink, as she stared him down. The neighbor tapped on her window, nearly over Cary's shoulder the houses were so close, and shouted through the glass that she was going to call the cops.

"What do you know about my life?" he asked. "Let me guess, you don't have any kids, do you? So how do you get off telling me anything?"

"I'm not."

"You get to sleep through the night. I don't. I got nine of them. A little brat that won't go to bed when he's supposed to, gets me up four times during the night and his voice is always in my head, and on top of that wants breakfast before sunrise. Won't get dressed, then won't go to the school bus and makes me late for work, gets me fired. Take that times nine! Then you come tell me I fucked up. Then you stand on my lawn to tell me how I'm shit."

"I didn't say any of that."

"Yeah, you did."

Elisabeth must have wanted to correct him, to slug him. Elisabeth Holland wasn't a hypocrite, she wasn't judgmental, and it wasn't her fault Cary Junger had all those kids. She only wanted to see what made things happen the way they had, to experience it, the mildew, the cigarette stink that leached from the house, to hear his real voice, Cary's voice—a little deeper than she expected, gravelly and scratched, the battered voice of a construction worker, because that's what he was.

She had to look away from him, away from the tendons in his neck. Somehow it surprised her how his skin moved when he spoke, how his eyes followed her—she'd seen his face on the news so much, that one night when she peeked into the social worker's office, and now he was here, real, live, facing her. Elisabeth turned away to catch her breath.

Nick was on the sidewalk, halfway between her and the street. He said nothing. Elisabeth worried Nick would step between her and Cary Junger and pull her to the car, tell her to be smart. But that wasn't Nick.

Nick moseyed up the walk. Nick pulled his Camels from his pocket and lit one. Elisabeth and the father of those nine kids watching as he took a drag.

"Chief," Cary said, peeking around Elisabeth. "Can I get one of those?"

Nick fished one from the pack without thinking and held out the cigarette and his lighter, in case Cary needed a lighter. It was Nick's nature that made him do this. A guy asked Nick for a smoke, and Nick had one to spare.

Cary curved wide into the knee-high grass when he crossed Elisabeth. She watched him, the berth he gave her, how he came to congress with Nick to accept the cigarette. He said, "Thanks, buddy."

Maybe it looked like Elisabeth gave in when she laughed her loud laugh, not her cruel laugh, her *wow* laugh, and told Nick she was leaving. She waited for Nick to take a last drag and flick his cigarette into the grass—into the wild, dry grass—and she laughed again because everything was so stupid. Those two boys smoking, hoping a lady wouldn't yell at them. Those two twerps. Cary Junger staring at her as she walked by and her staring at him. What could she say to a man like that?

"They will never let you rest," she said.

She reversed the route. Fontenelle Boulevard, NW Radial, Saddle Creek, Farnam.

In the car she finally told him.

"You think you're the only one who runs from things? You think everything just goes along without you?"

"That's what happened, isn't it?" He leaned against the passenger door, as far away as he could get as she drove. "I don't appreciate how nobody told me. Three years and not a word."

She realized, hearing him, the tremble in his voice, that this was what Nick had come to say. She should have pulled over and stopped in the park until their emotions crested and washed away. She shouldn't have been operating a vehicle like that.

"Nobody knew where to find you."

"You could have asked. I *called* you."

"You did." She choked up remembering. Still driving, taking a right on red instead of stopping when the light conspired against her, so she didn't have to look at him. "You really think I could have told you about Caleb over the phone? How he died. That he died. Nick. You didn't even say hello. You never even said it was you who was calling."

"Who else would it have been?"

"I couldn't tell you. Don't you get it? If I'd told, you would have come back."

Nick looked sick, like his tongue swelled in his throat. It hit him. He might have never said another word again the rest of his life, it hit him so hard.

"I won't say I'm sorry," Elisabeth said. "You left. Why would I want you to come back to Chicago? What if you had? Then what?"

"You didn't want me to come back?"

"I tried to make you a better person. And after Caleb . . . Wasn't it best for everyone that you left? And after Caleb . . . I didn't have to wait for you."

Elisabeth making the turns, Elisabeth driving. She wasn't far from her apartment when a light finally stopped her, when she eased up to a yellow and didn't barrel through to keep moving. She let the light stop her, let it turn to red, to look at him.

"I didn't need you to save me."

"I want something of his," he said in the church parking lot. "The velveteen rabbit."

"Fine. Not the velveteen rabbit, but something else."

If he wanted to take something that touched Caleb once, three years ago, fine. She'd dig one out the closet if that's what would satisfy Nick. Up in her bedroom, even with Nick still in the doorway, Elisabeth wanted to crash. They'd laid their cards on the table. It was finished, whatever Nick had come to get from her. Once she gave him something, he'd leave.

The problem was that Elisabeth didn't want to lose anything special, and it was all special. Every stuffed animal she picked off the bed. The elephant, the penguin, the polar bear, the lamb, even the Ditka doll that she couldn't remember who gave it. She had to dig in the closet. There was a box at the back she never opened. She tore the packing tape off for the second or third time ever. Elisabeth knew what was in there, things she wanted to save forever when she packed up in Chicago. A pacifier. A newspaper clipping of the birth announcement from the *Chippewa Zeitung*. The growth charts the doctors gave her at Caleb's well-visit. He was a perfectly normal baby: 48th percentile height; 52nd, weight; 89th, head circumference, which Elisabeth had been so excited about in that geeky way that came out of her sometimes, Caleb's big brain. There was a framed picture of Nick holding Caleb, the two of them surrounded by sunlight from the window, Caleb in his baptismal gown.

That must have been the day her parents came to visit, when her mom made Caleb try on the gown—but it was only Nick and Caleb in the photo. Elisabeth had it framed after Nick left, before Caleb died. It was a good picture. Not the only one she had of them together, but this was the best. Underneath the picture was all the paperwork. Hospital invoices, the ambulance bill, the original death certificate and a few duplicates in case Elisabeth had to prove Caleb died, in legal proceedings, for the insurance company. There were the tiny velcro ID bracelets Caleb wore in the maternity ward. She kept those on him a week after he came home, she couldn't remember why.

She pressed the old packing tape over the tabs and slid the box back into its spot in the closet. Her face so drawn she could feel the skin drooping from her face, under her eyes, as much as she could feel anything.

Along with the framed photograph, Elisabeth decided she could part with the stuffed Ditka and snatched it off her bed.

When she returned to the alcove, Nick saw her face, her shaking. "Are you okay?"

She said she was fine, but he took the photo and doll from her and put his arm around her and walked her to the sectional couch where she could sit. He sat with her, arm over her shoulder, and waited for her to cry if she was going to cry, said, "Wait," and went to the kitchen. If Elisabeth heard him banging around in there, she showed no sign of caring. She stared at the open window, still shaking, still shivering, until Nick returned and set two mugs on the table. "Green tea," he said, then, "It's getting cold," the breeze from the window erasing the steam off the top of the tea. He closed the windows, latched the sashes, sat next to her so only their knees touched, held out her tea until she accepted, and sat with her, said, "Okay."

"I want you to stay," she said. "You can sleep on the couch."

"All right. If you want me to."

"The windows rattle when I'm alone."

"I'm happy to—" he started to say, but she was crying. Eyes forced shut, face bright red. Her body shaking, so he took her mug and set it on the table next to his. He put his arms around her. He slid next to her and held her.

"It's going to be okay," he said. He started to say more, but she told him to shut up.

He might have tried to explain it all to her. His leaving, his working on rails for three years without writing; how it was that he could go on without holding her body to his body in the deep dark of night; how it was he could stand without crumbling in shame now that he knew, that he hadn't been there to hold her arm when she had to bury Caleb in a little white box in a slim grave in Chippewa. But Nick didn't say another word. He let her cross her arms over his back, let her wet his shirt, and didn't insult her by patting her on the shoulder or whispering *shhhh* into her hair or *baby, rest your head*. He was just a body, a scent, a vessel that contained the last smoldering embers of a certain Lis Ahls she happened to have good memories about.

They lay on the couch, an hour or so. Her face near his, resting on her folded hands. She opened her eyes and let them wander to his mouth, his eyes, until he smiled at her. "You know," he murmured, but she shook her head. *Shut up.* Closed her eyes again, held the lids tight, and rubbed her head into his shoulder.

Nick stayed on the couch when she went to bed. She saw him through the doorway, from the light coming in the closed windows. Nick sat up straight and stared out at a greenish streetlamp light, to the motel-style apartments across the street, where two men boozed on lawn chairs. Nick's face was stone. A blanket wrapped around him even though it wasn't cold in the apartment anymore, it was warm. Elisabeth wondered what he was thinking just then. His expression gave no clues. His breathing even and soft. He was simply staring at the light, wasn't he? She would never get to ask what he was thinking, what unsolvable mystery he pondered that moment. His life? God's grace? If he took her seriously when she said she was afraid? If he hoped they might have a future together, for him to stay here with her, or if he'd already decided to leave?

She cried when he departed, early in the morning because they both worked Saturdays. Walking out the door on the ground floor of her building, she noticed how it rained overnight after she fell asleep, how it was foggy with only the hint of sun behind the apartments across the street. They should say good-bye, she supposed. Their cars were parked in opposite directions, his down the block, hers in the church lot.

The tears came before she even looked at him, out on the sidewalk. It wasn't quite real, his being there. The two of them in Omaha, a place they'd never been together. The feeling overtook her that she would never see him again—that if she said good-bye it would be the last time—but she was being silly. Why wouldn't she see him, if she wanted? It wasn't a trap. Nick had come back, hadn't he? They had to go to work, that was all. It was morning, one morning on the precipice of other mornings.

Neither could get out of work, they both said that, which wasn't true, they could have called in sick, as he'd done the day before—and Nick wouldn't have gone to work that day if they'd played hooky and stayed in her apartment. It was chilly for that time of year and the river was thick with fog, the bridges would be slick. But Elisabeth was being silly. He would come back that night, he promised. No matter what her gut told her, it was only fear bending her emotions, and that she was crying. Crying made everything worse. She wanted to go to work, if for no other reason than she would have to stop crying.

When she looked up, Nick was crying too. Her cowboy—a railroad man now—squinting to hold in what was tearing him up, cheeks going purple to hold in, lips sucked straight.

They didn't say good-bye, were too embarrassed to say anything. She waved, an infinitely small gesture, to which he nodded in agreement.

FILE 12

AGT FRANK SCHWALLER

04 Oct 08 to 05 Oct 08

05 May 09

Agent Schwaller was in his room at the Embassy Suites when he got the call about Nick. It was late morning. Schwaller was packing. He'd been in Omaha too long already and was anxious to return to Chicago, to his cubicle in the field office there, to his Loop apartment with a balcony, where there was an Irish bar on the ground floor and he knew the bartender, and every night a woman would sit alone at the end of the bar, a tourist or on business, who had only a few hours in the Windy City before she went home to San Diego or Minneapolis or Albany or Arkansas. As far as Schwaller was concerned, these were the finest kind of people to know. Woman or man—it didn't have to be sexual—with only a solitary night before they headed home.

Maybe coming to Omaha had been a waste of time. Schwaller didn't know for sure yet. He'd collected a lot of information, and, like he said from the start, trying to unearth a definitive Ahls family ignominy was a needle-in-a-haystack type of deal, as far as statute is concerned. There was a lot to find out, but no immediate matter of national security, which, nominally, was his purpose for coming here. Maybe nothing Agent Schwaller had done in Omaha was in the Bureau's charter, but whatever. Was there any point in tracking the every gesture and disgrace of these people? Sure there was. If you go by charter, knowing everything about the Ahls and their connections at least had the potential to make Americans safe, and that's the point of all points, the atom at the base of everything.

But were they up to anything? Elisabeth, Nick, Sandy, the Ahls?

Well, no. Not as much as you would hope. No more than anyone else, no more than you find in the life of any American, as it turns out.

Schwaller had to wrap up a few loose ends. Stop at the Omaha field office and put in some face time with the special agent in charge, let news travel up the ladder that there was still nothing to see in Nebraska. That night the agent would meet Sandy Laika at the hotel bar. He'd end things with her and didn't expect there to be any surprises. Maybe saying he was leaving would go better than anticipated, maybe Sandy also was intrigued by those who could promise only that they'd be gone by morning.

The call came from the Cass County sheriff's office shortly before lunch, when the agent was driving across town to the Omaha field office. The sheriff himself called, with the county attorney conferenced in.

—*This was flagged, this guy.*

—*What do you mean?*

—*Flagged to contact you at this number, if anything showed up on Nicholas Holland.*

That's how the sheriff explained himself, except it was Nick himself who showed up, in the morgue at a county hospital.

—*We got him. This is your courtesy call, if you want to know where to find him.*

—*Are you sure? I saw him two days ago.*

—*Pretty sure. Railroad guy? Fell off a bridge down here in Plattsmouth? Sound familiar?*

It was easy enough to connect with the foreman after that, find out where the accident happened, the precise location where Nick fell in the river, though Agent Schwaller already deduced that himself. He'd been there to watch Nick work. How Nick jumped from tie to tie and tossed off the straps. How the other repairmen thought Nick was an asshole. It wasn't much of a surprise to them that Nick fell.

Schwaller didn't bother following him out to the bridge that day or the day before. What was it worth to watch a man work another day? Especially a Saturday. Even then, Nick dead, Schwaller wasn't sure he was wrong about that. As it happened, Nick didn't even go to work the day before, he'd called in sick, so this was his first morning back on the bridge. The foreman told the agent this. Schwaller had taken off the tail and didn't know that Nick hadn't returned to his room at the Kellogg Rooming House the night before.

From what the foreman told, everything was normal. Nothing was extraordinary in the way Nick interacted with the other workers, with the foreman. Nick's file tells the exact time he showed up to the yard and when he arrived at the bridge. How he hardly talked to the other repairmen on site, only checked the charts to see what he missed when he was out sick, what they got done without him, and then he was out on the bridge. It was foggy. It rained that morning and was drizzling in Plattsmouth, according to the weather service. The other guys waited in the truck until conditions improved. But not Nick. He crossed to the tracks and charged out there with his tool belt to inspect repairs made the day before. He dropped down to smack the pylons with a mallet, and the other guys could hardly see him through the vapor off the river. One of them saw Nick fall. Said he saw a body drop from the bridge feetfirst through the fog.

The other guys, when Schwaller asked, they wouldn't say if it was an accident or if Nick jumped. That kind of speculation, the agent could never have enough information to determine anything with certainty. As far as Schwaller knew, Nick never ended up talking to his wife. Schwaller wished he kept a tail on Nick longer, but it was too hard to justify the budget. There was no reason to suspect Nick, not really. Still, the agent imagined: What if Nick had gone to his wife's apartment that night? Wouldn't that have been interesting to watch? The agent was a little sad, thinking he might have missed that, if it happened. It might make sense that Nick jumped if Elisabeth rebuffed him. It was hard to say. Maybe Nick falling was an accident. There was fog, the rain. That he went feet-first doesn't prove anything. Maybe he slipped, maybe he hung by his fingertips for five minutes and nobody noticed until he let go.

Did Nick have a bounce in his step that morning? A smile on his face? Happiness he couldn't contain? Or did he drag himself along, exhausted, defeated? Did it seem, from the way Nick carried himself, that he might struggle with some weight that caused him to jump in the river? Or did he simply fall?

The other men couldn't answer these questions the agent asked. If you worked for a railroad long enough, you got used to investigators trying to determine what was an accident and what was not. Usually it was cars stopped across the tracks until a freight arrived, but, sure, falling was the same idea. They didn't know Nick Holland all that well either.

Schwaller waited in the hallway outside the morgue until they were ready for him.

A nurse came out of the room, pale and calmer than Schwaller expected. It wasn't every day a dead man was brought into a little county facility like this, just a clinic really, connected to the sheriff's office. Schwaller watched the nurse—she was young, in her twenties—and speculated what kind of mangling farm accidents and boating misadventures she'd seen in her time here, which could only have been a few years.

The nurse asked the agent if he would step into the room, and could he identify the body.

"Where's the foreman?" Schwaller asked.

The foreman had left already. He couldn't deal with this. Nick just started on his crew, and the foreman didn't want to see the body. The foreman had been there when they pulled him from the river.

"How bad can it be?" Schwaller asked the nurse. He laughed a little, to be charming.

It's not like there was blunt trauma. The body hadn't been in the water for weeks, which the agent had seen before, bloated cadavers aerated by schools of minnows. But not Nick. He probably died when he hit the water; they pulled him out quickly without much ado; it was an efficient, mostly quiet way to die.

Schwaller entered the cooler where they had the body out on a slab. Nick's hair wet, sticking up. Scarlet blotches all over his skin, from shock. It wasn't so bad. What should the agent have said? He said, "That's him." That's all that was required, so the nurse covered the body again so Nick was just a dimpled ridge under a blue sheet, and that was all.

Schwaller sat on a bench in the hallway of the county facility to see if anybody else would show. He hoped someone would come, and that this someone would be Elisabeth. Maybe the agent was softhearted, after all, hoping he was wrong about the state of affairs between Elisabeth and Nick. It would have pleased him to know that they did in fact have contact, that through it all, their love didn't die.

Elisabeth didn't show. Schwaller waited three hours, and nobody. Finally a reporter from the *World-Herald* dropped in for comment. Some kid, a runner, an intern, maybe a fact-checker, because no senior reporter would trek down to Cass County to search for answers that would be addressed in a press release from Midland Pacific that evening. Schwaller stopped the kid, flashed his Bureau badge, and asked a few questions. The kid, a skinny redhead, a Jimmy Olsen, knew next to nothing about what happened. He wasn't even sure who he was supposed to talk to at the county facility, so Schwaller offered to help. He dictated a statement and made the kid write it down word for word.

Early this morning an employee of the Midland Pacific Railroad was performing maintenance on a bridge over the Missouri River. He became tangled in his equipment and dropped into the water and was drowned. No one can be blamed. Train traffic was not involved. The signal was clear in both directions, but the repairman was working in heavy fog and failed to attach his safety lines. Efforts to revive the man failed. He died at the scene.

The agent would see Sandy Laika once more, that evening.

"I'm leaving tomorrow. Don't act surprised."

"You got your suitcase packed. What's there to be surprised about?"

"I'm sorry I can't do anything for your mother. You understand. I only work for the government, I'm not the government."

"I understand."

"I can only do my job. I collect information. I talk to people and fill out questionnaires. Sometimes there's a big breakthrough, but not very often."

"That doesn't surprise me either."

Schwaller laughed. "Don't be angry. If anyone should be angry, it's me."

Her mouth dropped when the agent said that. She turned to the door in his room and wouldn't look at him, but she didn't leave.

"Look," he told her. "I'm sorry. Truly. Let's go downstairs and I'll buy you a drink."

"What was all this for?" Sandy asked him. "Do you even know why you came to Omaha? I mean, why did they have you ask all those questions about Tyler Ahls? You have no idea what you're supposed to be doing. That's what I think."

Schwaller grinned at the suggestion, not at all upset, just a little sore that Sandy was badgering him. He was trying to be practical about how everything turned out.

"Did Elisabeth know Nick was in Omaha?"

"What do you mean?"

"Come on. You knew Nick." Schwaller played with the end of his chin and watched Sandy squirm. "I wonder, did he know where she lives? I'm certain. He's just the type. He'd be watching her. Watching her go in and out of work. You sure you didn't know Nick?"

"I don't know him."

"A shitty thing that happened with him. Going in the river like that."

"What do you mean?"

"He died. Didn't you see? It's on the news. This morning. 'Rail Worker Drowns.'" Schwaller spread his hands in front of his face like a headline, then clapped them together, loud. "They let me see the body. Needed me to ID it because his foreman went to pieces. I had his file with me, some photos, had talked to him a few days before. It was him all right. Nick Holland, mystery man. Showed up in the morgue."

Sandy went dumb at the news. She cried, she couldn't help it.

"I didn't know," she said.

Schwaller saw this was true. She really didn't know what had happened to Nick.

"Have you heard?"

"I saw on the news. It was Nick who fell from the bridge, wasn't it?"

Elisabeth was pale with shock. Looked tired but not distraught. Maybe not so pale, when Agent Schwaller looked again. Elisabeth clicking through the screens of patient information at the nurses station. "You heard?"

"Yes," Elisabeth said. "Nick died."

"Then why are you at work? If you don't mind my asking."

She kept at it on the computer. The look on her face, like asking *what else should I do?* without having to say it. And Schwaller wondering, *Did she hear herself speak? Did she believe the news?*

The news that Nick died maybe wasn't so shocking to Elisabeth. She'd prepared herself long ago for such a thing to be revealed to her, maybe thought he died years before. It had been more shocking to see him still alive, in her apartment, to catch Nick picking up that velveteen rabbit to inspect it.

"Somebody ought to tell Nick's dad," she said. "I bet nobody told him what happened."

"The railroad took care of that. His father was listed as an emergency contact."

"Ah. That's good. I'm glad somebody thought to do it."

"They'll be calling you too, someday soon. You're the sole benefi-ciary of his AD&D."

She nodded, thought about what that meant, then looked back to her work.

Agent Schwaller stood straight on the other side of the counter. He had his luggage with him, his two roller suitcases that strapped one on top of the other and a laptop satchel, all of which he left by the eleva-tors. He took off his sunglasses and snuck them inside his jacket pocket. Sometimes when he took off his sunglasses it was to intimidate, but this time it was out of respect.

"Did you know Nick was in Omaha?" the agent asked. "You had to, right? There's no way this was the first you heard about him. You saw him at least. Tell me that. All those evenings he sat outside your building in his car."

She said nothing. Just clicked away at her terminal, playing soli-taire, though the agent couldn't see that.

"I don't want to badger you about this, and I won't. You can tell me. I get it's a sensitive topic, that you're probably in shock. It's some fucked-up stuff. So just nod if you saw him. If you knew he was here."

Nothing. She was a stone wall.

Elisabeth didn't know anything about what happened with her brother or Nick. Not where they spent the previous years, or even why they left. What she knew the whole time was that they were gone. There was no point in torturing her about it.

"I've got a plane to catch." Agent Schwaller pulled a calling card from his pocket, from the brass case where he kept his calling cards, and laid it on the counter. "For later, if you want to talk."

"Safe travels."

"I don't know if this helps at all. It will be out soon, I think. But the videos they released, the Tyler Ahls videos. CIA had them four months before they said anything. Haqqani didn't send it to CNN—CIA intercepted the video, then released it. That was all arranged. There hasn't been another one since."

"What does that mean?"

"They more than likely won't find your brother. Somebody should tell you that. If you have your hopes up, you shouldn't."

"Why did they lie about the tape?"

"It's not lying," Schwaller said. "To see what happened, that's why, if the threat was legit, if there were more Tyler videos out there, at first, then if anyone came out of the woodwork once the video was released."

"Did anyone come out of the woodwork?"

"Nobody."

He swallowed hard, admitting that, which he wasn't supposed to do. That's the kind of man Schwaller was, uncomfortable, pinching the end of his long nose, looking around sort of clueless—but he wanted to help her, his job was to help Americans.

"Personally, I don't get it," he said. "Playing all these games. Maybe it's a waste of time, all the cat-and-mouse stuff."

"You? I figured that would be your favorite part."

Schwaller shrugged, checked his wristwatch, then glanced to the elevators to see if his baggage was still in sight.

Elisabeth stood, inexplicably shook his hand, looked him in the eye. "Since you're being honest, will you tell me the truth about a few things?"

"Absolutely."

"Does anybody know where Tyler is?"

"No."

"Does anybody know if he made that video of his own free will?"

"No."

"Do they know if Tyler is still alive?"

"No."

"Good-bye, Agent Schwaller."

[05 May 09; seven months after Agt Schwaller left Omaha]

There's an asphalt track next to the field office in Chicago, inside the wrought-iron fences, on lush grounds that encircle the ten-story glass tower, among pine trees and bluegrass. Many agents like to run the track, early in the morning, over lunch, in the evening. There's stationary equipment tucked outside one of the bends in the asphalt—pull-up bars, push-up bars, Jack LaLanne kind of stuff, weather permitting. Sure, there's a full gym inside the building, but running on the track, blowing off steam by doing push-ups, sit-ups, letting UIC nursing students watch, those waiting at the bus stop outside the fence, it's better than repping iron in a salty basement compartment. Plus, it's life-affirming to get outside in spring, in Chicago.

Even if he wasn't going for a run, Agent Schwaller liked being out on the track. Walking circles helped him think through things, what the Romans called solvitur ambulando, going along slow, still in his suit and tie while other agents sprinted past in gym shorts and tees. Schwaller contemplating important stuff. Schwaller glancing skyward over the pine trees to see the Sears Tower in the distance, what he would always call the Sears Tower. He'd think back through his time with the Bureau—the majority of his adult life. Some of his successes, his coup in the UNABOM investigation, white-slavery rings he busted, etc.,

etc. Those days Schwaller must have spent a lot of time enumerating his vitae in the back of his mind, as he hardly ever left the field office. Not that he didn't work hard, he did. But the prestige he was angling for when he went to Omaha never materialized. It had nothing to do with him, the agent was certain. He'd done his job well enough, even if some force in the higher-ups was going to see him suffer for fixating on Tyler Ahls. (There were two bombings in Pakistan on October 10 that killed fifty people, mere days after the agent spent a workweek following leads in Nebraska. Those deaths weren't on him, it wasn't his fault—and those who died weren't Americans, it is noted—but his methods came off as philistine given the lives lost. He was seen as frivolous and never again would there be time for frivolity.) Schwaller suspected he'd be put out to pasture, his work marginalized. As he walked the asphalt track, the fear started to sneak in, the kind of fear he kept at bay for thirteen years, that he would be transferred somewhere provincial, to Ohio or somewhere worse than Ohio, if such a place could exist in the mind of Agent Schwaller. Surely, though, he would make the best of whatever hand he was dealt, like he'd tried to do in Omaha. Schwaller was nothing if he wasn't an agent for the Bureau of Investigation; he always did his part. What else did they want out of him?

It was such a dumb case, really. His time in Omaha.

He thought about it from time to time. More than he should. There was no practical reason the case should bother him. He'd done nothing wrong; as it turned out, there was no looming attack specifically related to Tyler Ahls and the videos that featured him so prominently. There was no case to solve, and maybe that's why it galled Agent Schwaller. That it was merely life. Normal people doing normal things, for the most part. The way Elisabeth Holland returned to work the day after her husband died, because there was only work and after-work and worrying about people you love. There was mystery in these stories of other people's lives but no crime the agent was able to detect.

Of course, Schwaller kept tabs on them, from time to time, because he came to see them as his people. That's the way it went after an investigation. It wasn't so easy to give them back to the world.

How Sandy Laika kept making inquiries on behalf of her mother. Sandy was persistent, she was clever, and eventually she was able to make peace with an immigration official to clarify that Peggy Laika wasn't really a sponsor of terrorism, that she only wanted to hurt Russia when she helped those Chechens with a small donation. The official was able to arrange for Mrs. Laika to be added to a roster of citizenship test takers, and strongly urged that the old woman make it to the exam on time, prepared to pass, as she had overlooked opportunities before.

It was in Chicago where Peggy passed her citizenship exam, where she'd been added to the roster and that official had been harangued into unflagging the old woman in their files. Going to Chicago for the exam wasn't the easiest way this could have been handled, but Sandy convinced her mother it was for the best. Sandy even came along on the trip. They went on a boat tour and drank wine while floating on the Chicago River, ate dinner at Pizzeria Due, rode the El together to the immigration field office on Congress Parkway. As Sandy's credit receipts show, they had a nice couple days there. It was an agreeable capstone to their troubles.

Did Sandy think about calling Agent Schwaller while she was in Chicago? She might have thought about it. Did she get in contact with the agent? Did she meet him? She did not. After all, maybe Sandy Laika actually did have an affinity for strangers who came into her life and left just as quickly.

By the time Agent Schwaller left Omaha, no final call had been made on Tyler Ahls, but it certainly looked like it was him being held in a cave in Afghanistan, and that he disappeared after that. None of the Bureau's intelligence sources came up with anything. Neither did CIA's. The Bureau would keep looking, keep listening, of course (what else could they do except their jobs?) but no new recordings popped up, no new photos of Tyler with so-called freedom fighters.

In fact, Schwaller discovered it was a State Department official who escalated the suspicion of Tyler Ahls—someone going up the chain about an adventure hiker gone missing in a war zone. This was months before that video clip was discovered. Who tipped off the guy in State? It was Gerry Ahls, as a matter of fact. When Ahls tried to get State to find his lost son, he engaged a bigger apparatus. How's that for funny? Later, a tip came from one of CIA's fixers in Pakistan, a private investigator: he was hired to look for an American in the Khyber Pass region. Of course, Khan Khalili was selling information to both CIA and, it turns out, the Ahls family—so it was in his financial interest to tell CIA this all looked suspicious; and it was in the interest of his personal safety to tell the Ahls that he hadn't turned up anything and, no, he wouldn't go to Khyber Pass to look for an American. Not for what the Ahls were paying him.

Was there anything to Tyler Ahls's disappearance? Did Tyler go to Asia looking to join al-Qaeda, or was he truly a missionary, an apostle, who was abducted and forced to say nasty things about the United States and its government on camera? Schwaller suspected Tyler would turn up within a decade, long-bearded and gray, looking like he'd aged twenty years in that time, and tell everyone a personal account of what he was doing at the Khyber Pass. That he was kidnapped by the Haqqani network and forced to make those videos and demand an impossible ransom; that they held him prisoner in bunkers and fed him spiced lentils and the guards were careful to never get drawn into conversation because it was known that Tyler spoke Urdu and some Pashto, that he called himself *al-Masīḥ*; that it was his pamphlets that caught the attention of Haqqani, that Tyler was a heretic, an invader;

that some of the guards took pity on Tyler, because even they came to understand how he had a hard time growing up, that he couldn't handle the torrent of faith that streamed through him, that he should take it easy, which was a weird thing to hear from a Muslim extremist; that they moved him from site to site every few months, gagged and bagged in the trunk of a car as an asset, until he was discovered by Pakistani security forces at a checkpoint, years later, and given to CIA. Then his body would be freed.

Maybe Tyler would show up someday and tell this tale. Or he'd never show up.

Is it true that Elisabeth Holland went to her husband's funeral? That she was the only one there?

Yes, she went; no, she wasn't alone during the ceremony. It wasn't exactly a funeral, more like a burial, that's all. Her parents were there, Gerry and Deb Ahls, and Nick's dad. And, yes, this was the first time the Ahls had met Harry Holland. It was the first time Elisabeth had met him too, if you believe that.

Midland Pacific took care of the arrangements, as Schwaller promised Elisabeth they would. When they called Harry Holland to notify him of the accident, there was protocol to follow, a burial site to be determined. It didn't really matter to Harry—there was no Holland family plot, so wherever was fine, so long as Harry could be there. Of course, Midland Pacific would buy the plot and see to the details; it was covered by their insurance. Were there particular religious rites the ceremony should adhere to? No, they weren't religious, neither father nor son. Was Mr. Holland sure he wouldn't prefer to have his son buried nearer to him, say, up there in Jackson County? No. *I don't care, so long as I can see him.*

It will be an open casket, won't it? Yes, Mr. Holland, they would arrange for the casket to be open.

Then, fine.

It was nearly two weeks between Nick dying and his burial. There was red tape with insurance companies, the mortician, the coroner, the sheriff and state law enforcement, OSHA, Midland Pacific's internal investigation; most every file related to Nick Holland's life was flagged for review by one federal agency or another by then, and each time the file changed, somebody had to look into it—if you think about it that way, it's a minor miracle he was interred so quickly. In his memos, in emailed responses to investigators, the clerk in the morgue in Cass County joked that Nick Holland's remains might never be buried.

You wonder about Elisabeth's state of mind those two weeks. Did she go to the morgue in that little county facility to see the body? She did not.

She went about her business, worked the rest of that week at Saint Wenceslaus like always. Did she talk to reporters? Only one, from the *Omaha World-Herald.* As it read in the paper on October 6, they'd been estranged a long time by then. *We haven't talked in years,* she told the reporter, *since we lived in Chicago.* And wasn't it odd that they ended up in the same city after all that time and didn't know? *Wasn't it romantic, in a way?* the reporter asked. *It's odd,* Elisabeth answered, and that's what they printed.

Maybe she isn't the type to lie, but sometimes there are exceptions.

After the first week, her parents arrived and stayed in a budget hotel close to Saint Wenceslaus—there weren't any hotels near where she lived. That was fine. They ate dinner together in the evenings when Elisabeth's shift ended. It was only fast food, at an Applebee's once, but Deb Ahls wanted to see Elisabeth every day, and Gerry made sure dinner was his treat. (And no, they never told her that Nick visited them in Chippewa a few months before. And no, she never told them that Nick visited her apartment in Omaha.) Elisabeth always looked ashamed when she sat with her parents at a restaurant, like she was a teenager beneath her shell of adulthood, like she still found them ugly.

Elisabeth, the Ahls, Harry Holland, the cemetery attendant and his backhoe, the foreman from the railroad—they all met at the burial site, a Cass County cemetery called L'Eau Qui Court, where the railroad bought a plot and casket and saw to the details. The foreman only stayed long enough to offer condolences and mumble an anecdote, one he didn't think Elisabeth would care about either way, but she might— how the morning he died, Nick put in a request to make his transfer to Omaha permanent. "The paperwork's still on my desk," the foreman said. Elisabeth clutched her chest as she took in this information, as the foreman retreated to his car, her breathing slow all of a sudden, struggling a moment, quiet, not saying a thing when her mother put a hand on her back and asked what was wrong. Her mother, her father, they waited for Elisabeth to catch her breath, for the color to return to her face, because they figured they knew why she struggled.

The Ahls must have recognized Harry Holland the moment they spotted him. A tall man with narrow hips, in straight jeans, checkered shirt, boots. He was old—Elisabeth might have forgotten that Nick explained how his father didn't become a parent until later in life, that he was a bachelor farmer until he was thirty-five, which is late to start a family in those parts—but Harry moved like he was strong and able, if a little sore, as he crossed the cemetery to join them, as he stretched his long cowboy legs over gravestones and swung from his hand a strange bouquet (something that looked like a cornstalk with rusty-red buds clustered at the top) and a stuffed Mike Ditka doll the railroad sent him that was found in Nick's car. Elisabeth would have seen Nick in his father's face—the same sly smile, his wide and bright eyes—though Harry's skin was sunbaked and mottled, covered over with what were more barnacles than freckles. She could hear Nick: *That's what working outside your whole life will do to you.*

"You're Harry, aren't you?" Elisabeth asked, holding out her hand to shake.

He smiled, took her hand, said, "It's a pleasure to meet you." There was coffee and cigarettes on his breath, on his teeth.

He still held her hand as he looked to where the casket was held aloft by a metal apparatus and canvas straps. The lid was closed, but the attendant had been instructed to open the lid if the bereaved wanted it opened, which he'd been told they would. There hadn't been a wake, no funeral, so this was it.

Elisabeth gasped when she saw him, when the attendant scuttled between them to the casket and released a clasp so the lid would open, and it was Nick, after all. There was so much makeup on him, his skin pale and pastel, except on his cheeks where they'd blushed a sunburn, because he was sunburned in the photo the beautician had to work from. His lips and eyelids were shriveled, his hair so thin from the gel combed through that he looked bald. But it was Nick.

She wasn't alone in her gasping—isn't that a moment of change for everyone, that moment when there's no hope of a mistake having been made, when it's truly done, for whomever is laid there? Deb Ahls leaned into Gerry's arms, bent her updo out of shape putting her head on his shoulder; Gerry wrapped an arm around Deb, his back straightening, his chin rising as he looked over and beyond the casket, one glimpse enough for him.

"Well, shit," Harry said, gazing into the box, into Nick's face. He croaked like a frog, the sound of him gulping a sob back into his chest and holding it there.

Harry stepped forward, put his hand in the box and rubbed the back of a hand along Nick's jaw. He shook his head when he felt the stone of Nick's skin, the ice. "It's okay," he whispered. "My boy." He put his hand on Nick's shoulder and squeezed until he could feel the bone there, the actual shoulder beneath the pad of the suit jacket his son had been put in.

"He didn't belong to me, I always told him that. He was his own property, because he was smart. I believed he'd do important things." Harry stepped back and looked to Elisabeth, moved the hand that had been on Nick's shoulder to hers. "I was never a good dad, not like, I don't know, not like yours."

"He never complained about you. He said he liked being a boy. Having freedom."

"You do what you think is right. Maybe it is. You get what's coming. I would have liked to seen him more, but I guess not seeing him was my reward for how I lived."

Harry turned to the casket to put the doll and the flowers on the closed part, where Nick's legs were. The bouquet was so large, he worked a moment to angle it right so it didn't fall. The peculiar bouquet, its long, sharp leaves, its rusty buds that resembled small beetles up close.

"What are those?" Deb asked.

"It's milo," Harry said. "Milo is beautiful."

"You grow milo on your farm?"

"Yes, we do."

"Since there's no pastor," Gerry Ahls said, "I'll say a few words." Clearing his throat, "There's no simple path through life. I think we realize that, whether we want to or not. But there are directions that sustain us, guideposts. Faith, labor, gratitude, family, grace—"

"Thank you," Elisabeth interrupted. "Please don't."

"Can we at least sing?" Deb Ahls asked.

"No," Elisabeth said.

Harry looked baffled by all that. "We were never very religious. Me and his mom were both baptized Evangelical, but we didn't do that for Nick. I wouldn't have minded, but after his mom was gone, it seemed like it was too late, he was so old."

"He wasn't baptized?" Deb Ahls asked. She and Gerry looked to each other. "I could have sworn he was."

Elisabeth twisted away when the attendant closed the lid and clasped the clasp to seal it. The attendant was going to lower it into the ground when they were finished—Elisabeth, Harry, the Ahls—but they could stay as long as they wanted.

In the middle distance, at the road, Elisabeth saw a man watching from his car. She recognized him: the black sedan, black wayfarer shades, and black suit, how the agent sat low in the seat of his rental to watch her, a blank expression on his face, looking how an agent should look. But Schwaller couldn't help himself, rising behind the steering wheel to lean his head out the open window, showing that maybe it was he who had trouble letting go of others, after all, of those missing. That it was he who was invested in these people—in his way—that he offered a crucial part of himself and needed something in return. He watched expectant, fingertips gripped over the edge of the doorframe, when Elisabeth noticed him in his rental, as he waited to see if she would acknowledge him, if she would wave or even nod her head.

Did Elisabeth mind that Schwaller was watching her, even then, at Nick's burial?

She showed no offense. She only glanced, granted merely a moment more of her attention. The agent could take nothing from her.

ACKNOWLEDGMENTS

My sincere thanks to those who helped make this book possible. First and foremost to Nicole, Madeleine, and Clara for being the best old building-and-loan pals anyone could ask for. To all Wheelers and Wests, for making and keeping me real. To Stephanie Delman for her authenticity, fidelity, and unfailing enthusiasm as a literary partner; Vivian Lee for her impeccability, understanding, and clarity; Hafizah Geter for being a pinch hitter extraordinaire; and all the unsung heroes at Little A, like Kristin Lunghamer, Sarah Shaw, Gabby Trull, and Emma Reh, for their contributions big and small.

Also, my travel companions, sleeper agents, and confidants: Darren Keen, Amy O'Reilly, Tahir Khan, Bill Sedlak, Brent Spencer, Drew Justice, Ryan Borchers, Kassandra Montag, Felicity White, Jeff Alessandrelli, Bob Churchill, Ryan Norris, Doug Rice, Jonis Agee, Sam Slaughter, Jean-Baptiste Joly, Amina Gautier, Lydia Kang, Dave Mullins, Trey Moody, Jason Lee Brown, Pastor Marta, Natalie Wheeler, Robert Muelleman, Tammy Block, University of Nebraska Medical Center Emergency Department, Disquiet International Literary Program, University of Nebraska at Omaha Writers' Workshop, and the amazing crew of librarians and book advocates at the Omaha Public Library.

Akademie Schloss Solitude and the creative writing program at Creighton University played essential roles in this book becoming reality by supporting me throughout its early stages.

ABOUT THE AUTHOR

Photo © 2019 Patrick Mainelli

Theodore Wheeler is the author of the novel *Kings of Broken Things* and *Bad Faith*, a collection of short fiction. His work has appeared in publications including *New Stories from the Midwest*, the *Southern Review*, the *Kenyon Review*, *Narrative* magazine, and *Boulevard*, and he has been recognized with a Marianne Russo Award from the Key West Literary Seminar and a fellowship from Akademie Schloss Solitude in Stuttgart, Germany. A graduate of the creative writing program at Creighton University, Wheeler teaches at the University of Nebraska at Omaha, covers a civil-law beat for a national news service, codirects Omaha Lit Fest, and sidelines as a bookseller for the Dundee Book Company roving book cart, one of the world's smallest bookstores. For more information, visit www.theodore-wheeler.com.